W9-BKL-411

WARRIORS

RISING
STORM

WARRIORS

WARRIORS

RISING STORM

ERIN HUNTER

HARPERCOLLINS*PUBLISHERS*

Rising Storm
Copyright © 2004 by Working Partners Limited
Series created by Working Partners Limited

Library of Congress Cataloging-in-Publication Data
Hunter, Erin.
    Rising Storm / Erin Hunter.—1st ed.
       p.   cm.—(Warriors ; bk. 4)
    Summary: Fireheart, the warrior cat, faces many challenges in his new
role of ThunderClan deputy as his apprentice, Cloudpaw, resists following
the warrior code, Bluestar weakens, and Tigerclaw continues to haunt the
forest seeking revenge.
    ISBN 0-06-000005-8 — ISBN 0-06-052562-2 (lib. bdg.)
    [1. Cats—Fiction. 2. Fantasy.] I. Title.
PZ7.H916625 Ri 2004   2003006982
[Fic]—dc21

Typography by Karin Paprocki

4   5   6   7   8   9   10

❖

First Edition

To Denise—this is as close to a song as I could get

Special thanks to Kate Cary

WARRIORS

RISING
STORM

ALLEGIANCES

THUNDERCLAN

LEADER

BLUESTAR—blue-gray she-cat, tinged with silver around her muzzle

DEPUTY

FIREHEART—handsome ginger tom
APPRENTICE, CLOUDPAW

MEDICINE CAT

YELLOWFANG—old dark gray she-cat with a broad, flattened face, formerly of ShadowClan
APPRENTICE, CINDERPELT—DARK GRAY SHE-CAT

WARRIORS

(toms, and she-cats without kits)

WHITESTORM—big white tom
APPRENTICE, BRIGHTPAW

DARKSTRIPE—sleek black-and-gray tabby tom
APPRENTICE, FERNPAW

LONGTAIL—pale tabby tom with dark black stripes
APPRENTICE, SWIFTPAW

RUNNINGWIND—swift tabby tom

MOUSEFUR—small dusky-brown she-cat
APPRENTICE, THORNPAW

BRACKENFUR—golden-brown tabby tom

DUSTPELT—dark brown tabby tom
APPRENTICE, ASHPAW

SANDSTORM—pale ginger she-cat

APPRENTICES

(more than six moons old, in training to become warriors)

SWIFTPAW—black-and-white tom

CLOUDPAW—long-haired white tom

BRIGHTPAW—she-cat, white with ginger splotches

THORNPAW—golden-brown tabby tom

FERNPAW—pale gray with darker flecks, she-cat, pale green eyes

ASHPAW—pale gray with darker flecks, tom, dark blue eyes

QUEENS

(she-cats expecting or nursing kits)

FROSTFUR—beautiful white coat and blue eyes

BRINDLEFACE—pretty tabby

GOLDENFLOWER—pale ginger coat

SPECKLETAIL—pale tabby, and the oldest nursery queen

WILLOWPELT—very pale gray she-cat with unusual blue eyes

ELDERS

(former warriors and queens, now retired)

HALFTAIL—big dark brown tabby tom with part of his tail missing

SMALLEAR—gray tom with very small ears; the oldest tom in ThunderClan

PATCHPELT—small black-and-white tom

ONE-EYE—pale gray she-cat, the oldest cat in ThunderClan; virtually blind and deaf

DAPPLETAIL—once-pretty tortoiseshell she-cat with a lovely dappled coat

SHADOWCLAN

LEADER   **NIGHTSTAR**—old black tom

DEPUTY   **CINDERFUR**—thin gray tom

MEDICINE CAT   **RUNNINGNOSE**—small gray-and-white tom

WARRIORS   **STUMPYTAIL**—brown tabby tom
APPRENTICE, BROWNPAW

WETFOOT—gray tabby tom
APPRENTICE, OAKPAW

LITTLECLOUD—very small tabby tom

WHITETHROAT—black tom with white chest and paws

QUEENS   **DAWNCLOUD**—small tabby

DARKFLOWER—black she-cat

TALLPOPPY—long-legged light brown tabby she-cat

WINDCLAN

LEADER   **TALLSTAR**—black-and-white tom with a very long tail

DEPUTY   **DEADFOOT**—black tom with a twisted paw

MEDICINE CAT   **BARKFACE**—short-tailed brown tom

WARRIORS

MUDCLAW—mottled dark brown tom
APPRENTICE, WEBPAW

TORNEAR—tabby tom
APPRENTICE, TAWNYPAW

ONEWHISKER—brown tabby tom
APPRENTICE, WHITEPAW

RUNNINGBROOK—light gray tabby she-cat

QUEENS

ASHFOOT—gray queen

MORNINGFLOWER—tortoiseshell queen

RIVERCLAN

LEADER

CROOKEDSTAR—huge light-colored tabby with a twisted jaw

DEPUTY

LEOPARDFUR—unusually spotted golden tabby she-cat

MEDICINE CAT

MUDFUR—long-haired light brown tom

WARRIORS

BLACKCLAW—smoky black tom
APPRENTICE, HEAVYPAW

STONEFUR—gray tom with battle-scarred ears
APPRENTICE, SHADEPAW

LOUDBELLY—dark brown tom

GRAYSTRIPE—long-haired gray tom, formerly of ThunderClan

QUEENS

MISTYFOOT—dark gray she-cat

MOSSPELT—tortoiseshell she-cat

ELDERS

GRAYPOOL—thin gray she-cat with patchy fur and a scarred muzzle

CATS OUTSIDE CLANS

BARLEY—black-and-white tom that lives on a farm close to the forest

BLACKFOOT—large white tom with huge jet-black paws, formerly ShadowClan deputy

BOULDER—silver tabby tom, formerly of ShadowClan

PRINCESS—light brown tabby with a distinctive white chest and paws; a kittypet

RAVENPAW—sleek black cat who lives on the farm with Barley

SMUDGE—plump, friendly black-and-white kitten who lives in a house at the edge of the forest; a kittypet

TIGERCLAW—big dark brown tabby tom with unusually long front claws, formerly of ThunderClan

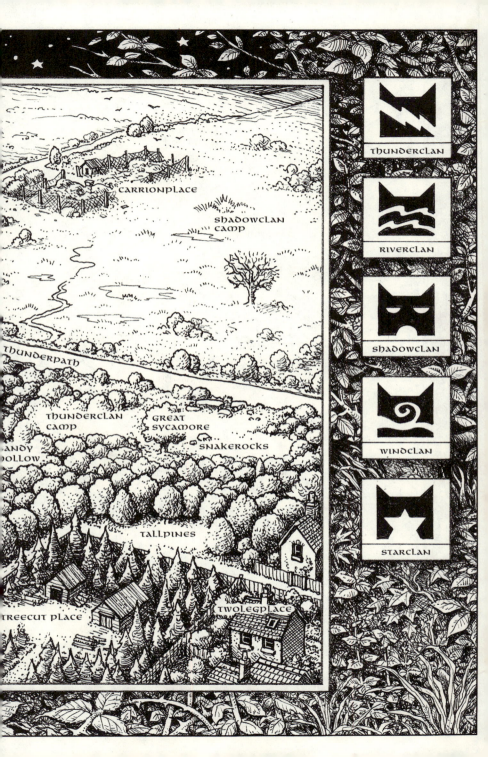

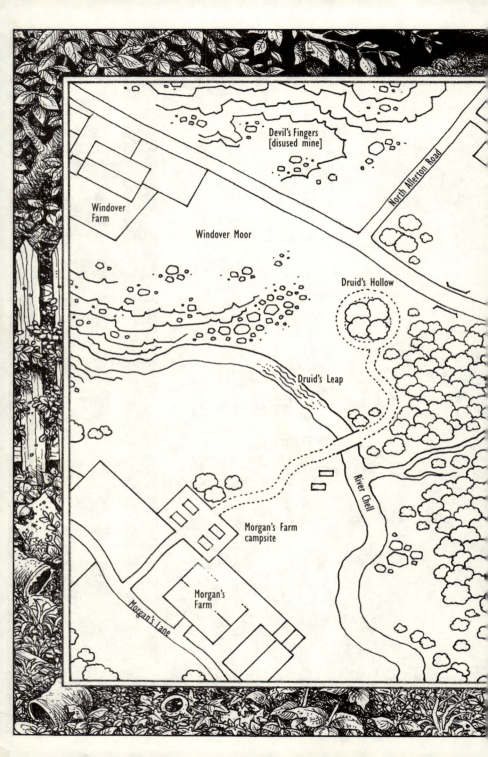

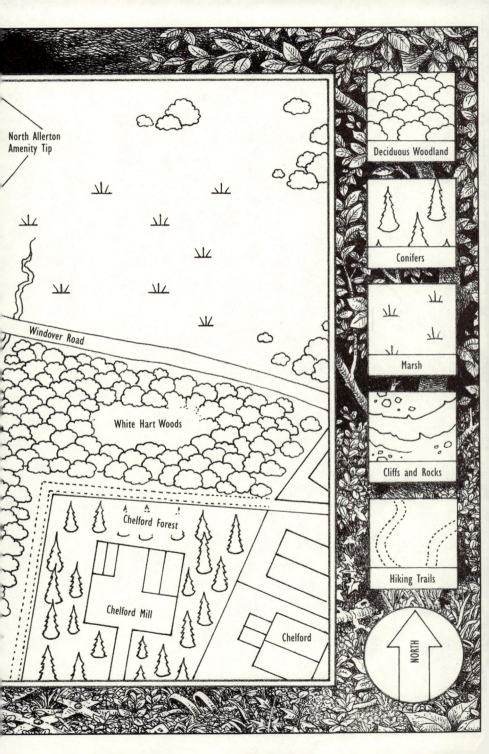

PROLOGUE

An agonized groan echoed across the moon-bleached floor of a forest clearing. Two cats crouched in the shadows under one of the bushes at the edge. One of them writhed in pain, lashing his long tail. The other cat raised himself to his paws and bowed his head. He had been a medicine cat for many long moons, and yet he could only watch helplessly as the leader of his Clan was overpowered by the sickness that had already claimed so many lives. He knew of no herb that would ease the cramps and fever this sickness brought, and his patchy gray fur bristled with frustration as the leader convulsed again and then fell exhausted into the moss-lined nest. Fearfully, the medicine cat leaned forward and sniffed. There was still breath in the leader's body, but it was foul and shallow, and the tom's thin flanks heaved with every gasp.

A screech ripped through the woods. Not a cat this time, but an owl. The medicine cat stiffened. Owls brought death to the forest, stealing prey and even kits that had strayed too far from their mothers. The medicine cat raised beseeching eyes to the sky, praying to the spirits of his warrior ancestors that the owl's call was not an ill omen. He stared through the branches that formed the roof of the den, searching the dark sky for Silverpelt. But the swathe of stars where StarClan lived was hidden by clouds, and the medicine cat shivered with fear. Had their warrior ancestors abandoned them to the sickness that ravaged the camp?

Then the wind stirred the trees, rattling the brittle leaves. High above, the clouds shifted and a single star sent a frail beam of light through the roof of the den. In the shadows, the leader drew in a long, steady breath. Hope leaped like a fish in the medicine cat's heart. StarClan was with them after all.

Weak with relief, the medicine cat lifted his chin, giving silent thanks to his warrior ancestors for sparing the life of his leader. As he narrowed his eyes against the shaft of starlight, he heard spirit-voices murmuring deep inside his head. They whispered of glorious battles to come, of new territories, and of a greater Clan rising from the ashes of the old. The medicine cat felt joy surge in his chest and pulsate through his paws. This star carried much more than a message of survival.

Suddenly, without warning, a wide gray wing swept across the ray of starlight, plunging the den into darkness. The medicine cat shrank back and pressed his belly to the floor as the owl screeched down and raked the roof of the den with its talons. It must have smelled the sickness that weakened the leader, and swooped in search of easy prey. But the branches were too thick for the owl to break through.

The medicine cat listened to the slow beating of wings as the owl flew away into the forest, then sat up, heart hammering, and searched the night sky once more. Like the owl, the star was gone. In its place was only blackness. Dread crawled beneath the medicine cat's pelt and clutched at his heart.

"Did you hear that?" a tom called through the entrance of the den, his voice high-pitched with alarm. The medicine cat squeezed quickly out into the clearing, knowing the Clan would be waiting for an interpretation of the omen. Warriors, queens, and elders—those well enough to move from their nests—huddled in the shadows on the far side of the clearing. The medicine cat paused for a moment, listening to the Clan murmuring anxiously to one another.

"What's an owl doing here?" hissed a mottled warrior, his eyes glinting in the darkness.

"They never come so close to the camp," wailed an elder.

"Did it take any kits?" demanded another warrior, turning his broad head to the cat beside him.

"Not this time," replied the silver queen. She had lost three of her kits to the sickness, and her voice was dull with pain. "But it might come back. It must smell our weakness."

"You'd think the stench of death would keep it away." A tabby warrior limped into the clearing. His paws were clotted with mud and his fur ruffled. He had been burying a Clan mate. There were more graves to be dug, but he was too weak to go on that night. "How's our leader?" he asked, his voice tight with fear.

"We don't know," replied the mottled tom.

"Where's the medicine cat?" whined the queen.

The cats peered around the clearing and the medicine cat saw their frightened eyes gleaming in the dark. He could hear the rising panic in their voices and knew they needed to be soothed, assured that StarClan had not abandoned them completely. Taking a deep breath, the cat forced the fur to lie flat on his shoulders and padded across the clearing.

"We don't need a medicine cat to tell us the owl's screech spoke of death," whimpered an elder, his eyes brimming with fear.

"How do you know?" spat the mottled warrior.

"Yes," agreed the queen, glancing at the elder. "StarClan doesn't speak to you!" She turned as the medicine cat reached them. "Was the owl an omen?" she mewed anxiously.

Shifting his paws uncomfortably, the medicine cat avoided a direct reply. "StarClan has spoken to me tonight," he announced. "Did you see the star shine between the clouds?"

The queen nodded, and around her the other cats' eyes flickered with desperate hope. "What did it mean?" asked the elder.

"Will our leader live?" called the tabby warrior.

The medicine cat hesitated.

"He cannot die now!" cried the queen. "What about his nine lives? StarClan granted them only six moons ago!"

"There is only so much strength StarClan can give," answered the medicine cat. "But our ancestors have not forgotten us," he went on, trying to push aside the image of the owl's dark wing as it blotted out the thin ray of light. "The star brought a message of hope."

A high-pitched moan sounded from a dim corner of the camp, and a tortoiseshell queen sprang up and hurried toward the sound. The others continued to stare at the medicine cat with eyes that begged for comfort.

"Did StarClan speak of rain?" asked a young warrior. "It's been so long since it rained, and it might cleanse the camp of the sickness."

The medicine cat shook his head. "Not of rain, but of a great new dawn that awaits our Clan. In that ray of light, our warrior ancestors showed me the future, and it will be glorious!"

"Then we'll survive?" mewed the silver queen.

"We'll do more than survive," the medicine cat promised. "We shall rule the whole forest!"

Murmurs of relief flickered through the cats, the first purrs that had been heard in the camp for nearly a moon. But the medicine cat turned his head away to hide his trembling whiskers. He prayed that the Clan would not ask again about the owl. He dared not share the dreadful warning StarClan had added when the bird's wing had obscured the star—that the Clan would pay the highest possible price for their great new dawn.

CHAPTER 1

Warm shafts of sun shine streamed through the canopy of leaves and flickered over Fireheart's pelt. He crouched lower, aware that his coat would be glowing amber among the lush green undergrowth.

Paw by paw, he crept beneath a fern. He could smell a pigeon. He moved slowly toward the mouthwatering scent until he could see the plump bird pecking among the ferns.

Fireheart flexed his claws, his paws itching with anticipation. He was hungry after leading the dawn patrol and hunting all morning. This was the high season for prey, a time for the Clan to grow fat on the forest's bounty. And although there had been little rain since the newleaf floods, the woods were rich with food. After stocking the fresh-kill pile back at camp, it was time for Fireheart to hunt for himself. He tensed his muscles, ready to leap.

Suddenly a second scent wafted toward him on the dry breeze. Fireheart opened his mouth, tipping his head to one side. The pigeon must have smelled it too, for its head shot up and it began to unfold its wings, but it was too late. A rush of white fur shot out from under some brambles. Fireheart stared in surprise as the cat pounced on the startled bird, pinning it to the ground with his front paws before finishing it off with a swift bite to the neck.

The delicious smell of fresh-kill filled Fireheart's nostrils. He stood up and padded out of the undergrowth toward the fluffy white tom. "Well caught, Cloudpaw," he meowed. "I didn't see you coming until it was too late."

"Nor did this stupid bird," crowed Cloudpaw, flicking his tail smugly.

Fireheart felt his shoulders tense. Cloudpaw was his apprentice as well as his sister's son. It was Fireheart's responsibility to teach him the skills of a Clan warrior and how to respect the warrior code. The young tom was undeniably a good hunter, but Fireheart couldn't help wishing that he would learn a little humility. Deep down, he sometimes wondered if Cloudpaw would ever understand the importance of the warrior code, the moons-old traditions of loyalty and ritual that had been passed down through generations of cats in the forest.

But Cloudpaw had been born in Twolegplace to Fireheart's kittypet sister, Princess, and brought to ThunderClan by Fireheart as a tiny kit. Fireheart knew from his own bitter experience that Clan cats had no respect for kittypets. Fireheart had spent his first six moons living with Twolegs, and there were cats in his Clan that would never let him forget the fact that he was not forest-born. He twitched his ears impatiently. He knew he did everything he could to prove his loyalty to the Clan, but his stubborn apprentice was a different matter. If Cloudpaw was going to win any sympathy from his Clanmates, he was going to have to lose some of his arrogance.

"It's just as well you're so quick," Fireheart pointed out. "You were upwind. I could *smell* you, even if I couldn't see you. And so could the bird."

Cloudpaw's long snowy fur bristled and he snapped back, "I *know* I was upwind! But I could tell this dumb dove wasn't going to be hard to catch whether he smelled me or not."

The young cat stared defiantly into Fireheart's eyes, and Fireheart felt his annoyance turning to anger. "It's a pigeon, not a dove!" he spat. "And a true warrior shows more respect for the prey that feeds his Clan."

"Yeah, right!" retorted Cloudpaw. "I didn't see Thornpaw show much respect for that squirrel he dragged back to camp yesterday. He said it was so dopey, a kit could have caught it."

"Thornpaw is just an apprentice," Fireheart growled. "Like you, he still has a lot to learn."

"Well, I caught it, didn't I?" grumbled Cloudpaw, prodding the pigeon with a sullen paw.

"There's more to being a warrior than catching pigeons!"

"I'm faster than Brightpaw and stronger than Thornpaw," Cloudpaw spat back. "What more do you want?"

"Your denmates would know that a warrior never attacks with the wind behind him!" Fireheart knew he shouldn't let himself be drawn into an argument, but his apprentice's stubbornness infuriated him like a tick on his ear.

"Big deal. You might have been downwind like a good warrior, but *I* got to the pigeon first!" Cloudpaw raised his voice in an angry yowl.

"Be quiet," Fireheart hissed, suddenly distracted. He lifted his head and sniffed the air. The forest seemed strangely silent, and Cloudpaw's loud meows were echoing too loudly through the trees.

"What's the matter?" Cloudpaw glanced around. "I can't smell anything."

"Neither can I," Fireheart admitted.

"So what are you worried about?"

"Tigerclaw," Fireheart answered bluntly. The dark warrior had been prowling through his dreams since Bluestar had banished him from the Clan a quarter moon ago. Tigerclaw had tried to kill the ThunderClan leader, but Fireheart had stopped him and exposed his long-hidden treachery to the whole Clan. There had been no sign of Tigerclaw since, but Fireheart felt icy claws of fear pricking at his heart now as he listened to the stillness of the forest. It seemed to be listening too, holding its breath, and Tigerclaw's parting words echoed in Fireheart's mind: *Keep your eyes open, Fireheart. Keep your ears pricked. Keep looking behind you. Because one day I'll find you, and then you'll be crowfood.*

Cloudpaw's mew broke the silence. "What would Tigerclaw be doing around here?" he scoffed. "Bluestar exiled him!"

"I know," Fireheart agreed. "And only StarClan knows where he went. But Tigerclaw made it clear that we'd not seen the last of him!"

"I'm not scared of that traitor."

"Well, you should be!" hissed Fireheart. "Tigerclaw knows

these woods as well as any cat in ThunderClan. He'd tear you to shreds if he got the chance."

Cloudpaw snorted and circled his catch impatiently. "You've been no fun since Bluestar made you deputy. I'm not hanging around if you're just going to waste the morning trying to scare me with nursery tales. I'm meant to be hunting for the Clan elders." And he dashed away into the brambles, leaving the lifeless pigeon lying on the earth.

"Cloudpaw, come back!" Fireheart yowled furiously. Then he shook his head. "Let Tigerclaw have the young mouse-brained idiot!" he muttered to himself.

Lashing his tail, he snatched up the pigeon and wondered whether to carry it back to camp for Cloudpaw. *A warrior should be responsible for his own fresh-kill*, he concluded, and tossed the pigeon into a thick clump of grass. He padded after it and flattened down the green stalks to cover the fat bird, wishing he could be sure that Cloudpaw would return and take it back with the rest of his catch to the hungry elders. *If he doesn't bring it home with him, he can go hungry until he does*, Fireheart decided. His apprentice had to learn that even in greenleaf, prey should never be wasted.

The sun rose higher, scorching the earth and sucking moisture from the leaves on the trees. Fireheart pricked his ears. The forest was still eerily quiet, as if its creatures were hiding till the evening shade brought relief from another day of glaring heat. The stillness unnerved him, and a flicker of doubt tugged at his belly. Perhaps he should go and find Cloudpaw after all.

You tried to warn him about Tigerclaw! Fireheart could almost hear the familiar voice of his best friend, Graystripe, echoing in his head, and he winced as bittersweet memories flooded through him. It was exactly the sort of thing the former ThunderClan warrior would say to him right now. They had trained together as apprentices and fought beside each other until love and tragedy had torn them apart. Graystripe had fallen in love with a she-cat from another Clan, but if Silverstream had not died in her kitting, perhaps Graystripe would have stayed with ThunderClan. Once more Fireheart remembered Graystripe carrying his two kits into RiverClan territory, taking them to join their dead mother's Clan. Fireheart's shoulders sagged. He missed the companionship of Graystripe and still silently shared words with him almost every day. He knew his old friend so well, it was always easy to imagine what Graystripe would say in reply.

Fireheart shook away the memories with a flick of his ears. It was time he got back to camp. He was the deputy of ThunderClan now, and there were hunting parties and patrols to organize. Cloudpaw would have to manage alone.

The ground was dry underpaw as Fireheart raced through the woods to the top of the ravine where the camp lay. He hesitated for a moment and enjoyed the surge of pride and affection he always felt as he approached his forest home. Even though he had spent his kithood in Twolegplace, he had known since the first time he had ventured into the forest that this was where he truly belonged.

Below him, the ThunderClan camp was well hidden by thick

brambles. Bounding down the steep slope, Fireheart followed the well-worn path to the gorse tunnel that led into the camp.

The pale gray queen, Willowpelt, lay at the entrance to the nursery, warming her swollen belly in the morning sun. Until recently she had shared the warriors' den. Now she lived in the nursery with the other queens while she waited for her first litter to be born.

Beside her, Brindleface affectionately watched her two kits as they tussled on the hard earth, scuffing up small clouds of dust. They had been Cloudpaw's adopted littermates. When Fireheart had brought his sister's firstborn into the Clan, Brindleface had agreed to suckle the helpless kit. Cloudpaw had recently been made an apprentice, and it would not be long before Brindleface's own kits were ready to leave the nursery too.

A murmur of voices drew Fireheart's gaze toward the Highrock, which stood at the head of the clearing. A group of warriors was gathered in the shadows beneath the rock on which Bluestar, the leader of ThunderClan, normally stood to address her Clan. Fireheart recognized Darkstripe's tabby pelt, the lithe shape of Runningwind, and Whitestorm's snowy head among them.

As Fireheart padded silently across the baked earth, Darkstripe's querulous meow sounded above the other voices. "So who's going to lead the patrol at sunhigh?"

"Fireheart will decide when he returns from hunting," Whitestorm answered calmly. The elderly warrior was clearly reluctant to be stirred by Darkstripe's hostile tone.

"He should be back by now," complained Dustpelt, a brown tabby who had been an apprentice at the same time as Fireheart.

"I *am* back," Fireheart announced. He shouldered his way through the warriors to sit down beside Whitestorm.

"Well, now that you're here, are you going to tell us who's going to lead the patrol at sunhigh?" meowed Darkstripe. The silver tabby turned a cold gaze on Fireheart.

Fireheart felt hot under his fur, in spite of the shade cast by the Highrock. Darkstripe had been closer to Tigerclaw than any other cat, and Fireheart couldn't help wondering about the depth of his loyalty, even though Darkstripe had chosen to stay when his former ally was exiled. "Longtail will lead the patrol," Fireheart meowed.

Slowly Darkstripe switched his gaze from Fireheart to Whitestorm, his whiskers twitching and his eyes glittering with scorn. Fireheart swallowed nervously, wondering if he had said something stupid.

"Er, Longtail's out with his apprentice," explained Runningwind, looking awkward. "He and Swiftpaw won't be back till evening, remember?" Beside him, Dustpelt snorted scornfully.

Fireheart gritted his teeth. *I should have known that!* "Runningwind, then. You can take Brackenfur and Dustpelt with you."

"Brackenfur'll never keep up with us," meowed Dustpelt. "He's still limping from the battle with the rogue cats."

"Okay, okay." Fireheart tried to disguise his mounting agitation, but he couldn't help feeling he was just plucking names at random as he ordered, "Brackenfur can go hunting with Mousefur and . . . and . . ."

"I'd like to hunt with them," Sandstorm offered.

Fireheart blinked gratefully at the orange she-cat and went on. ". . . and Sandstorm."

"What about the patrol? It'll be past sunhigh if we don't decide soon!" meowed Darkstripe.

"You can join Runningwind on patrol," snapped Fireheart.

"And the evening patrol?" Mousefur asked mildly. Fireheart stared back at the dusky brown she-cat, his mind suddenly blank.

Whitestorm's rusty mew sounded beside Fireheart. "I'd like to lead the evening patrol," he meowed. "Do you think Swiftpaw and Longtail would like to come with me when they return?"

"Yes, of course." Fireheart looked around the circle of eyes and was relieved to see that they all seemed satisfied.

The cats moved away, leaving Fireheart alone with Whitestorm. "Thanks," he meowed, dipping his head to the old warrior. "I guess I should have planned the patrols before now."

"It'll get easier," Whitestorm reassured him. "We have all grown used to Tigerclaw telling us exactly what to do and when."

Fireheart glanced away, his heart sinking.

"They're also bound to be more edgy than usual," Whitestorm went on. "Tigerclaw's treachery has shaken the whole Clan."

Fireheart looked at the white warrior and understood that Whitestorm was trying to encourage him. It was easy to forget that Tigerclaw's actions had come as a massive shock to the rest of the Clan. Fireheart had known for a long time that Tigerclaw's hunger for power had driven him to murder and lies. But the other cats had found it hard to believe that the fearless warrior would turn against his own Clan. Whitestorm's words reminded Fireheart that, even if he did not yet have Tigerclaw's confident authority, he would never betray his Clan as Tigerclaw had done.

Whitestorm's voice interrupted his thoughts. "I must go and see Brindleface. She said there was something she wanted to talk to me about." He dipped his head. The warrior's respectful gesture took Fireheart by surprise, and he nodded awkwardly in reply.

As he watched Whitestorm leave, Fireheart's belly growled with hunger and he thought of the juicy pigeon Cloudpaw had caught. Whitestorm's ginger-and-white apprentice, Brightpaw, sat outside the apprentices' den, and Fireheart wondered if she'd brought the elders any fresh-kill. He padded over to the old tree stump where she was washing her tail. She lifted her head and mewed, "Hello, Fireheart."

"Hi, Brightpaw. Been hunting?" Fireheart asked.

"Yes," replied Brightpaw, her eyes shining. "It's the first time Whitestorm's let me out by myself."

"Catch much?"

Brightpaw looked shyly at her paws. "Two sparrows and a squirrel."

"Well done," Fireheart purred. "I bet Whitestorm was pleased."

Brightpaw nodded.

"Did you take it straight to the elders?"

"Yes." Brightpaw's eyes clouded with worry. "Was that okay?" she mewed anxiously.

"That was great," Fireheart assured her. If only his own apprentice were so reliable. Cloudpaw should have been back by now. The elders would need more than two sparrows and a squirrel to fill their bellies. He decided to visit them to check that they were not suffering too much from the green-leaf heat. As he approached the fallen oak where the elders made their den, voices drifted up from behind its bare branches.

"Willowpelt's kits will be born soon." That was Speckletail. She was the oldest queen in the nursery, and her single kit was weak and small for its age after a bout of whitecough.

"New kits are always a good omen," purred One-Eye.

"StarClan knows we could do with a good omen," Smallear muttered darkly.

"You're not still fretting about the ritual, are you?" croaked Patchpelt. Fireheart could imagine the old black-and-white tom flicking his ears impatiently at Smallear.

"The what?" meowed One-Eye.

"The naming ceremony for the new Clan deputy," Patchpelt explained loudly. "You know, when Tigerclaw left, a quarter moon ago."

"It's my ears that don't work as well as they used to, not my mind!" snapped One-Eye. She went on, and the other cats listened in silence because One-Eye was respected for her wisdom in spite of her bad temper. "I don't think StarClan would punish us just because Bluestar failed to name the new deputy before moonhigh. The circumstances were very unusual."

"But that just makes it worse!" fretted Dappletail. "What will StarClan think of a Clan whose deputy turns against it, and whose new deputy was named *after* moonhigh? It looks as if we can't keep our cats loyal, or even carry out the proper ceremonies."

Fireheart felt an icy ripple along his spine. When Bluestar had learned about Tigerclaw's treachery and banished him from the Clan, she had been too upset to carry out the proper rituals for appointing a new deputy. Fireheart had not been named as Tigerclaw's successor until the following day, and to many cats this was a very bad omen.

"Fireheart's naming broke with Clan ritual for the first time I can remember," meowed Smallear in a grave tone. "I hate to say it, but I can't help feeling that his deputyship will be a dark time for ThunderClan."

Patchpelt mewed in agreement, and Fireheart felt his heart pound as he waited for One-Eye to calm the others' fears with her wise words. But for once she remained silent. Above him the fierce sun continued to shine in a clear, blue sky, yet Fireheart felt chilled to the bone.

He turned away from the elders' den, unable to face them now, and paced anxiously along the edge of the clearing. As he approached the nursery, Fireheart stared at the ground, lost in thought. A sudden movement outside the nursery entrance made him look up. He froze, and his heart began to pound as he recognized Tigerclaw's amber eyes gleaming at him. Horrified by the familiar gaze, Fireheart blinked in alarm. Then he realized that it was not the fierce warrior he was looking at, but Bramblekit—Tigerclaw's son.

CHAPTER 2

❧

Fireheart saw a ripple of pale amber fur and looked up to see Goldenflower slip out of the nursery behind the dark tabby kit. A pale ginger kit dangled from her jaws, and she placed it gently on the ground next to Bramblekit. Fireheart knew at once that Goldenflower had seen his reaction, for the pale ginger queen wrapped her tail protectively around her kits and lifted her chin, as if she were challenging Fireheart to say something.

Fireheart felt a rush of guilt. What was he thinking of? He was the Clan deputy, for StarClan's sake! He knew he had to reassure Goldenflower that these kits would be cared for and respected like any other member's of ThunderClan. "Your . . . your kits look healthy," he stammered, but his fur prickled as the dark tabby kit stared up at him with unblinking amber eyes, the image of Tigerclaw's menacing glare.

Fireheart tried to push away the fear and anger that made him instinctively unsheathe his claws and press them against the hard ground. *It was Tigerclaw who betrayed ThunderClan*, he told himself. *Not this tiny kit.*

"It's Tawnykit's first time out of the nursery," Goldenflower told him. She glanced anxiously down at the little kit.

"They've grown quickly," Fireheart murmured.

Goldenflower leaned down and licked each kit on the head, then padded toward Fireheart. "I understand how you feel," she mewed quietly. "Your eyes have always betrayed your heart. But these are my kits and I will die to protect them if I have to." She looked up into Fireheart's eyes and he saw the intensity of her feeling in their yellow depths.

"I'm afraid for them, Fireheart," she went on. "The Clan will never forgive Tigerclaw—nor should they. But Bramble-kit and Tawnykit have done nothing wrong, and I will not let them be punished because of Tigerclaw. I'm not even going to tell them who their father was, just that he was a brave and powerful warrior."

Fireheart felt a pang of sympathy for the troubled queen. "They will be safe here," he promised, but the amber eyes of Bramblekit still made his paws prickle with unease as Goldenflower turned away.

Behind them Whitestorm squeezed out of the nursery. "Brindleface thinks her two remaining kits are ready to begin their training," he told Fireheart.

"Does Bluestar know?" Fireheart asked.

Whitestorm shook his head. "Brindleface wanted to share the news with Bluestar herself, but she hasn't visited the nursery in days."

Fireheart frowned. The Clan leader usually took an interest in every aspect of Clan life, especially the nursery. Every cat knew how important it was for ThunderClan to have fine, healthy kits.

"I suppose it's not surprising," Whitestorm continued. "She's still recovering from her wounds after the battle with the rogue cats."

"Shall I go and tell her now?" Fireheart offered.

"Yes. Some good news might cheer her up," Whitestorm remarked.

With a jolt, Fireheart realized that Whitestorm was as worried as he was about their leader. "I'm sure it will," he agreed. "ThunderClan hasn't had this many apprentices in moons."

"That reminds me," meowed Whitestorm, his eyes suddenly brightening. "Where's Cloudpaw? I thought he was fetching prey for the elders."

Fireheart glanced away awkwardly. "Er, yes, he is. I don't know what's taking him so long."

Whitestorm lifted a massive paw and gave it a lick. "The woods are not as safe as they once were," he murmured, as if he could read Fireheart's uneasy thoughts. "Don't forget WindClan and ShadowClan are still angry with us for sheltering Brokentail. They don't know yet that Brokentail is dead, and they might attack us again."

Brokentail had once been the leader of ShadowClan. He had nearly destroyed the other Clans in the forest with his greed for more territory. ThunderClan had helped to drive Brokentail out of his troubled Clan, but had later given him sanctuary as a blind and helpless prisoner—a merciful decision that had not been welcomed by his former enemies.

Fireheart knew that Whitestorm was warning him as carefully as possible—the warrior hadn't even mentioned the possibility that Tigerclaw might still be around—but his guilt at letting Cloudpaw go off alone made him defensive. "You let Brightpaw hunt alone this morning," he retorted.

"Yes. I told her to stay in the ravine and to be back by sunhigh." Whitestorm's tone was mild, but he stopped washing his paw and looked at Fireheart with concern in his eyes. "I hope Cloudpaw won't go too far from the camp."

Fireheart looked away and muttered, "I should go and tell Bluestar the kits are ready."

"Good idea," answered Whitestorm. "I can take Brightpaw out for some training. She hunts well, but her fighting skills need some work."

Silently cursing Cloudpaw, Fireheart padded away toward the Highrock. Outside Bluestar's den, he gave his ears a quick wash and put Cloudpaw out of his mind before calling a greeting through the lichen that draped the entrance. A soft "Enter" sounded from inside, and Fireheart pushed his way slowly in.

It was cool in the small cave, hollowed out of the base of the Highrock by an ancient stream. The sunlight that filtered through the lichen made the walls glow warmly. Bluestar sat hunched in her nest like a brooding duck. Her long gray fur was dirty and matted. *Perhaps her wounds are still too sore to wash properly*, Fireheart thought. His mind shied away from considering the other possibility—that his leader no longer wished to look after herself.

But the worry he had seen in Whitestorm's eyes pricked at him. Fireheart couldn't help noticing how thin Bluestar looked, and he remembered the half-eaten bird she'd abandoned last night, returning alone to her den instead of staying to share tongues with her senior warriors, as she'd used to.

The Clan leader raised her eyes as Fireheart entered, and he was relieved to see a faint spark of interest when she saw him.

"Fireheart," she greeted him, sitting up and lifting her chin. She held her broad gray head with the same dignity Fireheart had admired when he first met her in the woods near his old Twoleg home. It was Bluestar who had invited him to join the Clan, and her faith in him had quickly established a special bond between them.

"Bluestar," he began, respectfully dipping his head. "Whitestorm's been to the nursery today. Brindleface told him her kits are ready to begin their apprenticeships."

Bluestar slowly widened her eyes. "Already?" she murmured.

Fireheart waited for Bluestar to start giving orders for the apprentice ceremony. But the she-cat just stared at him.

"Er . . . who do you want to be their mentors?" he prompted.

"Mentors," echoed Bluestar faintly.

Fireheart's fur began to prickle with unease.

Suddenly a flinty hardness flared in her blue eyes. "Is there any cat we can trust to train these innocent kits?" she spat.

Fireheart flinched, too shocked to answer. The leader's eyes flashed once more. "Can *you* take them?" she demanded. "Or Graystripe?"

Fireheart shook his head, trying to push away the alarm that jabbed at him like an adder. Had Bluestar forgotten that

Graystripe was no longer part of ThunderClan? "I—I already have Cloudpaw. And Graystripe . . ." His words trailed away. He took a small, fast breath and began again. "Bluestar, the only warrior not fit to train these kits was Tigerclaw, and he has been exiled, remember? Any one of ThunderClan's warriors would make a fine mentor for Brindleface's kits." He searched Bluestar's face for a reaction, but she was staring unseeing at the floor of the den. "Brindleface is hoping to have a naming ceremony soon," he persisted. "Her kits are more than ready. Cloudpaw was their littermate, and he's been an apprentice for half a moon now."

Fireheart leaned forward, willing Bluestar to answer. At last the she-cat nodded her head briskly and lifted her eyes to Fireheart. With a wave of relief he saw the tension leave her shoulders. And although her gaze still seemed remote and icy, it was calmer now. "We'll have the naming ceremony before we eat this evening," she meowed, as if she had never doubted it.

"So who do you want to be their mentors?" Fireheart asked cautiously. He felt a tremor ripple through his tail as Bluestar stiffened again and her gaze darted anxiously around the cave.

"You decide."

Her reply was barely audible, and Fireheart decided not to press her any more. He dipped his head and meowed, "Yes, Bluestar," before backing out of the den.

He sat in the shade of the Highrock for a moment to gather his thoughts. Tigerclaw's treachery must have shaken her even more than he realized if she didn't trust any of her warriors now. Fireheart ducked his head to give his chest a reassuring lick. It was barely a quarter moon since the attack by the rogue cats. Bluestar would get over it, he told himself. Meanwhile, he had to hide her anxiety from the other cats. If the Clan was already uneasy, as Whitestorm had said, seeing Bluestar like this would only make them more alarmed.

Fireheart flexed his shoulder muscles and padded toward the nursery. "Hi, Willowpelt," he meowed as he reached the queen. The pale gray she-cat was lying on her side outside the thicket of brambles that sheltered the kits, enjoying the warmth of the sun.

She lifted her head as Fireheart stopped beside her. "Hi, Fireheart. How's life as a deputy?" Her eyes were gently curious and her voice was friendly, not challenging.

"Fine," Fireheart told her. *Or it would be, if I didn't have a pain in the neck for an apprentice*, he thought with frustration, *or the elders fretting about the wrath of StarClan, or a leader who can't even decide who should mentor Brindleface's kits.*

"Glad to hear it," purred Willowpelt. She twisted her head to wash her back.

"Is Brindleface around?" Fireheart asked.

"She's inside," Willowpelt meowed between licks.

"Thanks." Fireheart pushed his way into the brambles. It was surprisingly bright inside. Sunlight streamed through gaps in the twisted branches, and Fireheart told himself he would have to get the holes patched before the cold winds of leaf-fall.

"Hi, Brindleface," he meowed. "Good news! Bluestar says the naming ceremony for your kits will be this evening."

Brindleface was lying on her side while her two pale gray kits clambered over her. "Thank StarClan for that!" she grunted as the heavier of the kits, his fur speckled with dark flecks, sprang off his mother's flank and flung himself at his sister. "These two are getting too big for the nursery."

The kits tumbled over and rolled against their mother's back in a tangle of paws and tails. Brindleface gently shoved the kits away from her and asked, "Do you know who their mentors will be?"

Fireheart was already prepared for this question. "Bluestar hasn't decided yet," he explained. "Are there any warriors you'd prefer?"

Brindleface looked surprised. "Bluestar will know best; she should decide."

Fireheart knew as well as any cat that it was traditional for the Clan leader to select mentors. "Yes, you're right," he meowed heavily.

His fur prickled as the breeze carried the odor of Tigerclaw's tabby kit to his scent glands. "Where's Goldenflower?" he asked Brindleface, more sharply than he intended.

Her eyes widened. "She's taken her kits to meet the elders," she replied. She narrowed her eyes at Fireheart. "You recognize Tigerclaw in his son, don't you?"

Fireheart nodded uncomfortably.

"He has his father's looks, but that's all," Brindleface assured him. "He's gentle enough with the other kits, and his sister certainly keeps him in his place!"

"Well, that's good." Fireheart turned away. "I'll see you later at the ceremony," he meowed as he pushed his way back through the entrance.

"Does this mean Bluestar's decided when the naming ceremony should be?" Willowpelt called over to him when he appeared outside.

"Yes," he answered.

"Who will be their men . . . ?"

But Fireheart trotted away before he could hear the rest of Willowpelt's question. News of the naming ceremony would spread through the camp like forest fire, and every cat would want to know the same thing. Fireheart would have to decide soon, but his nostrils were still filled with the scent of Bramblekit, and his mind whirled as dark thoughts unfolded sinister wings within him.

Instinctively he headed for the fern tunnel that led to the medicine cat's clearing. Yellowfang's apprentice, Cinderpelt, would be there. Now that Graystripe had gone to live with RiverClan, Cinderpelt was Fireheart's closest friend. He knew that the gentle gray she-cat would be able to make sense of the confused emotions that seethed in his heart.

He quickened his pace through the cool ferns and emerged into the sunlit clearing. At one end loomed the flat face of a tall rock, split down the center. The niche in the middle of the stone was just large enough for Yellowfang to make her den and store her healing herbs.

Fireheart was about to call when Cinderpelt limped out

from the shadowy cleft in the rock. As ever, delight at seeing his friend was tempered by the pain of seeing the twisted hind leg that had prevented her from becoming a warrior. The young she-cat had been badly injured when she'd run onto the Thunderpath. Fireheart couldn't help feeling responsible, because Cinderpelt had been his apprentice when the accident happened. But as she recovered under the watchful eye of the Clan's medicine cat, Yellowfang had begun to teach her how to care for sick cats, taking her on as apprentice a moon and a half ago. Cinderpelt had found her place in the Clan at last.

A large bunch of herbs dangled from Cinderpelt's jaws as she limped into the clearing. Her face was creased in a worried frown, and she didn't even notice Fireheart standing at the tunnel entrance. She dropped the bundle on the sun-baked ground and began sorting fretfully though the leaves with her forepaws.

"Cinderpelt?" he meowed.

The little cat glanced up, surprised. "Fireheart! What are you doing here? Are you sick?"

Fireheart shook his head. "No. Is everything okay?"

Cinderpelt looked dejectedly at the pile of leaves in front of her, and Fireheart padded over and gave her a nuzzle. "What's the matter? Don't tell me you spilled mouse bile in Yellowfang's nest again?"

"No!" replied Cinderpelt indignantly. Then she lowered her eyes. "I should never have agreed to train as a medicine cat. I'm a disaster. I should have read the signs when I found that rotting bird!"

Fireheart remembered the moment that had happened after his naming ceremony. Cinderpelt had chosen a magpie from the fresh-kill pile to give to Bluestar, only to find that, beneath its soft feathers, it was crawling with maggots.

"Did Yellowfang think that was an omen about you?" Fireheart asked.

"Well, no," Cinderpaw admitted.

"So what makes you think you're not cut out to be a medicine cat?" He tried not to let his mind dwell on the fact that the rotting magpie could have been an omen about another cat—his leader, Bluestar.

Cinderpelt flicked her tail with frustration. "Yellowfang asked me to mix a poultice for her. Just a simple one for cleansing wounds. It was one of the first things she ever taught me, but now I've forgotten which herbs to put in it. She's going to think I'm an idiot!" Her voice rose to a wail and her blue eyes were huge and troubled.

"You're no idiot, and Yellowfang knows it," Fireheart told her robustly.

"But it's not the first dumb thing I've done lately. Yesterday I had to ask her the difference between foxglove and poppy seeds." Cinderpelt hung her head even lower. "Yellowfang said I was a danger to the Clan."

"Oh, you know what Yellowfang's like," Fireheart reassured her. "She's always saying things like that." Yellowfang had been ShadowClan's medicine cat and, although she had become part of ThunderClan after being exiled by their cruel leader, Brokentail, she still betrayed flashes of the fierce temper of a ShadowClan warrior. But one of the reasons she and Cinderpelt got on so well was that Cinderpelt was more than capable of standing up to Yellowfang's irritable outbursts.

Cinderpelt sighed. "I don't think I've got what it takes to become a medicine cat. I thought I was doing the right thing, becoming Yellowfang's apprentice, but it's no good. I just can't learn everything I need to know."

Fireheart crouched down until his eyes were level with Cinderpelt's. "This is about Silverstream, isn't it?" he meowed fiercely. He remembered the day at Sunningrocks when Graystripe's RiverClan queen had given birth before her time. Cinderpelt had tried desperately to save her, but Silverstream had lost too much blood. The beautiful silver tabby had died, although her newborn kits had survived.

Cinderpelt didn't reply, and Fireheart knew he was right. "You saved her kits!" he pointed out.

"But I lost *her*."

"You did everything you could." Fireheart leaned forward to lick Cinderpelt on her soft gray head. "Look, just ask Yellowfang what herbs to use in the poultice. She won't mind."

"I hope so." Cinderpelt sounded unconvinced. Then she gave herself a shake. "I need to stop feeling sorry for myself, don't I?"

"Yeah," Fireheart answered, flicking his tail at her.

"Sorry." Cinderpelt threw him a rueful look that glimmered with a hint of her old humor. "I don't suppose you've brought any fresh-kill with you?"

Fireheart shook his head. "Sorry. I just came to speak to you. Don't tell me Yellowfang's starving you?"

"No, but this medicine-cat thing is harder than you'd think," Cinderpelt replied. "I haven't had the chance to take any fresh-kill today." Her eyes flashed with curiosity. "What did you want to talk to me about?"

"Tigerclaw's kits." Fireheart felt the bleakness seep into his belly again. "Especially Bramblekit."

"Because he looks like his father?"

Fireheart winced. Were his feelings that easy to read? "I know I shouldn't judge him. He's just a kit. But when I saw him, it was as if Tigerclaw were looking at me. I . . . I couldn't move." Fireheart shook his head slowly, ashamed of his admission but glad of the chance to confide in his friend. "I don't know if I'll ever be able to trust him."

"If you see Tigerclaw every time you look at him, it's not surprising you feel like that," mewed Cinderpelt gently. "But you must look beyond the color of his pelt and try to see the cat inside. Remember, he's not just Tigerclaw's kit. There's some of Goldenflower in him too. And he will never know his father. It will be the Clan that raises him." She added, "You of all cats should know that you can't judge someone by the circumstances of their birth."

Cinderpelt was right. Fireheart had never let his kittypet roots interfere with his loyalty to the Clan. "Has StarClan spoken to you about Bramblekit?" he asked, knowing that Cinderpelt and Yellowfang would have studied Silverpelt at the moment of his birth.

His heart lurched uncomfortably as the gray cat looked away and murmured, "StarClan doesn't always share everything with me."

Fireheart knew Cinderpelt well enough to know she was holding something back. "But they shared *something* with you, right?"

Cinderpelt gazed up at him, her blue eyes steady. "His destiny will be as important as that of any kit born to ThunderClan," she mewed firmly.

Fireheart knew he wouldn't be able to make Cinderpelt reveal what StarClan had told her if she didn't want to. He decided to tell Cinderpelt about the other problem that was troubling him. "There's something else I wanted to talk to you about," he confessed. "I have to decide who should be the mentors for Brindleface's kits."

"Isn't that up to Bluestar?"

"She asked me to choose for her."

Cinderpelt lifted her head in surprise. "Why are you looking so worried, then? You should be flattered."

Flattered? Fireheart echoed silently, recalling the hostility and confusion in Bluestar's eyes. He shrugged. "Maybe. But I'm not sure who to pick."

"You must have some idea," Cinderpelt prompted him.

"Not a clue."

Cinderpelt frowned thoughtfully. "Well, how did you feel when I was named as your apprentice?"

Fireheart was caught off guard by the question. "Proud. And scared. And desperate to prove myself," he replied slowly.

"Which one of the warriors do you think wants to prove himself most?" Cinderpelt mewed.

Fireheart narrowed his eyes. An image of a brown tabby flashed in his mind. "Dustpelt." Cinderpelt nodded thoughtfully as he went on: "He must be dying to get his first apprentice. He was pretty close to Tigerclaw, so he'll want to prove his loyalty to the Clan now that Tigerclaw's been exiled. He's a good warrior, and I think he'll make a good mentor." Even as he spoke, Fireheart realized he had a more personal motive for choosing Dustpelt. The tabby's eyes had flashed enviously as Bluestar twice made Fireheart a mentor, first to Cinderpelt, then to Cloudpaw. Perhaps, Fireheart thought guiltily, giving Dustpelt an apprentice would soothe the warrior's jealousy and make him easier to get along with.

"Well, then, that's one chosen," Cinderpelt mewed encouragingly.

Fireheart looked down into the medicine cat's clear, wide eyes. She made it sound so simple.

"And what about the other?" asked Cinderpelt.

"The other what?" Yellowfang's rasping mew sounded from the fern tunnel, and the dark gray she-cat padded stiffly into the clearing. Fireheart turned to greet her. As usual, her long fur looked matted and dull, as if caring for the Clan left her no time for grooming, but her orange eyes gleamed, missing nothing.

"Bluestar's asked Fireheart to choose the mentors for Brindleface's kits," Cinderpelt explained.

"Oh, has she?" Yellowfang's eyes widened in surprise.

"Who've you come up with?"

"We've already chosen Dustpelt—" Fireheart began.

Yellowfang interrupted him. *"We've?"* she rasped. "Who's *we?*"

"Cinderpelt helped," he admitted.

"I'm sure Bluestar will be pleased that a cat who's barely begun her apprenticeship is making such important decisions for the Clan," Yellowfang remarked. She turned to Cinderpelt. "Have you finished mixing that poultice?"

Cinderpelt opened her mouth, then shook her head before wordlessly padding back to the pile of herbs in the middle of the clearing.

Yellowfang snorted as she watched her apprentice limp away. "That cat hasn't answered me back for days!" she complained to Fireheart. "There was a time when I couldn't get a word in edgewise. The sooner she gets back to normal, the better it'll be for both of us!" The old medicine cat frowned, then turned back to Fireheart. "Now, where were we?"

"Trying to decide who would be the second mentor to Brindleface's kits," Fireheart answered heavily.

"Who doesn't have an apprentice?" rasped Yellowfang.

"Well, Sandstorm," Fireheart replied. He couldn't help feeling it would be unfair to give Dustpelt an apprentice without giving Sandstorm one too. After all, the two cats had trained together and earned their warrior names at the same time.

"Do you think it would be wise to have two inexperienced mentors at the same time?" Yellowfang pointed out.

Fireheart shook his head.

"So is there a more experienced ThunderClan warrior who doesn't have an apprentice?" Yellowfang pressed him.

Darkstripe, Fireheart thought reluctantly. Every cat knew that Darkstripe had been one of Tigerclaw's closest friends, even if he had chosen to stay with the Clan when the traitor had been sent into exile. Fireheart realized that if he didn't choose Darkstripe to be a mentor, it might look as if he were taking revenge for the hostility that the warrior had shown him since he first came to ThunderClan. After all, Darkstripe was an obvious choice to take one of the apprentices.

Yellowfang must have seen the look of determination on Fireheart's face, for she meowed, "Right, that's sorted. Would you mind leaving me and my apprentice in peace now? We have work to do."

Fireheart pushed himself to his paws, his relief that he had found two mentors tempered by the uneasy feeling that, while the chosen cats' loyalty to the Clan was not in question, he was far less sure of their loyalty to him.

CHAPTER 3

"Have you seen Cloudpaw?" Fireheart emerged from the fern tunnel and called to Thornpaw, Mousefur's apprentice. The ginger tom was trotting toward the pile of fresh-kill with two mice dangling from his jaws. He shook his head, and Fireheart felt a flash of annoyance. Cloudpaw should have been back ages ago.

"All right. Take those mice straight to the elders," he ordered Thornpaw. The apprentice gave a muffled mew and padded quickly away.

Fireheart felt his tail bristle with anger at Cloudpaw, but he knew it was fear that made him so furious. *What if Tigerclaw has found him?* Feeling his alarm grow, Fireheart hurried to Bluestar's den. He would tell her his decision about the mentors and then he could go and look for Cloudpaw.

At the Highrock, Fireheart didn't pause to smooth his ruffled fur; he just called out and pushed his way through the lichen as soon as he heard Bluestar's reply. The ThunderClan leader was crouching in her nest where he had left her, staring at the wall.

"Bluestar," Fireheart began, dipping his head. "I thought Dustpelt and Darkstripe would be good mentors."

The elderly she-cat turned her head and looked at Fireheart, then heaved herself up onto her haunches. "Very well," she answered flatly.

A wave of disappointment broke over Fireheart. Bluestar looked as if she didn't care whom he chose. "Shall I send them to you so you can tell them the good news?" he asked. "They're out of the camp just now," he added. "But when they return, I can——"

"They're out of camp?" Bluestar's whiskers twitched. "Both of them?"

"They're on patrol," Fireheart explained uncomfortably.

"Where's Whitestorm?"

"Out training Brightpaw."

"And Mousefur?"

"Hunting with Brackenfur and Sandstorm."

"Are *all* the warriors out of camp?" Bluestar demanded.

Fireheart saw the muscles in her shoulders tense and his heart lurched. What was Bluestar afraid of? His thoughts darted back to Cloudpaw and the fear he had felt this morning in the silent forest. "The patrol's due back soon." Fireheart fought to stay calm as he tried to reassure his leader. "And I'm still here."

"Don't patronize me! I'm not some frightened kit!" spat Bluestar. Fireheart shrank back and she went on: "Make sure you stay in camp until the patrol returns. We've been attacked twice in the past moon. I don't want the camp to be left unguarded. In the future I want at least three warriors to remain in camp all the time."

Fireheart felt a chill shudder through his pelt. For once he did not dare meet his leader's eyes, afraid that he wouldn't recognize the cat he saw there. "Yes, Bluestar," he murmured quietly.

"When Darkstripe and Dustpelt return, send them to my den. I wish to speak to them before the ceremony."

"Of course."

"Now go!" Bluestar flicked her tail at him, as if she thought he was putting the Clan in danger by wasting time.

Fireheart backed out of the den. He sat down in the shade of the Highrock and twisted his head to lick the fur on his tail. What should he do? His pounding heart told him to race into the forest, find Cloudpaw, and bring him home to the safety of the camp. But Bluestar had ordered him to stay here until one of the patrols returned.

Just then he heard the crashing of cats through the undergrowth outside the camp and he smelled the familiar scents of Darkstripe, Runningwind, and Dustpelt on the warm air. Their pawsteps slowed as they trotted through the gorse entrance, Runningwind leading the way.

Fireheart sprang to his paws with relief. Now he could leave the camp and find Cloudpaw. He hurried across the clearing to meet them. "How did the patrol go?" he called.

"No signs of the other Clans," reported Runningwind.

"But we did smell your apprentice," added Darkstripe. "Near Twolegplace."

"Did you see him?" Fireheart meowed as casually as he could.

Darkstripe shook his head.

"I expect he was looking for birds in one of the Twoleg gardens." Dustpelt smirked. "They're probably more to his taste."

Fireheart ignored Dustpelt's kittypet jibe. "Was the scent fresh?" he asked Runningwind.

"Fairly. We lost his trail when we started to head back to camp."

Fireheart nodded. At least he had an idea where to begin looking for Cloudpaw. "Darkstripe and Dustpelt," he meowed, "Bluestar wants to see you in her den." As the warriors padded away, Fireheart wondered whether to go with them, just in case Bluestar was still acting strangely. Then he noticed that Runningwind was leading Thornpaw toward the camp entrance. "Where are you going?" he called anxiously. Bluestar wanted three warriors to remain in camp; he couldn't go and look for Cloudpaw if Runningwind was going out again.

"I promised Mousefur I'd teach Thornpaw how to catch squirrels this afternoon," Runningwind meowed over his shoulder.

"But I . . ." Fireheart's voice trailed away as the lean warrior eyed him curiously. He couldn't bring himself to admit how worried he was about Cloudpaw. He shook his head. "Nothing," he meowed, and Runningwind and Thornpaw disappeared into the gorse tunnel. A twinge of guilt shot through Fireheart as he watched Mousefur's apprentice padding obediently after the warrior. Why couldn't he inspire that sort of behavior in his own apprentice?

⚜   ⚜   ⚜

The rest of the afternoon dragged. Fireheart settled himself beside the nettle clump outside the warriors' den and strained his ears, scanning the sounds of the forest for any sign of Cloudpaw's return. But the fear that Bluestar had stirred in him had eased slightly since Darkstripe reported scenting only the young apprentice on the patrol, and no intruders in ThunderClan territory.

As the sun began to sink below the treetops, the hunting party returned. It was followed by Whitestorm and Brightpaw, drawn away from the training hollow, no doubt, by the scent of fresh-kill. Longtail and Swiftpaw returned soon afterward, but there was still no sign of Cloudpaw.

There was plenty of prey to go around, but no cat approached the pile. News of the naming ceremony had spread through the camp. Fireheart could hear Thornpaw, Brightpaw, and Swiftpaw whispering in excited mews outside their den until Bluestar padded out from her cave, when they hushed one another and looked up with huge, expectant eyes.

The ThunderClan leader leaped onto the Highrock in a single, easy bound. She had clearly recovered from her physical injuries after the battle with the rogue cats, but Fireheart didn't know whether to feel relieved or worried by this. Why hadn't her mind recovered as quickly as her body? His heart quickened as she raised her chin, preparing to call the Clan together. Her voice sounded dry and cracked, as if it had grown brittle from lack of use, but as she yowled the familiar words, Fireheart felt his confidence return.

The sinking sun glowed on his flame-colored fur, and he thought of his own naming ceremony, when he had first joined the Clan. Proudly squaring his shoulders Fireheart took the deputy's place at the head of the clearing below the Highrock, while the rest of the Clan gathered in a circle around the edge. Darkstripe sat calmly at the front, staring ahead with unblinking eyes. Dustpelt sat stiffly beside him, unable to suppress the excitement that shone from his eyes.

"We are here today to give two Clan kits their apprentice names," Bluestar began formally, glancing down to where Brindleface sat with a kit on either side of her. Fireheart hardly recognized the boisterous gray kits he'd seen wrestling in the nursery earlier. They looked much smaller out here, with their fur neatly groomed. One of them leaned toward its mother, its whiskers trembling with nervous excitement. The larger kit kneaded the ground with its paws.

An expectant hush fell over the rest of the Clan.

"Come forward," Fireheart heard Bluestar's voice command from above.

The kits padded side by side to the center of the clearing, their mottled gray coats bristling with anticipation.

"Dustpelt," rasped Bluestar. "You will be mentor to Ashpaw."

Fireheart watched as Dustpelt walked toward the larger gray kit and stood beside him.

"Dustpelt," Bluestar went on, "this will be your first apprentice. Share your courage and determination with him. I know you will train him well, but don't be afraid to turn to the senior warriors for advice."

Dustpelt's eyes gleamed with pride, and he leaned down to touch Ashpaw's nose with his own. Ashpaw purred loudly as he followed his new mentor to the edge of the circle.

The smaller kit remained in the center of the clearing, her eyes shining and her little chest quivering. Fireheart caught her eye and blinked warmly at her. The kit stared back at him as though her life depended on it.

"Darkstripe." Bluestar paused when she meowed the warrior's name. Fireheart's spine tingled as he saw a glimmer of fear flash in the leader's eyes. He held his breath, but Bluestar blinked away her doubt and went on. "You will be mentor to Fernpaw." The kit's eyes widened, and she spun around to see the big tabby warrior padding toward her.

"Darkstripe," meowed Bluestar, "you are intelligent and bold. Pass on all you can to this young apprentice."

"Certainly," promised Darkstripe. He bent to touch noses with Fernpaw, who seemed to shrink back for a heartbeat before stretching up to accept his greeting. As the new apprentice followed Darkstripe to the edge of the clearing, she cast an anxious look over her shoulder at Fireheart. He nodded back encouragingly.

The other cats began congratulating the two new apprentices, crowding around them and calling them by their new names. Fireheart was just about to join them when he caught sight of a white pelt slipping into the camp. Cloudpaw had returned.

Fireheart hurried to meet him. "Where have you been?" he demanded.

Cloudpaw dropped the vole that was clamped between his jaws. "Hunting."

"Is that all you could find? You caught more than that during leaf-bare!"

Cloudpaw shrugged. "It's better than nothing."

"What about the pigeon you caught this morning?" Fireheart asked.

"Didn't you bring that back?"

"It was *your* catch!" Fireheart spat.

Cloudpaw sat down and curled his tail over his front paws. "I suppose I'll have to fetch it in the morning," he mewed.

"Yes," agreed Fireheart, exasperated by Cloudpaw's indifference. "And until then you can go hungry. Go and put that"—he flicked his nose at the vole—"on the fresh-kill pile."

Cloudpaw shrugged again, picked up the vole, and padded away.

Fireheart turned, still furious, and saw Whitestorm standing behind him.

"He'll learn when he's ready," meowed the white warrior softly.

"I hope so," Fireheart muttered.

"Have you decided who's going to lead the dawn patrol?" Whitestorm asked, diplomatically changing the subject.

Fireheart hesitated. He hadn't even thought about it, or the rest of the patrols and hunting parties for the next day. He'd been too busy worrying about Cloudpaw.

"Give it some thought," meowed Whitestorm, turning away. "There's plenty of time yet."

"I'll lead the patrol," Fireheart decided quickly. "I'll take Longtail and Mousefur."

"Good idea," purred Whitestorm. "Shall I tell them?" He glanced over at the fresh-kill pile, where the cats were beginning to gather.

"Yes," answered Fireheart. "Thanks."

He watched the white warrior head toward the pile, feeling his own belly growl with hunger. He was about to follow when he noticed another white pelt, longer-haired and the color of fresh snow, mingling with the cats around the fresh-kill pile. Cloudpaw had obviously disobeyed Fireheart's orders to keep away from the sharing of prey. Fury flashed through Fireheart, but he stayed where he was, his paws as heavy as stone. He didn't want to argue with Cloudpaw in front of the rest of the Clan.

As Fireheart watched, Cloudpaw picked out a fat mouse and bumped into Whitestorm. Fireheart saw the white warrior glare sternly at Cloudpaw and heard him murmur something—he couldn't tell what, but Cloudpaw dropped the mouse at once and slunk back toward his den with his tail down.

Fireheart quickly turned his head away, embarrassed that he hadn't confronted Cloudpaw before the senior warrior. Suddenly he didn't feel hungry anymore. He saw Bluestar lying under a clump of ferns beside the warriors' den and longed to share his worries about his disobedient apprentice with his old mentor. But the haunted look had returned to her eyes as she picked halfheartedly at a small thrush. Fireheart felt a sadness like ice in his heart as he watched the ThunderClan leader heave herself to her paws and walk slowly toward her den, leaving the thrush untouched.

CHAPTER 4

Soft paws padded through Fireheart's dreams that night. A tortoiseshell she-cat emerged from the forest beside him, her amber eyes glowing. Fireheart gazed at Spottedleaf and felt the familiar ache in his heart. The pain of the medicine cat's death, so many moons ago, was as raw as ever. He waited eagerly for her gentle greeting, but this time Spottedleaf didn't press her nose to his cheek as she usually did. Instead she turned from him and walked away. Surprised Fireheart began to follow, breaking into a run to chase the dappled cat through the woods. He called out to her, but even though her pace hadn't seemed to quicken, she stayed ahead of him, deaf to his cries.

Without warning, a dark gray shape loomed out from behind a tree. It was Bluestar, and the eyes of the ThunderClan leader were wide with fear. Fireheart swerved to avoid her, desperately trying to keep Spottedleaf in sight, but then Cloudpaw leaped at him from the ferns that lined the other side of the path, knocking him over. Lying winded for a moment, Fireheart could feel Whitestorm's eyes burning through his fur as the white warrior watched him from the branches of a tree.

Fireheart scrambled to his paws and raced after Spottedleaf

once more. She was still several fox-lengths ahead, padding steadily on without even turning to see who called her. Now the rest of ThunderClan had gathered along Fireheart's path. As he dodged and weaved through them, they called out to him—he couldn't make out their words, but their voices formed a deafening chorus of mews, questioning, criticizing, begging for help. The meows grew louder and louder until they drowned out his own cry so that even if she were listening, Spottedleaf could not have heard.

"Fireheart!" One voice sounded above the others. It was Whitestorm. "Mousefur and Longtail are waiting to leave. Wake up, Fireheart!"

Half-dreaming, clouded with sleep, Fireheart pulled himself to his paws. "W-what?" he meowed groggily.

Early morning light was streaming into the warriors' den. Whitestorm stood beside him in the empty nest where Graystripe used to sleep. "The patrol is waiting," he repeated. "And Bluestar wants to see you before you go."

Fireheart shook his head to clear his mind. The dream had frightened him. Spottedleaf had always been closer to him in dreams than she had been even in life. Her behavior last night stung like the bite of an adder. Was the gentle medicine cat abandoning him?

Fireheart leaned back to stretch, his legs trembling beneath him. "Tell Mousefur and Longtail I'll be as quick as I can." He slipped quickly past the slumbering bodies of the other warriors. Brindleface was sleeping near the wall of the den with Frostfur curled beside her; both she-cats had returned to their lives as warriors now that their kits had left the nursery.

Fireheart pushed his way out into the clearing. It was already warm even though the sun had not yet risen over the treetops, and the woods looked green and inviting at the top of the ravine. As he sniffed the familiar scents of the forest, the pain of Fireheart's dream began to fade, and he felt his fur relax on his shoulders.

Longtail and Mousefur were waiting at the camp entrance. Fireheart nodded to them as he headed toward Bluestar's den. What could the ThunderClan leader want so early in the day? Did she have a special mission for him? Fireheart couldn't help feeling it was a sign that Bluestar was feeling more like her old self, and he called a cheerful greeting through the lichen.

"Come in!" The Clan leader sounded excited, and Fireheart's hopes soared. Inside, Bluestar was pacing up and down the sandy floor. She didn't stop when Fireheart entered, and he had to press himself against the wall to keep out of her way.

"Fireheart," she began without looking at him. "I need to share dreams with StarClan. I must travel to the Moonstone." The Moonstone was a glittering rock that lay deep underground beyond WindClan territory, where the sun set.

"You want to go to Highstones?" Fireheart exclaimed, surprised.

"Do you know of another Moonstone?" retorted Bluestar impatiently. She was still pacing, her paws echoing in the den.

"But it's such a long way; are you sure you're up to it?" Fireheart stammered.

"I must speak with StarClan!" Bluestar insisted. She stopped dead and narrowed her eyes at her deputy. "And I want you to come. Whitestorm can take charge while we're gone."

Fireheart's unease was growing rapidly. "Who else is coming with us?"

"No one," answered Bluestar grimly.

Fireheart shivered. He felt bewildered by the dark intensity in Bluestar's tone; it sounded as if she thought her life depended on making this journey. "But isn't it a bit dangerous to travel by ourselves?" he ventured.

Bluestar turned an icy gaze on Fireheart. His mouth turned dry as the she-cat hissed at him, "You want to bring others? Why?"

Fireheart tried to keep his voice steady. "What if we're attacked?"

"You will protect me," Bluestar rasped in a low whisper. "Won't you?"

"With my life!" Fireheart promised solemnly. No matter what he thought about Bluestar's behavior, his loyalty to his leader was unshaken.

His words seemed to reassure Bluestar, and she sat down in front of him. "Good."

Fireheart tipped his head to one side. "But what about the threat from WindClan and ShadowClan?" he meowed hesitantly. "You mentioned it yourself yesterday."

Bluestar nodded slowly. Fireheart went on; "We'd have to

travel through WindClan's territory to get to Highstones."

Bluestar leaped to her paws. "I *must* speak with StarClan," she spat, the fur on her shoulders bristling. "Why are you trying to dissuade me? Either you come with me or I will go alone!"

Fireheart looked back at her. He had no choice. "I'll come," he agreed.

"Good." Bluestar nodded again, her voice softening a little. "We'll need traveling herbs to keep our strength up. I'll go and see Yellowfang about them." She swept past Fireheart and pushed her way out of the cave.

"Are we going *now*?" Fireheart called.

"Yes," Bluestar replied, without stopping.

Fireheart bounded out of the den after her. "But I'm meant to lead the dawn patrol," he protested.

"Send them off without you," ordered Bluestar.

"Okay." Fireheart stopped and watched the she-cat disappear into the ferns that led to Yellowfang's clearing. He felt very uneasy as he padded toward the camp entrance where Longtail and Mousefur were waiting. Longtail was flicking his tail impatiently, while Mousefur had settled onto her belly and watched Fireheart approach through half-closed eyes.

"What's going on?" Longtail demanded. "Why's Bluestar going to see Yellowfang? Is she okay?"

"She's going to get traveling herbs. Bluestar needs to share with StarClan, so we're going to the Moonstone," Fireheart explained.

"That's a long way," remarked Mousefur, slowly sitting up.

"Is it wise? Bluestar's probably still weak from the rogue cats' attack." Fireheart couldn't help noticing that she tactfully avoided mentioning Tigerclaw's part in the attack.

"She told me that StarClan has summoned her," he answered.

"Who else is going?" asked Longtail.

"Just me and Bluestar."

"I'll come too, if you like," offered Mousefur.

Fireheart shook his head regretfully.

Longtail's mouth twisted into a sneer. "You think you can protect her alone, do you? You may be deputy, but you're no Tigerclaw!" he hissed.

"And it's a good thing he's not!" Relief washed over Fireheart as he heard Whitestorm's voice behind him. The white warrior must have heard the whole conversation, because he went on: "Fireheart and Bluestar are less likely to be noticed if they travel together like this. Quite apart from the fact that they're allowed safe passage to Highstones any-way, they're more likely to appear like a raiding party to WindClan if there's more than two of them."

Mousefur nodded, but Longtail turned his head away. Fireheart blinked gratefully at Whitestorm.

"Yellowfang!" Bluestar's agitated meow sounded from the medicine cat's den.

"Go to her," meowed Whitestorm quietly. "I'll lead the patrol."

"But Bluestar wants you to take charge of the Clan while we're gone," Fireheart told him.

"In that case, I'll stay here and organize today's hunting parties. Mousefur can lead the patrol."

"Yes," agreed Fireheart, trying not to show how flustered he felt. He turned to Mousefur. "Take Thornpaw with you," he ordered.

Mousefur dipped her head as Fireheart turned and ran across the clearing to the medicine cat's den.

"I suppose you'll be wanting some traveling herbs too," remarked Yellowfang as Fireheart emerged from the tunnel. The old medicine cat was sitting calmly in the clearing while Bluestar paced restlessly around, lost in her own thoughts.

"Yes, please," answered Fireheart.

Cinderpelt limped out of the den in the split rock and made straight for Yellowfang without stopping to greet Fireheart. "Which one is chamomile?" she whispered into the medicine cat's ragged ear.

"You must know that by now!" Yellowfang hissed crossly.

Cinderpelt's ears twitched. "I thought I knew, and then I wasn't sure. I just thought I'd check."

Yellowfang snorted, heaved herself to her paws, and went over to the foot of the rock, where several small piles of herbs were lying in a row.

Fireheart glanced at Bluestar. She had stopped pacing and was staring up at the sky, warily sniffing the air. Fireheart padded after Yellowfang. "Chamomile's not a traveling herb," he meowed under his breath.

Yellowfang narrowed her eyes. "Bluestar needs something

to soothe her heart as well as to give her physical strength."
She glanced scathingly at Cinderpelt and added, "I was hoping to add it to the traveling herbs without telling the whole
camp!" She pushed one of the piles with a heavy paw. "That's
chamomile."

"Yes, I remember now," Cinderpelt mewed meekly.

"You shouldn't have forgotten in the first place," scolded
Yellowfang. "A medicine cat has no time for doubt. Put your
energy into *today* and stop worrying about the past. You have
a duty to your Clan. Stop dithering and get on with it!"

Fireheart couldn't help feeling sorry for the young cat. He
tried to catch her eye, but Cinderpelt wouldn't look at him.
Instead she busied herself with preparing the traveling con-
coction, pawing small amounts from each pile of herbs and
mixing them together while Yellowfang watched with a concerned frown.

Behind them Bluestar had begun to pace the clearing
again. "Aren't they ready yet?" she meowed irritably.

Fireheart padded over to Bluestar's side. "Nearly," he told
her. "Don't worry. We'll make it to Highstones by sunset."
Bluestar blinked at him as Cinderpelt limped up with a bundle
of herbs.

"These are yours," she mewed, dropping the mixed leaves
at Bluestar's paws. She jerked her head toward the rock.
"Yours are over there," she told Fireheart.

He was still swallowing to wash the bitter taste of the herbs
from his mouth when Bluestar headed out of the clearing,

nodding to Fireheart to follow her. Around them, the camp was beginning to stir. Willowpelt had just squeezed out of the nursery and was blinking in the bright sunlight, while Patchpelt was stretching his old limbs in front of the fallen oak. Both cats glanced curiously at Bluestar and Fireheart, then carried on with their morning routine.

"Hey!"

Fireheart heard a familiar voice behind him and his heart sank. It was Cloudpaw, scampering out of his den with his fur standing on end, ungroomed after a night's sleep. "Where are you going? Can I come?"

Fireheart paused at the tunnel entrance. "Don't you have a pigeon to collect?"

"The pigeon can wait. I bet some owl's flown off with it by now anyway," answered Cloudpaw. "Let me come with you, please!"

"Owls eat *live* prey," Fireheart corrected him. He caught sight of Runningwind padding sleepily out of the warriors' den and called across the clearing to the brown tom. "Runningwind, will you take Cloudpaw hunting this morning?" He caught a flash of resentment in the warrior's eyes as Runningwind nodded unenthusiastically. Fireheart remembered how willingly Runningwind had taken Thornpaw out to catch squirrels the day before; clearly the warrior wasn't as fond of Cloudpaw, and frankly Fireheart didn't blame him. His apprentice wasn't trying hard enough to earn the respect of these Clan cats.

"That's not fair," whined Cloudpaw. "I went hunting yesterday. Can't I come with you?"

"No. Today you will hunt with Runningwind!" Fireheart snapped. Before Cloudpaw could argue any more, he turned and raced after Bluestar.

CHAPTER 5

The ThunderClan leader had reached the top of the ravine by the time Fireheart caught up with her. She paused to sniff the air before padding into the forest. Fireheart noticed with relief how relaxed she seemed now that they were out of the camp, nosing her way through the undergrowth toward the RiverClan border.

Fireheart glanced in surprise at the she-cat. This wasn't the quickest route to Fourtrees and the uplands beyond, but he didn't question her. He couldn't help feeling excited at the thought that he might catch a glimpse of Graystripe across the river.

The two cats met the RiverClan border above Sunning-rocks and followed the scent markers upriver. A warm breeze carried the faint heather scent of the moor down to them. Fireheart could hear the river flowing past on the other side of the ferns. He craned his neck and saw the water glimmering in the dappled light under the trees. Above his head the leaves glowed green and flashed at the edges where the sunlight pierced the thick roof of the forest. Even in the shade, Fireheart felt hot. He wished he could plunge into the water like a RiverClan cat, to cool himself down.

Finally the river bent away, deeper into RiverClan territory, and Bluestar carried straight on, following the markers along the border between ThunderClan and RiverClan. Fireheart couldn't stop glancing across the scentline, searching the woods beyond for any sign of RiverClan cats, wary of being spotted by a patrol but ever hopeful of seeing his old friend. Bluestar was leading them recklessly close to the border, even crossing it occasionally as they weaved through the under-growth. Fireheart had no idea how RiverClan would react if they found them here. The two Clans had nearly come to conflict over Silverstream's kits, and battle was averted only when Graystripe took his kits back to their mother's Clan.

Suddenly Bluestar stopped and lifted her muzzle, opening her mouth to taste the air. She dropped into a crouch, and Fireheart, trusting Bluestar's warrior instincts, flattened himself too, ducking behind a patch of nettles.

"RiverClan warriors," Bluestar warned in a whisper.

Fireheart could smell them now. He felt his hackles rising as the scent grew stronger and he heard the swish of fur dis-turbing the undergrowth ahead of them. He raised his head very slowly and peered through the trees, his heart thumping as he searched for a familiar gray pelt. Beside him, Bluestar's eyes were wide and her flanks barely moved as she took silent, shallow breaths. *Was she hoping to see Graystripe too?* Fireheart wondered. It hadn't occurred to him before now that Bluestar might also want to run into some RiverClan cats. It would certainly explain why she had come this way.

But Fireheart couldn't believe that it was Graystripe she wanted to see. Yesterday, in her confusion, she'd forgotten that the gray warrior had left the Clan, and Fireheart sensed that Bluestar's mind was spinning with other thoughts. Then it hit him like a fledgling dropping into his paws: her kits. Many moons ago, the ThunderClan leader had given birth to two kits that had been raised in RiverClan. She'd entrusted them to their RiverClan father when they were barely old enough to leave their nest. Bluestar's ambition and loyalty to her Clan had made it impossible for her to raise the kits herself. Now they lived as RiverClan warriors, unaware that their real mother came from ThunderClan. But Bluestar had never forgotten them, although only Fireheart knew her secret. It must be Stonefur and Mistyfoot that Bluestar was scanning the undergrowth for.

A glimpse of tawny mottled fur in the distance made Fireheart duck down again. That wasn't Graystripe, or either of Bluestar's offspring. A vaguely familiar scent confirmed to Fireheart the identity of the warrior. It was Leopardfur, the RiverClan deputy.

Fireheart glanced at Bluestar; she still had her head up, peering through the trees. The rustling of ferns warned Fireheart that Leopardfur was getting nearer. He felt his breath quicken. What would happen if she saw the ThunderClan leader so close to the RiverClan border?

Fireheart froze as the rustling in the bushes grew louder. He heard the RiverClan deputy stop, and her silence told him she had detected something. Staring desperately at Bluestar he was about to signal to her with his tail when she dropped her head and hissed in his ear, "Come on; we'd better head deeper into our own territory."

Fireheart sighed with relief as the ThunderClan leader crept silently away. Keeping his ears flat and his belly to the ground, Fireheart followed her away from the scent markers and into the safety of ThunderClan's woods.

"That Leopardfur moves so loudly, I should think even ShadowClan heard her coming," remarked Bluestar once they were away from the border. Fireheart's whiskers quivered with surprise. He had begun to wonder if Bluestar had forgotten how fiercely the Clans defended their boundaries, especially in these difficult times.

"She's a good warrior, but too easily distracted," Bluestar went on calmly. "She was more interested in that rabbit upwind than looking for enemy warriors."

Fireheart couldn't help feeling cheered by his leader's confidence. Now that he thought about it, there had been the scent of rabbit on the breeze, but he'd been too worried about Leopardfur to take any notice of it.

"This reminds me of the days I used to take you for training," purred Bluestar as she padded through the sun-dappled woods.

Fireheart ran to catch up with her. "Me too," he replied.

"You were a fast learner. I chose well when I invited you into my Clan," Bluestar murmured. She looked back over her shoulder at Fireheart, and he saw pride in her eyes. He blinked gratefully at her.

"All the Clans have much to thank you for," Bluestar continued. "You drove Brokentail out of ShadowClan, brought WindClan home from exile, helped RiverClan when they were flooded, and saved ThunderClan from Tigerclaw." Fireheart began to feel a little overwhelmed by her praise as she went on: "No other warrior has your sense of fairness or loyalty or courage. . . ."

Fireheart's fur pricked uneasily. "But all the ThunderClan cats respect the warrior code as I do," he pointed out. "Every one of them would sacrifice themselves to protect you and the Clan."

Bluestar stopped in her tracks and turned to look at Fireheart. "You are the only cat who dared oppose Tigerclaw," she reminded him.

"But I was the only one who knew that he killed Redtail!" Fireheart had still been an apprentice when he had found out that the ThunderClan warrior had been responsible for the death of Bluestar's loyal deputy. But he had been unable to prove Tigerclaw's murderous secret until the traitor had led the rogue cats against his own Clan.

A fiery resentment flashed in Bluestar's eyes. "Graystripe knew too. It was only you who saved me!"

Fireheart looked away, lost for words. His ears twitched uncomfortably. It looked as if Bluestar didn't trust any of her warriors except him and maybe Whitestorm. Fireheart realized that Tigerclaw had done more damage than any of the Clan could possibly imagine. The dark warrior had poisoned their leader's judgment and drained away all her confidence in her warriors.

"Come on!" snapped Bluestar.

Fireheart watched the gray she-cat stalk away through the forest, her shoulders stiff and her tail fluffed up. He shivered. Although the sky was still bright overhead, he felt as if a black cloud had blotted out the sun and cast an ominous shadow over their journey.

They reached Fourtrees as the sun broke through the leaves at the top of the trees. Fireheart followed Bluestar down the slope into the valley, where the four great oaks stood, guarding the place where the Clans met each full moon under a single night's truce. The two cats passed the Great Rock where the leaders of each Clan stood to address the Gathering, and headed up the far side of the valley.

As the grassy hill turned steeper and rockier, Fireheart noticed that Bluestar was struggling to keep up the pace. She grunted each time she jumped onto the next rock, and Fireheart had to slow down so that he didn't pass her.

At the top of the slope, Bluestar stopped and sat down, wheezing.

"Are you okay?" Fireheart asked.

"Not so young . . ." panted Bluestar.

Fireheart felt a pang of worry. He had assumed that her physical injuries from the battle had healed. Where had this sudden weakness come from? It made her seem older and more vulnerable than ever. *Perhaps it's just climbing in this heat,* he thought hopefully. *After all, her pelt is thicker than mine.*

While Bluestar caught her breath, Fireheart peered nervously across the stunted gorse and heather that covered the uplands. This was WindClan territory, stretching away from them under the cloudless sky. He felt even uneasier here than on the RiverClan border. WindClan was still angry with ThunderClan because they had given sanctuary to the former ShadowClan leader, and it was Bluestar herself who had decided to take in the blinded Brokentail. What would a WindClan patrol do if they found the ThunderClan leader on their territory, with only one warrior to guard her? Fireheart wasn't sure if he could protect his leader against a whole patrol.

"We must be careful not to be spotted," he whispered.

"What did you say?" called Bluestar. The breeze was stronger up here, and even though it did nothing to ease the sun's burning heat, it carried Fireheart's words away.

"We must be careful they don't see us!" Fireheart reluctantly raised his voice.

"Why?" Bluestar demanded. "We're traveling to the Moonstone. StarClan has granted us the right to travel safely!"

Fireheart realized it would be a waste of time to argue. "I'll lead the way," he offered.

He knew the uplands well, better than most ThunderClan cats. He'd been here many times before, but he'd never felt as exposed and vulnerable as he did now. Quickly he led

Bluestar into the sea of heather, praying that StarClan had as much belief in their right to travel here as Bluestar did, and that their warrior ancestors would protect them from any passing WindClan patrols. He also hoped that Bluestar had enough sense to keep her ears and tail low.

The sun was reaching its highest point as they neared the swathe of gorse at the heart of WindClan's territory. Fourtrees was far behind them, but there was still a long way to go before they reached the slope at the edge of the moor that ran down into Twoleg farmland. Fireheart paused. A hot breeze was blowing toward him, as stifling as the breath of a sick cat, and he knew their scent would be carried back through WindClan territory. He just hoped the perfume of the honey-rich heather would mask it. Beside him, Bluestar signaled with a flick of her tail and vanished into the gorse.

An angry yowl sounded from behind them. Fireheart spun around and backed away, wincing as the gorse pricked his haunches. Three WindClan cats faced him, their fur bristling and their ears flattened.

"Intruders. Why are you here?" hissed a mottled dark brown tabby. Fireheart recognized Mudclaw, one of the senior warriors. A gray tabby warrior called Tornear was beside him, his back arched and his claws unsheathed. Fireheart had grown to know and respect these cats when he had escorted WindClan back from their exile in Twoleg territory, but all traces of their former alliance had vanished now. He didn't recognize the smallest cat—an apprentice, perhaps, but every bit as fierce-looking and wiry as his Clanmates.

The fur rose along Fireheart's spine and his heart began to pound, but he tried to stay calm. "We're just traveling through——" he began.

"You are on our land," spat Mudclaw. His eyes shone angrily as he stared at Fireheart.

Where was Bluestar? Fireheart thought desperately, half wanting her support, half hoping she hadn't heard Mudclaw's yowl and was heading safely through the gorse toward Twoleg territory.

A snarl at his side told him she had returned for him. He glanced quickly to see Bluestar standing at the edge of the gorse with her head held high and her eyes blazing with fury. "We are traveling to Highstones. StarClan grants us safe passage. You have no right to stop us!"

Mudclaw didn't flinch. "You gave up your rights to StarClan's protection when you took Brokentail into your Clan!" he retorted.

Fireheart could understand the WindClan cats' anger. He had seen for himself the misery they had endured when they were driven out by Brokentail's Clan warriors. With a surge of pity he remembered the tiny WindClan kit he'd helped to carry home—it had been the only one of its litter to survive. The former ShadowClan leader had nearly destroyed the Clan with his cruelty.

Fireheart stared into Mudclaw's fierce gaze. "Brokentail is dead," he told him.

Mudclaw's eyes glittered. "You killed him?" he demanded.

As Fireheart hesitated, Bluestar growled menacingly from his side. "Of course we didn't kill him. ThunderClan aren't murderers."

"No," Mudclaw spat back. "You just protect them!" The WindClan warrior arched his back aggressively.

Disappointed, Fireheart felt his mind whirl as he tried to think of another way to convince WindClan.

"You will let us pass!" Bluestar hissed. Fireheart froze as he saw his leader flexing her claws and raising her hackles, ready to attack.

CHAPTER 6

❧

"StarClan grants us safe passage," Bluestar repeated stubbornly.

"Go home!" snarled Mudclaw.

Fireheart's paws tingled as he sized up their opponents. Three strong cats against him and the unfit ThunderClan leader. They would not escape a fight without serious injury, and there was no way he could risk Bluestar's losing a life—not when he knew that she was on the last of her nine lives, which were granted by StarClan to all Clan leaders.

"We should go home," Fireheart hissed at Bluestar. The she-cat swung her head around and stared at him in disbelief. "We're too far from safety and this isn't a battle we can fight," he urged her.

"But I must speak with StarClan!" meowed Bluestar.

"Another time," Fireheart insisted. Bluestar's eyes clouded with indecision and he added, "We'd not win this battle."

He twitched with relief as Bluestar retracted her claws and let the fur on her shoulders relax. The ThunderClan leader turned back to Mudclaw and meowed, "Very well, we'll go home. But we will return. You cannot cut us off from StarClan forever!"

Mudclaw flattened his back and replied, "You've made a wise decision."

Fireheart growled at Mudclaw. "Did you hear what Bluestar said?" Mudclaw narrowed his eyes threateningly, but Fireheart went on: "We will leave this time, but you will never again stop us from traveling to the Moonstone."

Mudclaw turned away. "We'll escort you back to Fourtrees."

Fireheart tensed, afraid of how Bluestar would react to the suggestion that the WindClan warrior did not trust the ThunderClan cats to leave his territory. But she simply padded forward, brushing past the WindClan cats as she headed back the way they had come.

Fireheart walked after her, followed at a distance by the WindClan cats. He was aware of them rustling through the heather behind him, and when he looked over his shoulder he caught glimpses of their lithe, brown shapes among the purple flowers. Frustration pricked at his paws with every step. He would not let WindClan block their way again.

They reached Fourtrees and began to climb back down the rocky slope, leaving the WindClan warriors at the top watching them with hostile, narrowed eyes. Bluestar was starting to look very tired. With each leap she landed heavily and grunted. Fireheart was frightened the she-cat would slip, but she kept her footing until they reached the grass at the bottom. Fireheart looked back up the hill to see the three WindClan cats silhouetted against the wide, glaring sky before they turned and vanished back into their own territory.

As the ThunderClan cats passed the Great Rock, Bluestar

let out a long moan. "Are you all right?" Fireheart asked, stopping.

Bluestar shook her head impatiently. "StarClan does not want to share dreams with me," she muttered. "Why are they so angry with my Clan?"

"WindClan stood in our way, not StarClan," Fireheart reminded her. But he couldn't help feeling that StarClan could have brought them better luck. Smallear's words echoed through his mind: *Fireheart's naming broke with Clan ritual for the first time since before I was born.*

Fireheart felt his head spin with alarm. Were the warrior ancestors really angry with Thunderclan?

From the surprised murmurs that greeted their news when Fireheart and Bluestar padded back into camp, Fireheart guessed that the Clan shared his fears. Never before had a leader been turned back on a journey to the Moonstone.

Bluestar padded unsteadily to her den, her eyes fixed on the dusty ground as she crossed the clearing. Fireheart watched her with a heavy heart. Suddenly the sun felt too hot to bear beneath his thick coat. He headed for the shade at the edge of the clearing, and noticed Dustpelt padding toward him from the gorse tunnel, Ashpaw at his heels.

"You're back early," meowed the tabby warrior. He circled Fireheart as Ashpaw stood wide-eyed and looked up at the two warriors.

"WindClan wouldn't let us pass," Fireheart explained.

"Didn't you tell them you were going to Highstones?"

asked Dustpelt, sitting down beside his apprentice.

"Of course," snapped Fireheart.

He saw Dustpelt's eyes flick toward the gorse tunnel and turned to see Darkstripe and Fernpaw enter the camp. Fernpaw looked exhausted as she ran to keep up with her mentor, her fur clumped and dusty.

"What are you doing back?" Darkstripe asked, narrowing his eyes at Fireheart.

"WindClan wouldn't let them pass," Dustpelt announced. Fernpaw looked up at Dustpelt, her pretty green eyes round with surprise.

"What? How dare they?" Darkstripe meowed, his tail bristling angrily.

"I don't know why Fireheart let them boss him around," commented Dustpelt.

"I didn't have much choice," Fireheart growled. "Would *you* have risked your leader's safety?"

Runningwind's meow sounded across the clearing. "Fireheart!" The lean warrior was trotting toward him, looking agitated. Darkstripe and Dustpelt glanced at each other and led their apprentices away. Runningwind reached Fireheart and asked, "Have you seen Cloudpaw anywhere?"

"No." Fireheart felt his heart lurch. "I thought he was going out with you this afternoon."

"I told him to wait till I'd washed." Runningwind seemed more angry than worried. "But when I'd finished, Brightpaw told me he'd gone hunting by himself."

"I'm sorry," Fireheart apologized, sighing inwardly. The

last thing he needed right now was Cloudpaw's disobedience. "I'll speak to him when he gets back."

Runningwind's eyes glittered with annoyance and he looked unconvinced by Fireheart's promise. Fireheart was about to apologize again when he saw Runningwind's expression turn to disbelief as Cloudpaw scampered into the camp, a squirrel grasped in his jaws. The apprentice's eyes shone with pride at the catch, which was almost as big as he was. Runningwind snorted with exasperation.

"I'll sort it out," Fireheart meowed quickly. He sensed Runningwind had plenty more to say about Cloudpaw, but the warrior just nodded and padded away.

Fireheart watched the white cat carry his squirrel to the fresh-kill pile. Cloudpaw dropped it and wandered toward the apprentices' den without taking any food for himself, even though there was plenty of prey. With a sinking feeling, Fireheart guessed that Cloudpaw had already eaten while out hunting. *How many times could Cloudpaw break the warrior code in a single day?* he wondered irritably.

"Cloudpaw!" called Fireheart.

Cloudpaw looked up. "What?" he mewed.

"I want to talk to you."

As Cloudpaw padded slowly toward him, Fireheart was uncomfortably aware of Runningwind watching from outside the warriors' den.

"Did you eat while out hunting?" he demanded as soon as Cloudpaw neared.

Cloudpaw shrugged. "So what if I did? I was hungry."

"What does the warrior code tell us about eating before the Clan is fed?"

Cloudpaw looked at the treetops. "If it's anything like the rest of the code, it'll tell me I can't," he muttered.

Fireheart pushed away his rising exasperation. "Did you fetch that pigeon?"

"I couldn't. It was gone."

With a shock Fireheart realized he didn't know if he believed Cloudpaw or not. He decided there was no point pursuing it. "Why didn't you go hunting with Runningwind?" he asked instead.

"He was taking too long to get ready. Anyway, I prefer hunting alone!"

"You're still just an apprentice," Fireheart reminded him sternly. "You'll learn better if you hunt with a warrior."

Cloudpaw sighed and nodded. "Yes, Fireheart."

Fireheart had no idea if Cloudpaw had really listened or not. "You'll never be given your warrior name if you carry on like this! How do you think you'll feel watching Ashpaw's and Fernpaw's naming ceremonies when you're still an apprentice?"

"That'll never happen," Cloudpaw argued.

"Well, one thing's for certain," Fireheart told him. "*You'll* be staying at camp while *they* go to the next Gathering."

Finally Fireheart seemed to have Cloudpaw's attention. The white-haired apprentice stared up at him in disbelief. "But——" he began.

"When I report this to Bluestar, I think she'll agree with

me," Fireheart interrupted him fiercely. "Now, go away!"

Tail down, Cloudpaw padded off toward the other apprentices, who were watching from outside their den. Fireheart didn't even bother looking to see if Runningwind had witnessed the scene. Right now he didn't care what the Clan thought of his apprentice. The opinions of the other cats seemed to pale into insignificance next to his growing fear that Cloudpaw would never become a true warrior.

CHAPTER 7

❧

"Bluestar, it's been a quarter moon since we returned from the uplands." Fireheart carefully avoided mentioning the Moonstone. Even though they were alone in her den, he still felt uncomfortable mentioning their fruitless expedition. "There's been no sign of WindClan in our territory, or ShadowClan." Bluestar narrowed her eyes disbelievingly but Fireheart pressed on. "There are so many apprentices in training, and the woods are so full of prey, that it is hard to keep three warriors in camp all the time. I . . . I think two would be plenty."

"But what if we're attacked again?" Bluestar fretted.

"If WindClan really intended to harm ThunderClan," Fireheart pointed out, "Mudclaw wouldn't have let you leave the uplands. . . ." *alive,* he finished silently, letting his words trail away.

"Okay." Bluestar nodded, her eyes clouded with an unreadable emotion. "Only two warriors need stay in camp."

"Thanks, Bluestar." This was going to make the task of organizing all the guards, hunting parties, and apprentice training much easier. "I'll go and sort out tomorrow's patrols."

Fireheart dipped his head respectfully and left the den.

Outside the warriors were waiting for him. "Whitestorm, you lead the dawn patrol," Fireheart ordered. "Take Sandstorm and Ashpaw with you. Brackenfur, Dustpelt, you'll guard the camp while I'm hunting with Cloudpaw." He looked around at the remaining warriors, realizing how much more confident he felt about arranging the patrols. He'd had a lot of practice since Bluestar stayed in her den so much nowadays. Pushing away the unsettling thought, Fireheart went on: "I'll leave it up to the rest of you whether you train your apprentices or take them hunting, but I want the fresh-kill pile as full as it is today. We're getting used to eating well!" An amused purr ran through the group of warriors. "Darkstripe, you lead tomorrow's sunhigh patrol. Runningwind, you take sunset. You can choose who you take with you; just be sure to let them know so they can be ready in time."

Runningwind nodded, but Darkstripe's eyes glittered and he asked, "Who will be going to the Gathering tonight?"

"I don't know," Fireheart admitted.

Darkstripe narrowed his eyes. "Didn't Bluestar tell you, or hasn't she decided yet?"

"She hasn't discussed it with me," Fireheart answered. "She'll tell us when she's ready."

Darkstripe turned his head and stared into the shadowy trees. "She'd better tell us soon. The sun is starting to set."

"Then you should be eating," Fireheart told him. "You'll need your strength for the Gathering, if you're going." Darkstripe's tone made him uneasy, but he refused to let it ruffle his fur. He sat down and waited for the warriors to move away. Only when they had all gone did he turn back to Bluestar's den. She hadn't mentioned the Gathering, and he'd been too busy worrying about tomorrow's patrols to remember it.

"Ah, Fireheart." Bluestar met him as she was pushing her way out through the lichen. She looked as if she'd just finished washing, and her pelt glowed in the dusky light. Fireheart felt a jolt of relief that she seemed to be taking care of herself once more. "When you've eaten, call the warriors together for the Gathering."

"Er . . . who shall I call?" Fireheart asked.

Bluestar looked surprised. She listed the names so easily—leaving out Cloudpaw and including Ashpaw, as he'd requested several days earlier—that Fireheart wondered if perhaps she'd already told him, and he'd forgotten.

"Yes, Bluestar," he answered. He dipped his head and padded across the clearing to the fresh-kill pile. A fat pigeon had been left on the heap. He decided to leave it for Bluestar. Perhaps this might tempt her to eat more than two mouthfuls. He picked up a vole, not feeling very hungry himself. He was too unsettled by Bluestar's shifting, patternless moods.

As Fireheart carried the vole back to his favorite eating place, a shiver ran along his spine. Instinctively he looked over his shoulder, and he felt a prickle of apprehension as he saw Bramblekit watching him. He recalled Cinderpelt's words: *He will never know his father. It will be the Clan that raises him.* Fireheart forced himself to nod at the kit, then turned away and padded to the clump of nettles to eat.

When he'd finished his meal, Fireheart glanced around the clearing. The rest of the Clan was sharing tongues as night stretched out the shadows and brought a welcome coolness to the camp. The days had been so hot lately that Fireheart had found himself wishing more and more that he could swim like the RiverClan cats. He looked over at the apprentices' den, wondering if Cloudpaw would remember that he wasn't going to the Gathering because he had eaten while out hunting.

Cloudpaw was crouched on the tree stump outside his den entrance, play-fighting with Ashpaw, who was scrabbling at him from below. Fireheart was pleased that at least Cloudpaw was getting on with his denmates. He wondered if Graystripe would be at Fourtrees tonight. It seemed unlikely, as he had been in RiverClan for barely a moon. But he had given them Silverstream's kits. The RiverClan leader, Crookedstar, must have been grateful—after all, Silverstream had been his daughter, so the kits were his kin. And even though it would confirm his friend's acceptance into another Clan, Fireheart found himself hoping that Graystripe would be granted the privilege of joining the Gathering.

Fireheart pushed himself to his paws and called the cats together for the ThunderClan patrol. As he ran through the list of names that Bluestar had given him—"Mousefur, Runningwind, Sandstorm, Brackenfur, Brightpaw, Ashpaw, and Swiftpaw"—he realized with growing unease that Darkstripe, Longtail, and Dustpelt weren't among them. The three warriors had all been close allies of Tigerclaw, and Fireheart wondered if Bluestar had left them out deliberately. An uncomfortable shiver rippled through his fur as the three cats exchanged glances, then fixed their gazes on him. There was an unmistakable gleam of anger in Darkstripe's eyes. Unnerved, Fireheart turned away and joined the other cats to wait for Bluestar.

She was sharing tongues with Whitestorm outside her den, and only when the gathered warriors began kneading the ground with anticipation did she get up and cross the clearing.

"Whitestorm will be in charge of the camp while we're away," she announced.

"Bluestar," Mousefur addressed her leader cautiously. "What are you going to say about the way that WindClan stopped you from traveling to Highstones?"

Fireheart's shoulders tensed. Mousefur clearly wanted to know if the ThunderClan cats should prepare themselves for hostility.

"I shall say nothing," Bluestar answered firmly. "WindClan knows that what they did was wrong. It's not worth risking their aggression by pointing it out in front of the other Clans."

The ThunderClan warriors greeted her response with reluctant nods, and Fireheart couldn't help wondering whether they saw weakness or wisdom in their leader's decision as they followed her through the gorse tunnel and out into the moonlit forest.

Dirt and pebbles showered down as the cats scrambled up

the side of the ravine. The lack of rain had left the forest as dry as crushed bones, and the sun-scorched ground seemed to turn to dust beneath their paws. Once in the woods, Bluestar ran on ahead. Fireheart dropped to the rear of the group as the cats raced silently through the trees, ducking beneath brittle ferns and swerving past brambles.

Sandstorm measured her pace until she matched Fireheart stride for stride, clearing a fallen branch in a single fluid leap. As they landed, she turned to Fireheart and murmured, "Bluestar seems to be feeling well again."

"Yes," Fireheart agreed guardedly, concentrating on threading his body between some prickly bramble stalks.

Sandstorm went on, keeping her voice low so it didn't carry to the other cats. "But she seems distant. She doesn't seem to be as . . ." She hesitated, and Fireheart didn't try to fill the silence that followed. His worst fears were being confirmed. The other ThunderClan cats were beginning to notice Bluestar was not herself.

"She's changed," Sandstorm finished.

Fireheart didn't look at the ginger she-cat. Instead he veered away to avoid a thick clump of nettles while Sandstorm leaped over them, springing up and through the stinging leaves to land on the forest floor beyond.

Fireheart ran faster to catch up. "Bluestar's still shaken," he said, panting. "Tigerclaw's treachery was a huge shock."

"I don't understand why she never suspected him."

"Did *you* ever suspect Tigerclaw?" countered Fireheart.

"No," Sandstorm admitted. "No cat did. But the rest of the

Clan has recovered from the shock. Bluestar still seems . . ." Again she seemed lost for words.

"She's leading us to the Gathering," Fireheart pointed out.

"Yes, that's true," answered Sandstorm, brightening.

"She's still the same Bluestar," Fireheart assured her. "You'll see."

The two warriors quickened their pace. They leaped over a stream that had been too swollen to cross during the newleaf floods. Now it trickled along a stony bed, so dry that it was almost impossible to imagine the water had ever flowed higher.

The rest of the group was only just ahead of them by the time they neared Fourtrees. Fireheart led Sandstorm along their trail, the undergrowth still trembling where the cats had passed, as if the leaves shared the Clan's anticipation of the Gathering.

Bluestar had stopped at the head of the slope and was staring down into the valley. Fireheart could see lithe feline shapes slipping through the shadows, greeting each other with muted purrs. From the scents on the still air, he could tell that ThunderClan was the last to arrive. Fireheart watched Bluestar gaze at the Great Rock in the center of the clearing and saw a shudder ripple along her spine. She seemed to take a deep breath before plunging down the slope.

Fireheart raced after her with his Clanmates. He slowed as he reached the clearing and scanned the other cats for a glimpse of Graystripe. The RiverClan deputy, Leopardfur, was talking with a ShadowClan warrior Fireheart didn't recognize. Crookedstar, the RiverClan leader, sat with Stonefur, looking silently around the clearing. Fireheart scented another RiverClan cat close by, but when he turned, he saw it was an apprentice moving to greet Brightpaw. There was no sign or scent of Graystripe. Fireheart wasn't surprised, but his tail still drooped with disappointment.

A gray ShadowClan apprentice joined Brightpaw as well. With one ear Fireheart listened idly to their conversation.

"Has your Clan seen any more of the rogues? Nightstar's worried that they're still roaming the forest."

Fireheart froze when he heard the ShadowClan cat's question. All of the Clans had been worried about the group of rogue cats that had been scented in their territories. What the other Clans didn't know was that ThunderClan's deputy, Tigerclaw, had befriended these rogues and used them to attack his own camp. Fireheart gave Brightpaw a cautionary glance, warning her to keep silent, but there was no need. The white-and-ginger she-cat replied coolly, "We've not scented them in our territory for nearly a moon."

Fireheart felt a jolt of relief as the RiverClan cat added, "Nor ours. They must have left the forest." Fireheart wished he could share the RiverClan cat's confidence, but his instincts told him that, if Tigerclaw were involved, the rogue cats would return one day.

Mudclaw, the WindClan warrior who had turned Fireheart and Bluestar away from Highstones, sat a foxlength away. Fireheart recognized the young WindClan warrior

Onewhisker standing at Mudclaw's side. He had made friends with this small brown tabby on the journey back from exile, but he didn't dare approach him now. Mudclaw was eyeing him coldly, and Fireheart knew this was no place to continue the argument they'd begun on their way to the Moonstone.

But he couldn't resist flexing his claws, still angry at the memory, and was angered further when Mudclaw leaned sideways to whisper something into his companion's ears with a meaningful glance at Fireheart. To Fireheart's surprise Onewhisker blinked sympathetically at him, then turned and walked away, leaving Mudclaw flicking his tail with annoyance. It looked as if there was at least one WindClan warrior who remembered the old debt of loyalty to ThunderClan. Fireheart couldn't stop his whiskers from twitching with satisfaction as he stalked past Mudclaw and headed toward Leopardfur and the ShadowClan warrior.

His confidence evaporated when he approached the RiverClan deputy. Although they were equals now in the hierarchy of their Clans, this she-cat had a fierce and commanding presence. Ever since ThunderClan and RiverClan cats had fought at the gorge and a RiverClan warrior, Whiteclaw, had fallen to his death, Fireheart had felt her unforgiving hostility as sharp as thorns. But he needed to find out how Graystripe was doing. He nodded respectfully, and Leopardfur dipped her head in return.

The ShadowClan warrior sitting beside Leopardfur started to rasp a greeting, but broke off, coughing and spluttering.

Fireheart noticed for the first time how ragged the warrior's pelt looked, as if he hadn't groomed himself for a moon.

Leopardfur gave her paws a lick and wiped her face as the ShadowClan warrior stumbled into the shadows.

"Is he all right?" Fireheart asked.

"Does he look all right?" retorted Leopardfur, her lip curling with distaste. "Cats shouldn't come to the Gathering riddled with disease."

"Shouldn't we do something?"

"Like what?" meowed Leopardfur. "ShadowClan has a medicine cat." She lowered her paw, her wet whiskers gleaming in the moonlight. Her eyes glittered with curiosity. "I hear you are ThunderClan's new deputy." Fireheart nodded, realizing that Graystripe must have shared this news with his new Clan. Leopardfur went on: "What happened to Tigerclaw? None of the other Clans seemed to know. Is he dead?"

Fireheart flicked his tail uncomfortably. He could imagine Leopardfur wasting no time in telling the other Clans that ThunderClan had replaced their distinguished deputy with a kittypet. "What happened to Tigerclaw is of no concern to RiverClan," he meowed, trying to match her cool tone. He wondered if Bluestar would say anything about her former deputy when she announced the news about Fireheart later on.

Leopardfur narrowed her eyes but didn't press the subject any further. "So," she meowed, "have you come to brag about your new title, or to find out about your old friend?"

Fireheart lifted his chin, surprised that she was giving him a clear opportunity to ask about Graystripe. "How is he?" he meowed.

"He'll do." Leopardfur shrugged. "He'll never be a true RiverClan warrior, but at least he's getting used to the water, which is more than I expected." Fireheart had to hold in his claws at her dismissive tone. "His kits are strong and clever," Leopardfur went on. "They must favor their mother."

Was this cat trying to annoy him on purpose? Fireheart was struggling to hold back a sharp reply when Mousefur trotted up behind him.

"Hello, Leopardfur," she greeted the RiverClan deputy. "Stonefur tells me there are new kits in your camp, besides Graystripe's."

"Yes, there are," Leopardfur meowed. "StarClan has blessed our nursery this greenleaf."

"He also said Mistyfoot's kits are about to begin their training," meowed Mousefur. "You know, the ones Fireheart saved from the floods," she added, her eyes sparkling with mischief. Fireheart noticed Leopardfur stiffen, but his mind was on Mistyfoot and her brother, Stonefur. He glanced around the clearing and saw Bluestar sitting alone beneath the Great Rock. Did she know her son was here? Had she heard that Mistyfoot's kits were ready for their apprenticeship? When he turned his gaze back to Leopardfur and Mousefur, the RiverClan deputy was stalking away.

Mousefur shot a look of sympathy at Fireheart. "Don't worry. You'll find her less intimidating when you get used to her. The rest of RiverClan seems happy to see us. They would not have survived the floods so well without the help of ThunderClan, and we did let them have Silverstream's kits without a fight."

"Graystripe was never Leopardfur's favorite ThunderClan cat, though," Fireheart reminded her. "Not since Whiteclaw fell into the gorge."

"She should learn to forgive and forget. Graystripe has given RiverClan two fine, healthy kits." Mousefur flicked her tail. "Did she ask you about Tigerclaw?"

"Yes."

"Everyone's desperate to know what happened to him."

"And why a kittypet has replaced him," Fireheart added bitterly.

"That too." Mousefur glanced briefly at him. "Don't take it personally, Fireheart. We'd be just as curious about a change of deputy in another Clan." Her attention wandered around the clearing for a moment before she observed, "Have you noticed how small ShadowClan's patrol is tonight?"

Fireheart nodded. "I've seen only a couple of ShadowClan warriors so far. One of them just had a nasty coughing fit."

"Really?" meowed Mousefur curiously.

"It is furball season," Fireheart pointed out.

"I suppose so."

A voice sounded from the Great Rock. Fireheart looked up and saw the RiverClan leader, Crookedstar, standing on top of the massive boulder, his thick pelt gleaming in the moonlight.

Bluestar sat on one side and Tallstar, the WindClan leader, on the other. And on the far side, half hidden by the shadow of an oak tree, sat Nightstar.

Fireheart was shocked by the ShadowClan leader's appearance. The black tom looked even scrawnier than a WindClan cat, who were kept lean by the rabbits they chased on the moor. But Nightstar didn't just look thin. He held his head low, and his shoulders were hunched. For a moment Fireheart wondered if he was sick, but then he remembered that Nightstar had already been an elder when he'd taken on the leadership of ShadowClan. Perhaps it wasn't surprising if he looked frail. He may have been granted the nine lives of a leader, but not even StarClan could turn back time.

"Come on," Mousefur murmured. Fireheart followed the dusky brown she-cat to the front of the cats and sat down beside her, with Mistyfoot at his other flank.

Crookedstar meowed from the Great Rock, "Bluestar wishes to speak first." He bowed his head to the ThunderClan leader as she stepped forward and raised her voice, sounding as strong as it always had.

"You may already have heard from WindClan, but for those of you who have not, Brokentail is dead!"

A satisfied murmur rippled through the crowd. Fireheart noticed Nightstar's ears and tail flicking restlessly. The ShadowClan leader seemed almost excited to know that his old enemy was dead.

"How did he die?" Nightstar rasped.

Bluestar didn't seem to hear him. "And ThunderClan has a new deputy," she went on.

"So it's true what RiverClan has been saying." The stunned mew of a WindClan warrior rose from the watching cats. "Something's happened to Tigerclaw!"

"Is he dead?" Mudclaw demanded to know. His words brought a barrage of concerned cries, and Fireheart couldn't help feeling a twinge of resentment when he realized how much Tigerclaw had been respected by the other Clans. He watched Bluestar anxiously as the cats bombarded her with questions.

"Did he die of sickness?"

"Was it an accident?"

Fireheart felt his Clanmates stiffen around him. They all shared Brightpaw's unwillingness to reveal the truth about their former deputy's disloyalty.

Bluestar's authoritative yowl silenced the questions. "Tigerclaw's fate is ThunderClan's business and does not concern anyone else!"

The cats fell into a disgruntled murmuring, their curiosity clearly not satisfied. Fireheart couldn't help wondering if Bluestar should warn the other Clans that Tigerclaw was still alive—that there was a dangerous traitor roaming the forest, unfettered by the warrior code.

But when Bluestar meowed again she made no mention of Tigerclaw. Instead she announced, "Our new deputy is Fireheart."

Dozens of heads turned to look at Fireheart, and he felt hot under their questioning stares. The silence seemed to pound in his ears. He kneaded the ground and soundlessly urged the leaders to carry on with the Gathering, aware only of the sound of breathing and the rows upon rows of unblinking eyes.

CHAPTER 8

Mews of alarm and the pounding of paws in the clearing roused Fireheart from sleep. He blinked against the glaring sunshine that streamed between the branches above the warriors' den.

A golden head appeared through the wall of leaves. It was Sandstorm, her pale green eyes gleaming with excitement. "We've captured two ShadowClan warriors!" she meowed breathlessly.

Fireheart leaped to his paws, instantly awake. "What? Where?"

"By the Owl Tree," Sandstorm explained, adding, "they were asleep!" Her voice betrayed her scorn at the ShadowClan cats' carelessness.

"Have you told Bluestar?"

"Dustpelt's telling her now." She ducked out of the warriors' den and Fireheart sprang after her, past Runningwind, who jerked up his head, startled awake by the commotion.

Fireheart had slept fitfully after returning from the Gathering, shaken by the loaded silence that had greeted the announcement of his deputyship. His dreams had been filled with unknown cats that recoiled from him as if he were an owl of ill omen flying through a forest of shadows. He thought he had left his days as an outsider behind him, but the challenging stares from the other cats had warned him that he was still not fully accepted into forest life. He just hoped they didn't find out about the broken naming ritual. That would only reinforce their uneasiness about a kittypet replacing a respected Clanborn deputy.

Now he faced yet another challenge. How would he deal with enemy cats captured on ThunderClan territory? Fireheart found himself hoping that Bluestar would be in a calm enough mood to guide him.

The dawn patrol was gathered in a circle in the middle of the clearing. Fireheart pushed his way through them and saw two ShadowClan cats crouching on the hard earth, their tails bushed out and their ears flattened.

He recognized one of the warriors at once. It was Littlecloud, a brown tabby tom. They'd met at a Gathering when Littlecloud was no more than a kit. He had been forced into apprenticeship by Brokentail when he was only three moons old. He was fully grown now, but still small-framed, and he looked in a bad way. His fur was matted and he stank of crowfood and fear. His haunches were bony, like feather-less wings, and his eyes were sunk into his head. The other one wasn't much better off. *These were hardly warriors to be afraid of,* Fireheart thought with a twinge of unease.

He looked at Whitestorm, who had led the dawn patrol. "Did they put up a fight when you found them?"

"No," Whitestorm admitted, flicking his tail. "When we woke them up, they begged us to bring them here."

Fireheart felt confused. "Begged you?" he echoed. "Why would they do that?"

"Where are these ShadowClan warriors?" yowled Bluestar, pushing her way through the audience of cats, her face twisted in fear and rage. Fireheart felt his belly tense. "Is this another attack?" she hissed at the two wretched cats.

"Whitestorm found them on patrol," Fireheart explained quickly. "They were sleeping in ThunderClan territory."

"Sleeping?" snarled Bluestar, her ears flat against her head. "Well, have we been invaded or not?"

"These were the only warriors we found," meowed Whitestorm.

"Are you sure?" demanded Bluestar. "It could be a trap."

As Fireheart looked at these two sorry creatures, his instinct told him that invasion was the last thing on their minds. But Bluestar had a point. It would be wise to make sure there were no other ShadowClan cats hiding in the woods, waiting for a signal to attack. He called to Mousefur and Dustpelt. "You two, take a warrior and an apprentice each. Start at the Thunderpath and work your way back to camp. I want every bit of the territory searched for signs of ShadowClan."

To Fireheart's relief the two warriors obeyed instantly. Dustpelt called Runningwind and Ashpaw, while Mousefur signaled to Swiftpaw and Brackenfur; then the six cats raced out of the camp and into the forest.

Fireheart turned back to the trembling captives. "What are

you doing in ThunderClan territory?" he asked. "Littlecloud, why are you here?"

The tabby tom stared up at Fireheart with round, frightened eyes, and Fireheart felt a stab of sympathy. The cat looked as lost and helpless as he'd been at that first Gathering, when he was a barely weaned kit.

"W-Whitethroat and I came here h-hoping you'd give us food and healing herbs," Littlecloud stammered at last.

Hisses of disbelief rose from the ThunderClan cats, and Littlecloud shrank back, pressing his scrawny body against the earth.

Fireheart stared at the prisoner in amazement. Since when did ShadowClan cats seek help from their bitterest enemy?

"Fireheart, wait." The voice of Cinderpelt sounded softly in Fireheart's ear. She was studying the two ShadowClan cats with narrowed eyes. "These cats are no threat to us. They are sick." She limped forward and touched Littlecloud's forepaw gently with her nose. "His pad is warm," she mewed. "He has a fever."

Cinderpelt was about to sniff the second cat's paw when Yellowfang forced her way through the throng of cats. "No, Cinderpelt!" she screeched. "Get away from them!"

Cinderpelt leaped around. "Why? These cats are sick. We must help them!" She twisted her head, looking pleadingly first at Fireheart, then at Bluestar.

Every cat turned expectantly to Bluestar, but the ThunderClan leader just stared, huge-eyed, at the captives. Fireheart could see the old gray she-cat struggling with bewilderment and fear, her eyes clouded with confusion. He realized he had to distract the cats' attention while the troubled leader gathered her thoughts.

"Why us? What made you come to our territory?" he asked the two prisoners again.

The other ShadowClan cat, Whitethroat, spoke this time. He was a black tom with paws and a chest that used to be white but were now stained with dust. "You helped ShadowClan before, when we drove out Brokentail," he explained quietly.

But ThunderClan also gave sanctuary to the ShadowClan leader, Fireheart thought with a ripple of unease. *Had Whitethroat forgotten that?* Then he realized that Brokentail had forced these cats into their apprenticeships when they were barely old enough to leave their mothers' sides. Banishing their cruel leader must have come as such a relief that what had happened to him afterward paled into insignificance. And now that Brokentail was dead, there was no threat to the ShadowClan warriors from the ThunderClan camp beyond normal Clan rivalry.

Whitethroat went on: "We hoped you would be able to help us now. Nightstar is sick. The camp is in chaos with so many cats ill. There are not enough herbs or fresh-kill to go around."

"What's Runningnose doing? He's your medicine cat. It's up to him to tend to you!" spat Yellowfang, before Fireheart could say anything.

Fireheart was taken aback by her tone. Yellowfang had once belonged to ShadowClan. Even though Fireheart knew her loyalties lay with ThunderClan now, he was surprised at her lack of compassion toward her former Clanmates.

"Nightstar seemed all right at the Gathering last night," Darkstripe growled.

"Yes," agreed Bluestar, narrowing her eyes suspiciously.

But Fireheart remembered how frail the ShadowClan leader had seemed, and he was not surprised when Littlecloud mewed, "He got worse when he returned to the camp. Runningnose was with him all night. He won't leave Nightstar's side. He let a kit die at its mother's belly without even a poppy seed to ease its journey to StarClan! We are afraid that he'll let us die too. Please help us!"

Littlecloud's plea sounded real enough to Fireheart. He looked hopefully at Bluestar, but her blue eyes still looked bewildered.

"They must leave," insisted Yellowfang in a low growl.

"Why?" Fireheart blurted out. "They're no threat to us in this state!"

"They carry a disease I've seen before in ShadowClan." Yellowfang began to circle the ShadowClan cats, studying them but keeping her distance. "It killed many cats last time."

"It's not greencough, is it?" Fireheart asked. Some of the ThunderClan cats began to edge slowly backward as Fireheart mentioned the sickness that had ravaged their own Clan during leaf-bare.

"No. It has no name," Yellowfang muttered, keeping her eyes fixed on the captives. "It comes from the rats that live on a Twoleg dump on the far side of ShadowClan territory." She glared at Littlecloud. "Surely the elders know those Twoleg rats carry sickness, and must never be taken as prey?"

"An apprentice brought the rat back," explained Littlecloud. "He was too young to remember."

Fireheart listened to the sick cat's labored breathing as the ThunderClan cats looked on in silence. "What should we do?" he asked Bluestar.

Yellowfang spoke up before she could answer. "Bluestar, it is not long since greencough devastated our Clan," she reminded her. "You lost a life then." The medicine cat narrowed her eyes, and Fireheart guessed what she must be thinking. Only he and Yellowfang knew that Bluestar was on her last life. If the disease spread into ThunderClan, she might die, and ThunderClan would be left without a leader. The thought turned Fireheart's blood to ice, and he shivered in spite of the hot morning sun.

Bluestar nodded. "You are right, Yellowfang," she meowed quietly. "These cats must leave. Fireheart, send them away." Her voice was flat and expressionless as she turned back to her den.

Reluctantly, his relief at reaching a decision tempered by pity for the sick cats, Fireheart meowed, "Sandstorm and I will escort the ShadowClan warriors back to their border." Mews of approval rippled through the other cats. Littlecloud stared at Fireheart, pleading with his eyes. Fireheart forced himself to look away. "Go back to your dens," he told his Clanmates.

The other cats slipped noiselessly into the undergrowth at

the edge of the clearing, until only Cinderpelt lingered next to Fireheart and Sandstorm. Whitethroat started to cough, his body racked with painful spasms.

"Please let me help them," begged Cinderpelt.

Fireheart shook his head helplessly as Yellowfang called from her tunnel, "Cinderpelt! Come here. You must wash their sickness from your muzzle."

Cinderpelt stared at Fireheart.

"Come now!" spat Yellowfang. "Unless you want me to add a few nettle leaves to the mixture!"

Cinderpelt backed away with a last reproachful glance at Fireheart. But there was nothing he could do. Bluestar had given him an order, and the Clan had agreed.

Fireheart glanced at Sandstorm and was relieved to find her eyes filled with sympathy. He knew she would understand his struggle between compassion for the sick cats and the desire to protect his Clan from the illness.

"Let's go," Sandstorm meowed softly. "The sooner they get back to their own camp, the better."

"Okay," Fireheart answered. He looked at Littlecloud, forcing himself to ignore the desperation on the small cat's face. "The Thunderpath is busy. There are always more monsters about in greenleaf. We'll help you cross."

"No need," whispered Littlecloud. "We can cross it ourselves."

"We'll take you there anyway," Fireheart told him. "Come on."

The ShadowClan warriors heaved themselves to their

paws and padded unsteadily to the camp entrance. Sandstorm and Fireheart followed without speaking, although Fireheart drew in his breath sharply as he watched the sick cats haul themselves painfully up the ravine.

As they made their way into the forest, a mouse scuttled across the path in front of them. The ShadowClan warriors' ears twitched but they were too weak to give chase. Without stopping to think, Fireheart shot ahead of Sandstorm and tracked the scent of the mouse into the undergrowth. He killed it and carried it back to the sickly ShadowClan cats, dropping it at Littlecloud's paws. As if they felt too ill to be grateful, they said nothing but crouched and nibbled at the fresh-kill.

Fireheart saw Sandstorm looking on doubtfully. "They can't spread sickness by eating," he pointed out. "And they'll need their strength to return to their camp."

"Looks like they don't have much appetite anyway," Sandstorm commented as Littlecloud and Whitethroat suddenly got up and stumbled away from the half-eaten mouse into the undergrowth. A moment later Fireheart heard them retching.

"A waste of prey," Sandstorm muttered, scraping dust over the remains of the mouse.

"I guess," answered Fireheart, disappointed. He waited till the two cats reappeared, then led Sandstorm after them.

Fireheart could smell the acrid fumes of the Thunderpath a few moments before the rumbling of the monsters reached them through the leaf-laden trees. Sandstorm meowed to the

ShadowClan cats, "I know you don't want our help, but we'll see you across the Thunderpath." Fireheart nodded in agreement. He was more concerned about their safety than suspicious that the cats would not leave ThunderClan territory.

"We'll cross alone," insisted Littlecloud. "Just leave us here."

Fireheart looked sharply at him, suddenly wondering if he should be less trusting. But he still found it hard to believe that these sick warriors posed any threat to his Clan. "Okay," he conceded. Sandstorm flashed him a questioning glance, but Fireheart gave a small signal with his tail and the orange she-cat sat down. Littlecloud and Whitethroat nodded farewell and disappeared into the ferns.

"Are we going to—" began Sandstorm.

"Follow them?" Fireheart guessed what she was going to say. "I suppose we should."

They waited a few moments for the sound of the ShadowClan cats to fade into the bushes, and then began to track them through the forest.

"This isn't the way to the Thunderpath," Sandstorm whispered as the trail veered toward Fourtrees.

"Perhaps they're following the route they came by," Fireheart suggested, touching his nose to the tip of a bramble stem. The fresh stench of the sick cats made his lip curl. "Come on," he meowed. "Let's catch up with them." Anxiety flashed through him. Had he been wrong about the ShadowClan cats? Were they heading back into ThunderClan territory in spite of their promise to leave? He quickened his pace and Sandstorm ran silently at his heels.

The noise of the Thunderpath hummed like sleepy bees in the distance. The ShadowClan cats seemed to be following a trail that ran parallel with the stinking stone path. Their scent led Fireheart and Sandstorm out of the cover of the forest ferns and onto a bare patch of ground. Just ahead, the ShadowClan cats had crossed the scentline that marked the border between the two territories and were ducking into a clump of brambles, unaware of their ThunderClan shadows.

Sandstorm narrowed her eyes. "Why are they going in there?"

"Let's find out," Fireheart replied. He hurried forward, swallowing a prickle of fear as he crossed the scentline. The rumble of the Thunderpath had grown much louder, and his ears twitched uncomfortably at the bruising din.

The ThunderClan warriors picked their way through the barbed stems. Fireheart was painfully aware they were on hostile territory now, but he had to be sure that the ShadowClan cats were returning to their camp. By the sound of it, the Thunderpath was only a few foxlengths in front of them now, and the scent of the sick cats was almost drowned by its fumes.

Suddenly the brambles ended and Fireheart found himself stepping out onto the filthy grass that edged the Thunderpath. "Careful!" he warned Sandstorm as she hopped out beside him. The hard gray path lay right in front of them, shimmering in the heat, and the ginger she-cat shrank back as a monster roared past.

"Where are the ShadowClan cats?" she asked.

Fireheart stared across the Thunderpath, screwing his eyes up and flattening his ears as more monsters screamed past, their bitter wind dragging at his fur and whiskers. The sick cats were nowhere to be seen, but they couldn't possibly have crossed already.

"Look," Sandstorm hissed. She pointed with her nose. Fireheart followed her wide-eyed stare along the dusty strip of grass. It was empty apart from a tiny flicker of movement where the tip of Whitethroat's tail was disappearing into the ground, underneath the stinking flat stone of the Thunderpath.

Fireheart's eyes grew round with disbelief. It was as if the Thunderpath had opened its mouth and swallowed the ShadowClan cats whole.

CHAPTER 9

♣

"Where have they gone?" Fireheart gasped.

"Let's have a closer look," suggested Sandstorm, already trotting toward the place where the ShadowClan cats had disappeared.

Fireheart hurried after her. As they neared the patch of grass that had swallowed up the black tail, he noticed a shadow where the earth dipped away sharply into a hollow beside the Thunderpath. It was the entrance to a stone tunnel that led under the Thunderpath, like the one he'd used with Graystripe on their journey to find WindClan. Sandstorm's pelt brushed against him as they crept down the slope and cautiously sniffed the gloomy entrance. Fireheart felt the rush of wind on his ears from the monsters roaring past above, but as well as the stench of the Thunderpath, he could smell the fresh scents of the ShadowClan cats. They had definitely come this way.

The tunnel was perfectly round, lined with pale cream stone about the height of two cats. The moss that grew halfway up the smooth sides told Fireheart that the tunnel ran with water during leaf-bare. Now it was dry, the bottom littered with leaves and Twoleg rubbish.

"Have you heard of this place before?" asked Sandstorm.

Fireheart shook his head. "It must be how ShadowClan crosses to get to Fourtrees."

"A lot easier than dodging the monsters," commented Sandstorm.

"No wonder Littlecloud wanted to be left to cross the Thunderpath alone. This tunnel is a secret ShadowClan would want to keep for themselves. Let's get back to the camp and tell Bluestar."

Fireheart dashed up the slope and back into the forest, glancing over his shoulder to make sure Sandstorm was with him. She came charging after him, and the two cats headed home. As they crossed the scentline, Fireheart felt the familiar relief of being back in the safety of ThunderClan territory; although, after hearing Littlecloud's news about the sickness in ShadowClan, he doubted if the rival Clan was in a fit state to keep up their border patrols anyway.

"Bluestar!" Hotter than ever and breathless after the run home, Fireheart went straight to Bluestar's den.

"Yes?" came the answer through the lichen.

Fireheart pushed his way in. The ThunderClan leader was lying in her nest with paws tucked neatly under her chest. "We found a tunnel just inside ShadowClan territory," he told her. "It leads under the Thunderpath."

"I hope you didn't follow it," growled Bluestar.

Fireheart hesitated. He had expected his leader to be

excited by this discovery; instead her tone was harsh and accusing. "N-no, we didn't," he stammered.

"You took too much risk entering their territory at all. We don't want to antagonize ShadowClan."

"If ShadowClan is as weak as the warriors said, I don't think they'd do anything about it," he pointed out, but Bluestar stared past him, apparently busy with her own thoughts.

"Have those two cats gone?" she asked.

"Yes. They went through the tunnel. That's how we found it," Fireheart explained.

Bluestar nodded distantly. "I see."

Fireheart searched the ThunderClan leader's eyes for some hint of compassion. Didn't she care about the sickness in ShadowClan at all? "Did we do the right thing, sending them back?" he couldn't help asking.

"Of course!" snapped Bluestar. "We don't want sickness in the camp again."

"No, we don't," Fireheart agreed heavily.

As he turned to leave, Bluestar added, "Don't tell anyone about the tunnel yet."

"Okay," Fireheart promised, slipping through the lichen. He wondered why Bluestar wanted to keep the tunnel a secret. After all, he had uncovered a weakness in ShadowClan's border that could become a strength for ThunderClan. Not that he felt ShadowClan deserved any sort of attack at the moment, but surely a better knowledge of the forest could only be a good thing? Fireheart sighed as Sandstorm dashed up to him.

"What did she say? Was she pleased we'd found the tunnel?" she demanded.

Fireheart shook his head. "She told me to keep it a secret."

"Why?" Sandstorm meowed in surprise.

Fireheart shrugged and kept going toward his den. Sandstorm trotted after him. "Are you okay?" she asked. "Is it Bluestar? Did she say anything else?"

Fireheart realized he was giving away too much of his anxiety about the ThunderClan leader. He bent to give his chest a quick lick, then lifted his head and meowed with forced brightness, "I must go. I promised I'd take Cloudpaw hunting this afternoon."

"Do you want me to come with you?" Sandstorm's eyes looked concerned, and she added, "It'll be fun. We haven't been hunting together for ages." She nodded toward the apprentices' den, where Cloudpaw was dozing in the sunshine. The apprentice's plump, furry belly rose and fell as he breathed. "He certainly needs the exercise," she added. "He's beginning to look like Willowpelt." She purred with amusement. "He must be quite a hunter! I don't think I've ever seen a Clan cat that fat."

There was no spite in Sandstorm's voice, but Fireheart felt his fur growing hot. Cloudpaw did look fat for such a young cat, much fatter than the other apprentices, even though they were all enjoying the plentiful prey of greenleaf. "I think I should take Cloudpaw out by myself," he meowed reluctantly. "I've been neglecting him a bit lately. Could we go out together another time?"

"Just let me know when," Sandstorm responded cheerfully. "I'll be there. I could catch us another rabbit." Fireheart saw mischief flash in her pale green eyes, and he knew she was referring to the time they'd hunted together in a snowbound forest that shimmered with frost, when she had surprised him with her speed and skill. "Unless you've finally learned how to catch them for yourself!" Sandstorm teased, flicking Fireheart's cheek with her tail as she trotted away.

Watching her go, Fireheart felt a strange, happy prickling in his paws. He shook his head and padded over to Cloudpaw. The sleepy apprentice arched his back and stretched, his short legs quivering with the effort.

"Have you been out of the camp today?" Fireheart asked.

"No," answered Cloudpaw.

"Well, we're going hunting," Fireheart informed him curtly. He felt ruffled by the way Cloudpaw seemed to think he could just lie about and enjoy the sunshine. "You must be hungry."

"Not really," replied Cloudpaw.

Fireheart felt puzzled. Had Cloudpaw been stealing from the fresh-kill pile? Apprentices were not allowed to take food until they had hunted for the elders, or gone training with their mentors. Fireheart dismissed the thought instantly. The apprentice couldn't have managed it without one of the Clan seeing him. "Well, if you're not hungry we'll start in the training hollow for some fighting practice," he meowed. "We can hunt afterward."

Without giving the young cat a chance to object, Fireheart

raced out of the camp. He heard Cloudpaw's pawsteps thumping after him, but he didn't look back or slow his pace until he reached the sheltered hollow where he had trained as an apprentice. He stopped in the middle of the sandy clearing. The air was so still that, even in the shade, the midday heat felt stifling. "Attack me," he ordered as Cloudpaw scrambled down the slope to join him, his paws sending up puffs of red dust that clung to his long white fur.

Cloudpaw stared at him, wrinkling his nose. "What? Just like that?"

"Yes," replied Fireheart. "Pretend I'm an enemy warrior."

"Okay." Cloudpaw shrugged and began racing halfheartedly toward him. His round belly slowed him down, making his small paws sink deep into the sand. Fireheart had plenty of time to prepare himself so that when Cloudpaw finally reached him, it was easy to dodge to one side and send the young apprentice rolling into the dust.

Cloudpaw clambered to his paws and shook himself, sneezing as the dust tickled his nostrils.

"Too slow," Fireheart told him. "Try again."

Cloudpaw crouched down, breathing hard, and narrowed his eyes. Fireheart stared back, impressed by the intensity of Cloudpaw's gaze—this time the apprentice looked as if he were actually thinking about the attack. Cloudpaw leaped and flew at Fireheart, twisting as he landed so that he could kick Fireheart with his hind legs.

Fireheart staggered but managed to keep his balance and send Cloudpaw flying with a swipe from his front paw. "Better," he puffed. "But you're not prepared for the counterstrike."

Cloudpaw lay unmoving in the sand.

"Cloudpaw?" Fireheart meowed. The blow from his front paw had been heavy, but surely not enough to hurt. The apprentice's ear twitched but he stayed where he was.

Fireheart padded over to him, his fur suddenly prickling with worry. He peered down and saw that Cloudpaw's eyes were wide open.

"You've killed me." The apprentice gasped mockingly, and rolled feebly onto his back.

Fireheart snorted. "Stop messing around," he snapped. "This is serious!"

"Okay, okay." Cloudpaw struggled to his paws, still panting. "But I'm hungry now. Can we go hunting?"

Fireheart opened his mouth to argue. Then he remembered Whitestorm's words: *He'll learn when he's ready.* Perhaps it was better to let Cloudpaw train at his own pace after all. So far arguing had been a complete waste of time.

"Come on then." Fireheart sighed and led Cloudpaw out of the training hollow.

As they trekked along the bottom of the ravine into the forest, Cloudpaw stopped and sniffed the air. "I smell rabbit," he mewed. Fireheart lifted his nose. The apprentice was right.

"Over there," whispered Cloudpaw.

A bright flicker in the bushes betrayed the white tail of a young rabbit. Fireheart dropped low against the ground. He tensed his muscles, ready to give chase. Beside him Cloudpaw dropped too, his belly bulging out sideways as he crouched. The rabbit's tail flickered again and Cloudpaw dashed toward it, his paws thudding heavily on the dry forest floor. The rabbit heard the noise at once and shot away into the undergrowth. Cloudpaw crashed after it while Fireheart followed on silent paws. The ferns trembled where Cloudpaw had charged through them, and Fireheart felt a stab of disappointment as Cloudpaw skidded, panting, to a halt ahead of him. The rabbit had disappeared.

"You hunted better than that when you were a kit!" Fireheart exclaimed. His sister's kit had once had the makings of a fine warrior, but the fluffy white apprentice seemed to be turning as soft as a kittypet. "Only StarClan knows how you got so fat with a hunting technique like that. Even a fit cat can't outrun a rabbit. You need to be much lighter on your paws if you want to catch one!" He was thankful Sandstorm hadn't come with them. He would have been embarrassed if she had seen what a poor hunter his apprentice had become.

For once Cloudpaw didn't argue. "Sorry," he muttered, and Fireheart felt a pang of sympathy for the young cat. It did look as if Cloudpaw had been trying his best this time, and he couldn't help feeling that he'd let his apprentice down by neglecting his training lately.

"Why don't I just go hunting by myself?" Cloudpaw suggested, looking down at his paws. "I promise I'll bring something back for the fresh-kill pile."

Fireheart studied him for a moment. Cloudpaw couldn't be such a poor hunter all the time, because he was looking more well fed than any of the cats in the Clan. Perhaps he fared better when he wasn't being watched. In a flash, Fireheart decided to follow his apprentice without him knowing and watch him hunt. "That's a good idea," he agreed. "Just make sure you're back by mealtime."

Cloudpaw brightened instantly. "Of course," he meowed. "I won't be late; I promise." Fireheart heard the apprentice's belly growl with hunger. *Perhaps that will sharpen his skills*, he thought.

As he listened to Cloudpaw's pawsteps fade away into the forest, he felt a flicker of guilt at the thought of spying on him. But he was only going to assess his apprentice's skills, he reminded himself, as any mentor would.

Tracking Cloudpaw through Tallpines was easy. The undergrowth was sparse beneath the shade of the towering pine trees, and Fireheart could see his apprentice's snowy pelt from a long way off. The woods here were alive with small birds, and he kept expecting Cloudpaw to stop and take advantage of the rich offerings.

But Cloudpaw didn't stop. He carried on at a surprisingly swift pace, considering the size of his belly, out of Tallpines and into the oak forest that backed onto Twolegplace. Fireheart felt an ominous prickle in his paws. Keeping low, he sped up so he didn't lose sight of Cloudpaw in the thick undergrowth. Then the trees thinned out and Fireheart caught a glimpse of the fences that bordered the Twoleg gardens up ahead. Was Cloudpaw going to visit his mother, Princess? Her Twoleg nest was near here. He couldn't blame

Cloudpaw for wanting to see her from time to time. He was still young enough to remember her warm scent. But why hadn't Cloudpaw mentioned Princess to Fireheart before now? And why did he say he was going hunting if he was going to visit his mother? Surely he knew that Fireheart, of all the Clan, would understand.

Fireheart's confusion grew as Cloudpaw turned away from Princess's fence and followed the line of Twoleg nests until Princess's home was far behind them. The apprentice padded steadily onward, even ignoring a fresh mouse-scent that crossed his path, until he reached a silver birch that stretched up beside a pale green garden fence. The small white cat heaved himself up the trunk of the birch and clambered on top of the fence, swaying as his belly dragged him off balance. Fireheart remembered Dustpelt's jibe and winced. Perhaps garden birds were more to Cloudpaw's taste after all. But he would have to tell Cloudpaw that Clan cats didn't hunt in Twolegplace. StarClan had given them the forest to provide their food.

Cloudpaw jumped down to the other side of the fence. Fireheart quickly scrambled up the birch, thankful that it was in full leaf as he sheltered behind its fluttering leaves. Below he could see Cloudpaw trotting across the carefully clipped grass, his tail and chin high. A sense of foreboding flowed through Fireheart as Cloudpaw ran straight past a small gang of starlings. The birds scattered upward in a flurry of wings, but Cloudpaw didn't even turn his head. Fireheart felt the blood begin to pound in his ears. If

Cloudpaw hadn't come to hunt garden birds, what was he doing here? Then he froze with horror as he watched Cloudpaw sit down outside the Twoleg nest and let out a shrill, pitiful wail.

CHAPTER 10

❧

Fireheart held his breath as the Twoleg door opened. He longed for Cloudpaw to turn and run away, but part of him knew that the apprentice had no intention of leaving. He leaned forward on his branch, willing the Twoleg to shout and chase Cloudpaw away. Forest cats were not usually welcomed in Twolegplace. But this Twoleg bent down and stroked Cloudpaw, who stretched up to press his head against its hand as the Twoleg murmured something to him. By the Twoleg's tone, it was clear they had greeted each other like this before. Disappointment as bitter as mouse bile pulsed through Fireheart's body as Cloudpaw trotted happily through the door and vanished into the Twoleg nest.

Fireheart stayed clinging to the slender branch of the birch long after the Twoleg door had shut. His apprentice was being tempted back into the life that Fireheart had turned his back on. Perhaps Fireheart had been completely wrong about him after all. Lost in thought, he stirred only when the sun began to dip behind the trees and sent a chill through his fur. He slid lightly down to the fence and dropped onto the ground outside.

Fireheart padded back through the forest, blindly follow-ing his own scent trail back the way he had come. Cloudpaw's actions felt like a terrible betrayal, yet it was hard to be angry with him. Fireheart had been so eager to prove to the Clan that kittypets were as good as forestborn cats, he hadn't even considered that Cloudpaw might prefer life with the Twolegs. Fireheart loved his life in the forest, but he had chosen it for himself. Only now did it occur to him that Cloudpaw had been given to the Clan by his mother, passed along as a kit before he was old enough to make his own decision.

Fireheart trekked onward, numb to the sights and scents of the forest, until he suddenly realized he had come to his sister's fence. He stared at it in surprise. Had his paws brought him here on purpose? He turned away, not yet ready to share his discovery with Princess. He didn't want to tell her what a mis-take she'd made in giving Cloudpaw to the Clan. With paws as heavy as stone, he started padding toward Tallpines and the camp.

"Fireheart!" the soft voice of a she-cat cried out behind him. *Princess!*

Fireheart froze, his heart sinking, but he couldn't walk away from his sister, not now that she had seen him. He turned back as Princess leaped down from her fence. Her tabby-and-white pelt rippled softly as she bounded toward him.

"I haven't seen you for ages!" she mewed, skidding to a halt. Her tone was sharp with worry. "Even Cloudpaw hasn't visited for a while. Is everything okay?"

"E-everything's fine," Fireheart stammered. He felt his voice tighten and his shoulders tense with the effort of lying.

Princess blinked gratefully, instantly trusting his words, and touched her nose to Fireheart's in greeting. He nuzzled her, breathing in the familiar smell that reminded him of his kithood. "I'm glad," she purred. "I was beginning to worry. Why hasn't Cloudpaw been to visit? I keep smelling his scent, but I haven't seen him for days." Fireheart couldn't think of what to say, and felt relieved when Princess carried on chattering. "I suppose you're keeping him busy with his training," she mewed. "Last time he visited he told me you were really impressed with his progress. He said he was way ahead of the other apprentices!" Princess sounded delighted and her eyes shone with pride.

She wants Cloudpaw to become a great warrior as much as I do, thought Fireheart. Guiltily he mumbled, "He shows great promise, Princess."

"He was my firstborn," purred Princess. "I knew he'd be special. I still miss him, even though I know how happy he is."

"I'm sure all your kits are special in their own way." Fireheart longed to tell his sister the truth, but he didn't have the heart to tell her that her sacrifice had been wasted. "I must go," he meowed instead.

"Already?" Princess exclaimed. "Well, come back and see me soon. And bring Cloudpaw next time!"

Fireheart nodded. He didn't want to return to the camp just yet, but this conversation was making him way too uncomfortable, as if he were confronting the impossible chasm between the forest and kittypet life.

Fireheart traveled the long way back to camp, letting the familiar greenness of the forest calm him. As he emerged from the trees at the top of the ravine, he found himself thinking yet again how much he missed having Graystripe around to confide in.

"Hi!" Sandstorm's voice surprised him. She was climbing out of the ravine and must have smelled his scent. "How was training? Where's Cloudpaw?"

Fireheart looked at the she-cat's sharp orange face. Her green eyes shone, and suddenly he knew that he could confide in her. He glanced anxiously around. "Are you alone?"

Sandstorm stared back at him curiously. "Yes. I thought I'd do a bit of hunting before mealtime."

Fireheart padded to the edge of the slope and stared down at the treetops that sheltered the camp below. Sandstorm sat beside him. She didn't speak, but pressed her flank to his sympathetically. Fireheart knew that he could even walk away now and she wouldn't ask any more questions.

"Sandstorm," he began hesitantly.

"Yes?"

"Do you think I made the wrong decision bringing Cloudpaw into the Clan?"

Sandstorm was silent for a few moments, and when she spoke, her words were careful and honest. "When I looked at him today, lying outside his den, I thought he looked more like a kittypet than a warrior. And then I remembered the day he caught his first prey. He was just a tiny kit, but he went out into a blizzard to catch that vole. He looked so unafraid, so proud of what he had done. He seemed like a Clan cat then, born and bred."

"So I made the right decision?" Fireheart meowed hopefully.

There was another heavy pause. "I think only time will tell," Sandstorm replied at last.

Fireheart didn't say anything. This wasn't the reassurance he'd been hoping for, but he knew she was right.

"Has something happened to him?" asked Sandstorm, her eyes narrowed with concern.

"I saw him go into a Twoleg nest this afternoon," Fireheart confessed flatly. "I think he's been allowing them to feed him for a while now."

Sandstorm frowned. "Does he know you saw him?"

"No."

"You should tell him," advised Sandstorm. "Cloudpaw needs to decide where he belongs."

"But what if he decides to return to a kittypet life?" Fireheart protested. Today had made him realize how much he wanted Cloudpaw to stay in the Clan. Not just for his own sake, or to show the other cats that warriors didn't have to be forestborn, but for Cloudpaw's sake too. He had so much to give to the Clan, and would be repaid more than enough by their loyalty. Fireheart felt his heart begin to pound at the thought of what Cloudpaw might be about to throw away.

"It's his decision," meowed Sandstorm gently.

"If only I'd been a better mentor—"

"It's not your fault," Sandstorm interrupted him. "You can't change what's in his heart."

Fireheart shrugged hopelessly.

"Just talk to him," urged Sandstorm. "Find out what he wants. Let him decide for himself." Her eyes were round with sympathy, but Fireheart still felt miserable. "Go and find him," she meowed. Fireheart nodded as Sandstorm stood up and padded away into the trees.

With a heavy heart he began to scramble down into the ravine, heading for the training hollow in the hope that Cloudpaw would return to camp the same way he'd left. He didn't want to confront his apprentice like this; he was afraid of pushing Cloudpaw away for good. But he also knew that Sandstorm was right. Cloudpaw could not stay in Thunder-Clan and keep one paw in the life of a kittypet.

Fireheart sat in the hollow as the sun dropped behind the trees. The air was still warm even though long shadows stretched across the sand. It would be time for the evening meal soon. Fireheart began to wonder if Cloudpaw would return at all. Then he heard the rustle of bushes and the padding of small paws and knew Cloudpaw was approaching even before he smelled his scent.

The apprentice trotted into the clearing with his tail high and his ears pricked. He was carrying a tiny shrew in his jaws, which he dropped as soon as he saw Fireheart. "What are you doing here?" Fireheart heard reproach in the young cat's voice. "I told you I'd be back by mealtime. Don't you trust me?"

Fireheart shook his head. "No."

Cloudpaw tipped his head to one side and looked hurt. "Well, I said I'd be back, and I am," he protested.

"I saw you," Fireheart meowed simply.

"Saw me where?"

"I saw you go into that Twoleg nest." He paused.

"So?"

Fireheart was shocked almost to speechlessness by Cloudpaw's lack of concern. Didn't he realize what he'd done? "You were supposed to be hunting for the Clan," he hissed, anger burning in his belly.

"I did hunt," answered Cloudpaw.

Fireheart looked scornfully at the shrew that Cloudpaw had dropped on the ground. "And how many cats do you think that will feed?"

"Well, I won't take anything for myself," mewed Cloudpaw.

"Only because you're stuffed with kittypet slop!" Fireheart spat. "Why did you come back at all?"

"Why wouldn't I? I'm just visiting the Twolegs for food." Cloudpaw sounded genuinely puzzled. "What's the problem?"

Seething with frustration, Fireheart growled, "I can't help wondering if your mother did the right thing in giving up her firstborn kit to be a Clan cat."

"Well, she's done it now," Cloudpaw hissed back. "So you're stuck with me!"

"I may be stuck with you as an apprentice, but I can keep you from becoming a warrior!" threatened Fireheart.

Cloudpaw's eyes widened in surprise. "You wouldn't! You couldn't! I'm going to become such a great fighter that you won't be able to stop me." He glared defiantly at Fireheart.

"How many times do I have to tell you, there's more to being a warrior than hunting and fighting. You have to know what you're hunting and fighting *for*!" Fireheart fought back the fury that rose in his chest.

"I know what I'm fighting for. The same as you—survival!"

Fireheart stared at Cloudpaw in disbelief. "I fight for the Clan, not myself," he growled.

Cloudpaw gazed steadily back at him. "Okay," he mewed. "I'll fight for the Clan, if that's what it takes to become a warrior. It's all the same in the end."

Fireheart felt like clawing some sense into the mouse-brained young cat, but he took a deep breath and meowed as calmly as he could, "You can't live with a paw in two worlds, Cloudpaw. You're going to have to decide. You must choose whether you want to live by the warrior code as a Clan cat, or whether you want the life of a kittypet." As he spoke, he recalled Bluestar saying exactly the same thing when Tigerclaw had spotted him talking to his old kittypet friend, Smudge, at the edge of the forest. The difference was that Fireheart had had no trouble recognizing where his loyalties lay. He had been a Clan cat from the moment he had stepped into the forest, in his own mind at least.

Cloudpaw looked taken aback. "Why must I choose? I like

my life the way it is, and I'm not going to change it just to make you feel better!"

"It's not just to make *me* feel better," Fireheart spat. "It's for the good of the Clan! The life of a kittypet goes against everything in the warrior code." He watched incredulously as Cloudpaw ignored him and picked up his shrew, then marched past him toward the camp. Fireheart took a long breath, resisting the urge to chase Cloudpaw out of ThunderClan territory once and for all. *Let him decide for himself.* He repeated Sandstorm's words under his breath as he followed his apprentice back to the camp. After all, he told himself desperately, Cloudpaw wasn't doing any harm by eating kittypet food. He just hoped none of the other cats found out.

As they neared the gorse tunnel, Fireheart heard the clatter of dirt cascading down the ravine. He stopped and waited, hoping it was Sandstorm returning from her hunt, but a warm scent on the early evening air told him it was Cinderpelt.

The small gray cat jumped awkwardly down from the last rock. Her jaws were full of herbs and she was limping heavily.

"Are you okay?" Fireheart asked.

Cinderpelt dropped the herbs. "I'm fine, honestly," she puffed. "My leg is playing up, that's all, and it took me longer than I thought to find the herbs."

"You should tell Yellowfang," Fireheart meowed. "She wouldn't want you overdoing it."

"No!" mewed Cinderpelt, shaking her head.

"Okay, okay," Fireheart agreed, surprised by the strength of her refusal. "At least let me carry these herbs for you."

Cinderpelt blinked gratefully at him. "May StarClan banish all the fleas from your nest," she purred, her eyes twinkling. "I didn't mean to snap. It's just that Yellowfang is very busy. Willowpelt began her kitting this afternoon."

Fireheart felt a flicker of anxiety. The last kitting he had seen had been Silverstream's. "Is she okay?"

Cinderpelt glanced away. "I don't know," she mumbled. "I offered to collect herbs instead of helping." A shadow crossed her face. "I . . . I didn't want to be there. . . ."

Fireheart guessed that she too was thinking of Silverstream. "Come on then," he meowed. "The sooner we find out how she's doing, the sooner we can stop worrying." He quickened his pace.

"Hold on!" winced Cinderpelt, limping after him. "You'll be the first to know if I make a miraculous recovery. But for now you'll have to slow down!"

As they entered the camp Fireheart knew instantly that Willowpelt's kitting had been a success. One-Eye and Dappletail were padding away from the nursery, their eyes soft with affection and their purrs audible even from this side of the clearing.

Sandstorm came dashing over to greet them with the good news. "Willowpelt had two she-cats and a tom!" she announced.

"How's Willowpelt?" asked Cinderpelt anxiously.

"She's fine," Sandstorm assured her. "She's feeding them already."

Cinderpelt broke into a loud purr. "I must go and see," she mewed, and hobbled toward the nursery.

Fireheart spat out his mouthful of herbs and looked around. "Where's Cloudpaw?"

Sandstorm narrowed her eyes mischievously. "When Darkstripe saw what a measly catch he'd brought back, he sent him off to clean out the elders' bedding."

"Good," Fireheart meowed, pleased for once with Darkstripe's interference.

"Did you speak to Cloudpaw?" asked Sandstorm, her tone turning more serious.

"Yes." Fireheart's happiness at Willowpelt's kitting disappeared like dew under the midday sun as he thought of his apprentice's indifference.

"Well?" prompted Sandstorm. "What did he say?"

"I don't think he even realizes he's done anything wrong," Fireheart meowed bleakly.

To his surprise, Sandstorm didn't seem troubled. "He's young," she reminded Fireheart. "Don't be too upset. Keep remembering his first catch, and that you share the same blood." She gave him a gentle lick on the cheek. "With any luck it'll show in Cloudpaw one day."

Dustpelt trotted up and interrupted them, his eyes glinting with barely disguised scorn. "You must be proud of your apprentice," he jeered. "Darkstripe tells me he made the smallest catch of the day." Fireheart flinched as the warrior added, "You're obviously a great mentor."

"Go away, Dustpelt," spat Sandstorm. "There's no need to

be spiteful. It doesn't impress anyone, you know."

Fireheart was surprised to see Dustpelt recoil as if Sandstorm had taken a swipe at him. The warrior turned and hurried away, flashing a resentful look at Fireheart over his shoulder.

"That's a neat trick," Fireheart meowed, impressed by Sandstorm's ferocity. "You'll have to teach me how you do it!"

"I'm afraid it wouldn't work for you." Sandstorm sighed, staring ruefully after Dustpelt. She had shared her apprenticeship with the tabby tom, but their friendship had faltered since Sandstorm had grown closer to Fireheart. "Never mind. I'll apologize later. Why don't we go and see the new kits?"

She led the way to the nursery, where Bluestar was just squeezing out of the entrance. The old leader's face was relaxed and her eyes were shining. As Sandstorm slipped inside, she declared triumphantly, "More warriors for ThunderClan!"

Fireheart purred. "We'll have more warriors than any Clan soon!" he meowed.

The leader's eyes clouded, and Fireheart felt a chill of unease spread across his fur. "Let's just hope we can trust our new warriors better than our old," Bluestar growled darkly.

"Are you coming?" Sandstorm called to him from the warm shadows of the nursery. Fireheart shrugged off his fears about Bluestar and pushed his way inside.

Willowpelt lay in a nest made of soft moss. Three kits squirmed in the curl of her body, still damp and blind as they kneaded their mother's belly.

Fireheart saw a new softness enter Sandstorm's expression. She leaned forward and breathed in the warm, milky scent of each kit in turn while Willowpelt looked on, her eyes sleepy but content.

"They're great," Fireheart whispered. It was good to see kits again, but he couldn't help feeling a thorn-sharp stab of sorrow. The last newborn kits he'd seen had been Silverstream's, and Fireheart's mind flew instantly to Graystripe. He wondered how his old friend was—whether he was still grieving, or whether his new life in RiverClan with his kits had helped to ease his sadness.

Fireheart felt his tail bristle as he picked up the scent of Tigerclaw's kit. He turned to see where it was, swallowing the distrust that rose like bile in his throat. Behind him, Goldenflower was curled in her nest, her eyes closed and the kits sleeping soundly at her side. The dark tabby kit looked as innocent as any of its nursery Clanmates, and Fireheart felt a pang of guilt at the resentment that ruffled his fur.

Fireheart awoke early the next day. Thoughts of Graystripe lay heavy at the edge of his mind like rain clouds. He missed his old friend even more now that he was so worried about Cloudpaw. Talking to Sandstorm had helped, but he longed to know what Graystripe would say. Fireheart lay in his nest for a few moments before he made up his mind: He would go to the river today to see if he could find his old friend.

He slipped out of the den and gave himself a long, satisfying stretch. The sun was only just showing on the horizon, and there was a powdery softness in the early morning sky. Dustpelt was sitting in the middle of the clearing talking with Fernpaw. Fireheart wondered grimly what the brown warrior wanted to share with Darkstripe's gentle apprentice. Was Dustpelt poisoning her mind with malicious gossip? But Dustpelt's fur lay smoothly on his broad shoulders, and Fireheart detected none of the usual arrogance in his tone, even though he couldn't hear what he was saying. In fact the warrior was talking to Fernpaw in a voice as soft as a wood pigeon.

Fireheart approached the pair. When Dustpelt saw him coming, his eyes hardened.

"Dustpelt," Fireheart greeted him, "will you take the sun-high patrol?"

Fernpaw's eyes sparkled with excitement. "Can I go too?"

"I don't know," Fireheart admitted. "I haven't spoken with Darkstripe about your progress yet."

"Darkstripe says she's doing well," meowed Dustpelt.

"Then perhaps you could speak to him about it," Fireheart suggested. He didn't want to provoke a scornful response, but this could be a chance to smooth out some of the hostility Dustpelt usually showed toward him. "But take Ashpaw and another warrior too."

"Don't worry," Dustpelt assured him. His eyes were filled with uncharacteristic concern. "I'll make sure Fernpaw's safe."

"Er . . . good," meowed Fireheart, padding away. He couldn't believe that he'd had a whole conversation with Dustpelt without the warrior uttering a single barbed jibe.

Once he was out of the ravine, Fireheart raced toward Sunningrocks. The ground was so dry that his paws threw up small clouds of dust where they pounded over the forest floor. When he reached the great stone slabs, he noticed that the plants growing between the cracks had shriveled and died, and it dawned on him with a shock that it had been almost two moons since it had rained.

He skirted the bottom edge of the rocks and headed for the scent markers at the edge of RiverClan territory. The forest thinned out and sloped down to the river here. The air was filled with birdsong and the whispering of wind-stirred leaves, and in the background Fireheart could hear the steady lap of water. He stopped and sniffed the air. There was no scent of Graystripe. If he was going to see his friend, Fireheart would have to venture into RiverClan territory. Determination made him more willing than usual to take the risk. Their dawn patrol would be out, but with any luck they would be patrolling the other borders now.

Fireheart crept cautiously across the scentline and pushed his way through the ferns to the edge of the water, feeling exposed and vulnerable. There was still no sign of Graystripe. Did he dare cross the river and try his luck deeper in RiverClan territory? It would be easy enough—the water was shallow now, so he could wade most of the way, apart from the deep channel in the middle, where the current was slow enough to swim without too much difficulty. After all, he'd grown more used to water than most ThunderClan cats during the terrible floods of newleaf.

An unexpected scent drifting into his half-open mouth made Fireheart stiffen in surprise. It was the stench of ShadowClan! What were ShadowClan cats doing so far from home? The whole of ThunderClan's territory lay between their land and the river.

Alarmed, Fireheart backed into the ferns. He inhaled deeply, trying to pinpoint where the smell came from. With a sickening feeling, he recognized more than the scent of ShadowClan. There was a rancid tang of illness to it that he had smelled recently, and it was coming from farther upriver.

Fireheart began to creep slowly through the ferns, their browning tips whispering against his fur. He could see the gnarled trunk of an ancient oak tree ahead of him, just inside the ThunderClan border. Its twisted roots stuck out of the forest floor, the earth under which they had once been buried long since eroded by wind and rain. Now there was a space underneath, a small cave walled by roots. Fireheart sniffed again. The smell was definitely coming from there, tainted by the unmistakeable stench of sickness.

Fear and the desire to protect his Clan made Fireheart instinctively unsheathe his claws. Whatever foulness was in that cave must be driven out of ThunderClan territory. Swallowing the bile that rose in his throat, Fireheart raced from the ferns. He arched his back and stood threateningly in the mouth of the root cave, ready for a fight. But he was met by a heavy silence, broken with shallow, rasping breaths.

He stared into the gloom, his hackles raised. As his eyes grew accustomed to the dim light, he blinked in surprise.

The last time he'd seen these cats, they'd been disappearing under the Thunderpath, back to their own territory. It was the two ShadowClan warriors who had sought help from ThunderClan—Littlecloud and Whitethroat.

"Why have you come back?" Fireheart spat. "Go home, before you infect every Clan in the forest!" He drew back his lips, baring his teeth, when a familiar voice sounded behind him.

"Fireheart, stop! Leave them alone!"

CHAPTER 11

"Cinderpelt! What are you doing here?" Fireheart spun around to face the medicine cat. "Did you know about this?"

A pile of herbs lay between Cinderpelt's paws. She lifted her chin defiantly. "They needed my help. There was nothing for them in their camp but sickness."

"So they came straight back!" Fireheart glared at her angrily. "Where did you find them?"

"Near Sunningrocks. I smelled their sickness when I was out collecting herbs yesterday. They were looking for a safe place to hide," explained Cinderpelt.

"And you brought them here." Fireheart snorted. "They probably only came back onto our land because they knew you'd take pity on them." Cinderpelt's concern for the ShadowClan cats had been obvious when they were in the ThunderClan camp. "Did you think you could treat them without any cat finding out?" Fireheart demanded. He couldn't believe that Cinderpelt had exposed herself—and the rest of the Clan—to such a risk.

Cinderpelt met his eyes, undaunted. "Don't pretend you're really angry with me. You felt just as sorry for them," she reminded him. "You couldn't have turned them away a second time either!"

Fireheart could see that she believed she had done the right thing, and he had to admit the truth in her words—he couldn't deny he felt sorry for the sick cats, and had felt uncomfortable with Bluestar's lack of compassion. "Does Yellowfang know?" he asked, his anger fading.

"No, I don't think so," answered Cinderpelt.

"How sick are they?"

"They're starting to recover." Cinderpelt allowed a hint of satisfaction to enter her voice.

"I still smell sickness," Fireheart meowed suspiciously.

"Well, they're not completely cured yet. But they will be."

Littlecloud's voice rasped from the shadows behind him. "We're getting better, thanks to Cinderpelt."

Fireheart could hear that Littlecloud's voice was already stronger than it had been in the ThunderClan camp, and the young warrior's eyes shone brightly in the gloom. "They do sound better," he admitted, turning back to the young medicine cat. "How did you do it? Yellowfang seemed to think this sickness was deadly."

"I must have found the right combination of herbs and berries," Cinderpelt replied happily. Fireheart noticed she spoke with a confidence he'd not heard in her for a while, and he recognized the spirit of the lively, strong-willed apprentice he had once trained.

"Well done!" he meowed. He thought instinctively of how Bluestar would relish the news that a ThunderClan cat might have found a cure for ShadowClan's strange sickness. But then he remembered that Bluestar was not the leader she had once been. It wouldn't be safe to tell her that Cinderpelt had been hiding ShadowClan cats in ThunderClan territory. Her judgment had been clouded by her obsession with the threat of attack.

Fireheart realized that as long as the ShadowClan cats remained here, they were in danger. He was afraid Bluestar would order them to be killed at once if she found out they were still on ThunderClan territory. "I'm sorry, Cinderpelt." He shook his head. "These cats must leave. It's not safe for them here."

Cinderpelt flicked her tail in frustration. "They're too ill to return to their own camp yet. I might be able to heal them, but I'm no good as a hunter. They haven't eaten properly for days."

"I'll catch them something now," Fireheart offered. "It should give them enough strength to travel home."

"But what about when we get back?" Whitethroat rasped from the shadows.

Fireheart couldn't answer that, but he couldn't risk their sickness finding its way into the ThunderClan camp. What if a ShadowClan patrol came into ThunderClan territory looking for their missing warriors? "I'll feed you; then you must go," he repeated.

Littlecloud's voice was hoarse and high-pitched as he pushed himself to a sitting position, his paws scrabbling on the hard earth. "Please don't send us back! Nightstar is so weak. It's as if the sickness takes a new life from him each day.

Most of the Clan thinks he's going to die."

Fireheart frowned. "Surely he has plenty of lives left."

"You haven't seen how ill he is!" cried Whitethroat. "The Clan is scared. There's no cat ready to take his place."

"What about Cinderfur, your deputy?" asked Fireheart. The two ShadowClan cats looked away and didn't answer. Did that mean that Cinderfur had died already, or that he was just too old to become a leader? Like Nightstar, Cinderfur had been an elder when Brokentail had been driven out. Fireheart felt his sympathy winning in spite of his better judgment. "Okay." He sighed reluctantly. "You can stay here until you're strong enough to travel."

"Thank you, Fireheart," Littlecloud meowed wheezily. His eyes glittered with gratitude. Fireheart dipped his head, realizing how hard it must be for these proud ShadowClan warriors to admit they were dependent on another Clan.

He turned away and padded past Cinderpelt. She whispered as he passed, "Thanks, Fireheart. I knew you would understand why I took them in." Her eyes brimmed with compassion. "I couldn't let them die. Even . . . even if they were from another Clan." And Fireheart knew she was thinking of Silverstream, the RiverClan queen she had not been able to save.

He licked her ear affectionately. "You are a true medicine cat," he purred. "That's why Yellowfang chose you as her apprentice."

It didn't take Fireheart long to catch a thrush and a rabbit for the ShadowClan cats. This part of the forest was rich in prey. He was careful not to stray across the RiverClan border, although it was tempting—the scent of prey was strong from there, and it had been a long time since Fireheart had tasted water vole. But he was pleased with the juicy rabbit he found beside Sunningrocks, and the thrush was an easy catch, too busy cracking open a snail to hear his stealthy approach.

Cinderpelt was crouched beside the ancient oak when he returned, chewing berries and spitting the pulp into her herb mixture. Fireheart nudged the fresh-kill into the root cave, but he didn't enter. The stench of sickness made him wary of going inside.

He looked at Cinderpelt as she worked, feeling a sudden tingle of fear for the small cat. She must have entered the cave many times. "Are you okay?" he meowed quietly.

Cinderpelt looked up from her herbs. "Yes, I'm fine," she replied. "And I'm glad you found out about these cats. I didn't like keeping secrets from the Clan."

Fireheart flicked his tail uneasily. "I think we should keep this to ourselves," he told her.

Cinderpelt narrowed her eyes. "Aren't you going to tell Bluestar?"

"Normally I would—" Fireheart began hesitantly.

"But she's still not over the Tigerclaw thing," Cinderpelt finished.

Fireheart sighed. "Sometimes I think she's getting better, but then she'll say something or . . ." He trailed away.

"Yellowfang says it will take time for her to recover," mewed Cinderpelt.

"Then she's noticed too?"

"To be honest," Cinderpelt murmured regretfully, "I think most of the Clan has."

"What are they saying?" Fireheart wasn't sure if he wanted to hear the answer.

"She has been a great leader for a long time. They are simply waiting for her to become like that again." Cinderpelt's reply soothed Fireheart. The Clan's faith was moving, and should be trusted. Of course Bluestar would recover.

"Are you coming back with me?" he meowed.

"I have to finish up here." Cinderpelt picked up another berry with her teeth and started to chew.

Fireheart felt strange as he walked away, leaving Cinderpelt alone with the two ShadowClan cats and a stench that made his fur creep. He wondered if he'd done the right thing by letting them stay.

Outside the ThunderClan camp, he sheltered beneath a leafy bush and gave himself a good wash. He screwed up his eyes at the stink of the sick ShadowClan cats. He wished he could wash away the taste with a drink from the stream behind the training hollow, but it had dried up days ago. He'd have to follow its course back toward the river if he were to find water, and it was time he returned, before his Clanmates started to wonder where he was. He would return to find Graystripe another day.

Sandstorm met him as he emerged from the gorse tunnel into the clearing. "Been hunting?" she asked.

"Looking for Graystripe, honestly." Fireheart decided to

admit to the easiest part of the truth.

"I don't suppose you found any signs of Cloudpaw then," Sandstorm meowed, apparently unconcerned by Fireheart's admission.

"He's not in camp?"

"He went out hunting first thing this morning."

Fireheart knew she suspected the same as he did—that Cloudpaw was paying another visit to the Twolegs. "What should I do?"

"Why don't we go and find him together?" suggested Sandstorm. "Perhaps if I talk to him too, we can make him see sense."

Fireheart nodded gratefully. "It's worth a try," he agreed.

He led the way through Tallpines, neither cat speaking as they ran lightly over the ground. The air was still, and the needles felt soft and cool beneath their paws. Fireheart was acutely aware that this trail was as familiar to him as the route to Fourtrees or Sunningrocks, but Sandstorm was more cautious, pausing every so often to sniff the air and check for scent markings.

As they padded out from the pine forest and into the green woods, Fireheart sensed that Sandstorm's anxiety was building. He glanced at her and saw the tension in her shoulders as the line of Twoleg nests loomed ahead of them.

"Are you sure this is the way he would have come?" she whispered, looking nervously from side to side. A dog barked and Sandstorm's fur bristled.

"It's okay, the dog won't leave its garden," Fireheart

assured her, feeling uncomfortable that he knew things like this. Sandstorm had taunted him about his kittypet origins when he had first joined the Clan, and now that she accepted him so completely as a forest cat, he was reluctant to remind her that he had been born somewhere different.

"Don't the Twolegs bring their dogs out here?" she asked.

"Sometimes," Fireheart admitted. "But we'll have plenty of warning. Twoleg dogs don't exactly creep through the woods. You'll hear them before you smell them, and their stench isn't subtle." He hoped his humor might help Sandstorm relax, but she remained as tense as ever.

"Come on," he urged. "Cloudpaw's scent is here." He rubbed his cheek against a bramble stem. "Does it smell fresh to you?"

Sandstorm leaned forward and sniffed the bramble. "Yes."

"Then I think we can guess where he was heading." Fireheart padded around the bramble, relieved that at least the trail was leading them away from Princess's garden. He had no desire for Sandstorm to meet his kittypet sister just yet. Since he had brought Cloudpaw to the camp, the Clan all knew that he visited her, but they had no real idea of the affection that bonded him to Princess, and he preferred to keep it that way. It was best to keep the other cats as certain as he was that his heart lay with the Clan, in spite of his friendship with his sister.

As they neared the fence that Cloudpaw had climbed the day before, Fireheart felt an ominous chill ripple through his pelt. There were new scents here, as well as Cloudpaw's.

Something had changed. He led Sandstorm to the silver birch and she followed him lightly up the smooth trunk and into its branches. Fireheart could see her whiskers twitching as she sniffed the air.

Fireheart peered through the windows in the Twoleg nest. The space inside looked curiously dark and empty. He jumped as a door slammed, making a strange echoing bang like a thunderclap. He began to feel alarmed.

"What is it?" asked Sandstorm nervously as Fireheart leaped down to the fence, his tail fluffed up.

"There's something strange going on. The nest is empty. Stay there," he ordered. "I'm going to have a closer look."

He crept across the garden, keeping low. As he neared the door to the Twoleg nest he heard pawsteps behind him. He spun around and saw Sandstorm, her face tense but determined. He nodded at her, silently agreeing she could stay with him if she wanted, then turned toward the door again.

Just then, the loud rumble of a monster started up. Fireheart slipped down the passage that skirted one side of the nest. His fur bristled with fear, but he kept going until he had reached the end of the pathway. He peered out from the shadows to where bright sunshine flooded a treeless maze of Twoleg nests and pathways.

He felt Sandstorm panting at his side, her pelt lightly brushing his. "Look," he hissed. A gigantic monster, almost as big as a Twoleg nest, stood on the Thunderpath. The deafening growl was coming from the belly of the monster.

Both cats flinched as another door to the nest clattered

shut just around the corner from them. Fireheart saw a Twoleg walking toward the monster with something swinging from its hand. It looked like a den woven from brittle dead stems. Through the hard mesh at one end of the den, Fireheart could see a soft white pelt. He peered closer, and felt his heart lurch as he recognized the face behind the mesh, its eyes stretched wide with terror.

It was Cloudpaw!

CHAPTER 12

❧

"Help! Don't let them take me!" Fireheart heard Cloudpaw's desperate yowling above the noise of the roaring monster.

The Twoleg took no notice. It clambered into the monster with Cloudpaw and slammed the door shut. In a cloud of choking fumes, the monster pulled away and headed up the Thunderpath.

"No! Wait!"

Fireheart ignored Sandstorm's cry as he dashed out of the passageway and pelted after the monster. The rough stone path tore at his pads, but as fast as he ran, the monster went faster, until it rounded a corner and disappeared from view.

Fireheart skidded to a halt, his paws stinging and his heart pounding. Sandstorm called to him again. "Fireheart! Come back!"

Fireheart glanced in despair at the empty Thunderpath where the monster had stood just moments before and then hurried back to Sandstorm. Numb with shock, he blindly followed Sandstorm as she led him along the passageway, past the nest, through the garden, and over the fence into the safety of the woods.

"Fireheart!" Sandstorm gasped when they landed on the leafy forest floor. "Are you okay?"

Fireheart couldn't answer. He stared at the blank fence, trying to take in what he had just seen. The Twolegs had stolen Cloudpaw! Fireheart couldn't block out the look of fear on the young cat's face. Where were they taking him? Wherever it was, Cloudpaw hadn't wanted to go.

"Your pads are bleeding," murmured Sandstorm.

Fireheart lifted a foreleg and turned over his paw to look. He gazed blankly at the oozing blood until Sandstorm leaned forward and began to lick the grit from his wounds. It stung, but Fireheart didn't protest. The rhythmic licks comforted him, stirring long-distant memories of kithood. Gradually the panic that had frozen his mind began to melt away. "He's gone," he meowed dismally. His heart felt like a hollow log, ringing with sorrow at every beat.

"He'll find his way home," Sandstorm told him. Fireheart looked at her calm green eyes and felt a flicker of hope.

"If he wants to," she added. Her words pierced him like thorns, but her eyes were full of sympathy, and Fireheart knew she was only speaking the truth. "Cloudpaw might be happier where he's going," she meowed. "You want him to be happy, don't you?"

Fireheart nodded slowly.

"Come on then; let's get back to camp." Sandstorm's mew became brisk, and Fireheart felt a surge of frustration.

"It's easy for you!" he argued. "You share Clan blood with the rest of them. Cloudpaw was my only kin. Now there's no one in the Clan that's close to me."

Sandstorm flinched as if he had struck her. "How can you say that? You have *me*!" she spat. "I've done nothing but try to help you. Doesn't that mean anything? I thought that our friendship was important to you, but clearly I was wrong!" She spun around, flicking Fireheart's legs with her tail before racing away into the trees.

He watched her disappear, bewildered by her response. His paws stung, and he felt more wretched than he could ever remember. He began to wander slowly through the woods, steering clear of Princess's fence. He couldn't even imagine how he would tell her what had happened to her kit.

With every step, the thorn-sharp worry about what Fireheart was going to say to the rest of the Clan added to his misery. He imagined how Darkstripe would gloat when he discovered Fireheart's kin had gone back to the soft life of a kittypet. *Once a kittypet, always a kittypet!* Perhaps the jibe that had haunted Fireheart for so long had an element of truth in it after all.

The scuttling of a mouse under the pine trees distracted him. The Clan still had to be fed. Fireheart crouched instinctively, but there was no joy in the hunt this time. He chased and caught the mouse with cold swiftness and carried it toward the camp.

The sun was touching the tips of the trees when he reached the gorse tunnel. He paused and took a steadying breath before he walked into the clearing, the mouse swinging between his jaws.

The Clan was sharing tongues around the clearing after their evening meal. Mousefur met him at the entrance and Fireheart wondered if she had been waiting for his return. "You've been gone a long time," she observed mildly. "Is everything okay?"

Fireheart glanced awkwardly away. He felt he should share his news about Cloudpaw with Bluestar first.

"Whitestorm organized the evening patrol in your absence," Mousefur went on.

"Er . . . good . . . thanks," Fireheart stammered. Mousefur dipped her head politely and padded away.

As Fireheart watched her go, he tried to tell himself that Cloudpaw's loss didn't mean he was alone in the Clan. Most of the cats seemed to accept him as deputy, despite the broken naming ritual. Fireheart just wished he could be sure that StarClan felt the same way, and his earlier fears clouded his mind like noisy fluttering crows. Was Cloudpaw's loss a sign that StarClan wanted to punish ThunderClan by depriving it of a potential warrior? Even worse, were the Clan's warrior ancestors signaling that kittypets didn't belong in the Clan?

Fireheart felt as if his legs were about to give way under the weight of his anxiety. He dropped his offering on the pile of fresh-kill and looked around. Sandstorm was lying beside Runningwind, a sparrow in her paws. Fireheart flinched as the ginger she-cat cast him a reproachful glance. He knew he would have to apologize, but first he had to tell Bluestar about Cloudpaw.

Fireheart crossed to the leader's den and called a greeting

at the entrance. He was surprised when Whitestorm's voice answered. He poked his head through the lichen and saw Bluestar curled in her nest, her head up and eyes shining as she shared tongues with Whitestorm. For once the ThunderClan leader looked like any other warrior, enjoying the company of a trusted friend. And as he saw the contented expression on Bluestar's face, Fireheart shied away from disturbing her with his bad news. He'd tell her later.

"Yes, what is it?" asked Bluestar.

"I . . . I just wondered if you were hungry," Fireheart stammered.

"Oh." Bluestar sounded puzzled. "Thank you, but Whitestorm brought me something." She dipped her head toward the half-eaten pigeon that lay on the floor of her den.

"Er . . . fine, I'll leave you to eat it then." Fireheart quickly backed out before she could ask what he had been up to. He returned to the fresh-kill pile, picked up the mouse he'd caught earlier, and carried it toward the nettle clump where Sandstorm and Runningwind lay.

Sandstorm looked away when she saw him coming and busied herself with tearing the wings off her fresh-kill. Fireheart dropped his mouse onto the ground.

"Hi, there," Runningwind greeted him. "I thought you were going to miss mealtime."

Fireheart tried to purr a friendly reply, but his answer came out hoarsely. "Busy day." Runningwind glanced at Sandstorm, who was still ignoring the Clan deputy, and Fireheart thought he saw the lean warrior's whiskers twitch.

"Sorry about earlier," Fireheart whispered to Sandstorm.

"So you should be," she muttered, not looking up.

"You've been a good friend," Fireheart persisted. "I'm sorry I made you think I don't appreciate you."

"Yeah, well, next time try thinking beyond your own whiskers!"

"Are we friends again?" Fireheart meowed.

"We always were," she replied simply.

Relieved, Fireheart lay down beside her and began to crunch on his mouse. Runningwind hadn't uttered a word, but Fireheart noticed that his eyes were glowing with amusement. His interaction with Sandstorm was obviously attracting attention from the other warriors. Fireheart felt a self-conscious prickle ripple through his fur, and he looked awkwardly around the clearing.

Darkstripe was sitting in front of the apprentices' den talking to Ashpaw. Fireheart wondered why he was speaking to Dustpelt's apprentice instead of sharing a meal with the other warriors. Ashpaw was shaking his head, but the dark tabby warrior carried on talking until Ashpaw lowered his eyes and began to pad across the clearing toward the nettle patch.

Fireheart's ears twitched. From the way Darkstripe was watching the young gray apprentice, he could tell something was up.

Ashpaw stopped in front of Fireheart, his small body stiff and his tail flicking nervously.

"Is something wrong?" Fireheart asked.

"I was just wondering where Cloudpaw was," mewed Ashpaw. "He said he'd be back by mealtime."

Fireheart gazed past the apprentice at the dark tabby who watching them closely, his amber eyes glinting with undisguised interest. "Tell Darkstripe that if he wants to know, he should ask me himself!" he snapped.

Ashpaw flinched. "I . . . I'm sorry," he stammered. "Darkstripe told me . . ." The apprentice shuffled his paws and suddenly looked up, staring Fireheart straight in the eye. "Actually, it's not just Darkstripe who wants to know. I'm worried, too. Cloudpaw promised he'd be back by now." The gray apprentice hesitated, glancing away, and finished, "Whatever else he might do, Cloudpaw always keeps his word."

Fireheart was amazed. It had never occurred to him that Cloudpaw could have earned the respect and loyalty of his denmates like any other warrior. But what did Ashpaw mean by "whatever else he might do"?

CHAPTER 13

"Is Cloudpaw okay?" asked Ashpaw.

Fireheart blinked while he searched for the right words to explain Cloudpaw's disappearance. "I believe Cloudpaw has left the Clan," he murmured at last. There was no point trying to hide what had happened.

Ashpaw's eyes grew wide with shock and bewilderment. "L-left?" he echoed. "But he . . . he would have told us. I mean, I never thought he'd *stay* there!"

"Stay where?" asked Runningwind sharply, sitting up. "What's going on?"

Ashpaw glanced guiltily at Fireheart, knowing he had betrayed his friend's secret.

"Go back to your supper," Fireheart meowed gently. "You can tell Darkstripe that Cloudpaw has returned to his kitty-pet life. There's no need for secrets anymore."

"I just can't believe he's actually left," mewed Ashpaw sadly. "I'll really miss him." He turned and plodded back to the apprentices' den, where Darkstripe sat waiting like a hungry owl. The news would be all through the camp by sunset.

"Where has Cloudpaw gone?" demanded Runningwind, turning to Fireheart.

"He's gone back to live with Twolegs," Fireheart replied, each word dropping like a stone into the sultry forest air. His ears still rang with Cloudpaw's heartbreaking cries for help, but Fireheart couldn't see that it would do any good to start making excuses for his errant apprentice. How could he convince the Clan that Cloudpaw had been taken against his will, when they would all remember that the apprentice had been growing fat from Twoleg offerings?

Runningwind frowned. "Darkstripe is going to enjoy hearing that."

The tabby warrior was already staring triumphantly across the clearing as he leaned down to listen to Ashpaw's news. With a sinking feeling Fireheart watched as he trotted over to Longtail and Smallear, and the news of Cloudpaw's disappearance began to spread through the Clan like tendrils of dark, clinging ivy. Smallear squeezed between the branches of the oak to share the news with the other elders, while Longtail nodded at his former mentor and headed toward the nursery. Just as Fireheart had feared, Darkstripe was making sure the whole camp knew that Fireheart's kin had returned to his kittypet roots.

"Aren't you going to do anything?" asked Sandstorm, her voice sharp with indignation. "Are you going to leave it to Darkstripe to tell the Clan about Cloudpaw?"

Fireheart shook his head. "How can I fight the truth?" he meowed sadly.

"You could speak to the Clan!" snapped Sandstorm. "Explain what really happened."

"Cloudpaw rejected Clan life as soon as he started accepting kittypet food," Fireheart pointed out.

"Well, you should at least tell Bluestar," Sandstorm urged.

"Too late," murmured Runningwind.

Fireheart followed the brown warrior's gaze and saw Darkstripe padding toward Bluestar's den. She was going to have her evening disturbed, when she needed peace more than anything else. Fireheart thrashed his tail at Darkstripe's selfish spite, although he knew that most of his anger was directed at Cloudpaw.

"Come on; you might as well eat your supper," meowed Sandstorm, more gently now. But Fireheart had no appetite left. He could only stare around the clearing, returning the glances of the other Clan cats—some anxious, some just greedily curious—as they learned of Cloudpaw's desertion.

Runningwind's tail flicked one of Fireheart's hind legs. "Look out."

Darkstripe was heading toward them with a smug expression he didn't even try to hide. "Bluestar wants to see you," he meowed loudly to Fireheart. With a resigned sigh Fireheart stood up and made his way to the ThunderClan leader's den.

He hesitated at the entrance, feeling a flicker of anxiety. It seemed inevitable that Bluestar would see Cloudpaw's disappearance as yet another betrayal by a ThunderClan cat. Did this mean she would start to doubt Fireheart as well, because of his kittypet origins?

"Come in, Fireheart," Bluestar called. "I can smell you lurking out there!"

He pushed through the lichen. Bluestar was curled in her nest with Whitestorm beside her, his eyes wide with curiosity. Fireheart pricked his ears, trying to stop them from twitching and betraying his nerves.

"So that's why you came to see me earlier," meowed Bluestar. "'Wondering if I was hungry, indeed!" Fireheart was caught off guard by the amused purr in her voice. "You only usually offer to bring food to my den if you think I'm dying. You had me thinking there was a rumor going around the camp that I was on my last legs!"

Fireheart couldn't believe that she was taking the news about Cloudpaw so calmly. "I-I'm sorry," he stammered. "I was going to tell you about Cloudpaw, but you seemed so . . . so peaceful. I didn't want to upset you."

"I may not have been feeling well lately," Bluestar acknowledged with a dip of her head, "but I'm not made of cobwebs." Her blue eyes grew serious as she went on. "I am still your leader, and I need to know everything that's going on in my Clan."

"Yes, Bluestar," answered Fireheart.

"Now, Darkstripe tells me that Cloudpaw has gone to live with Twolegs. Did you know this might happen?"

Fireheart nodded. "But not until recently," he added. "I only found out yesterday he was visiting a Twoleg nest for food."

"And you thought you could sort him out by yourself," murmured Bluestar.

"Yes." Fireheart glanced at Whitestorm, who watched in silence, his old eyes missing nothing.

"You can't tell a cat what his heart should feel," Bluestar warned. "If Cloudpaw's heart longed for a kittypet life, then not even StarClan could change him."

"I know," Fireheart agreed. "But it's not as simple as that." He didn't want to excuse Cloudpaw's behavior to the rest of the Clan, but he wanted Bluestar to know the whole story. Although whether that was for Cloudpaw's sake or his, he wasn't quite sure. "He was taken away by the Twolegs against his will."

"Taken away?" echoed Whitestorm. "What makes you say that?"

"I saw him being carried off inside a monster," Fireheart explained. "He was crying out for help. I chased after him, but there was nothing I could do."

"But he'd been accepting food from these Twolegs for some time," Bluestar reminded him, narrowing her eyes.

"Yes," Fireheart admitted. "I spoke to him about that yesterday, and I'm not sure he really wanted to live a kittypet life. He seemed to still think of himself as a Clan cat." Fireheart swallowed uncomfortably. "I don't think Cloudpaw understood how far he was breaking the warrior code."

"Are you sure he is the sort of warrior that ThunderClan needs?" asked Bluestar.

Fireheart lowered his eyes, ashamed of his apprentice and recognizing the truth in Bluestar's words. "He's still young," he meowed quietly. "I think he has the heart of a Clan cat, even if he doesn't realize it himself yet."

"Fireheart." Bluestar's mew was gentle. "ThunderClan needs loyal, brave cats, like you. If Cloudpaw was taken, then perhaps it was what StarClan intended. He may not be forest-born, but he has been part of our Clan long enough for our warrior ancestors to take an interest in him. Don't be too sad. Wherever he has gone, StarClan will make sure he finds happiness there."

Fireheart raised his eyes slowly to his old mentor. "Thanks, Bluestar," he meowed. He wanted to believe that StarClan had Cloudpaw's best interests at heart, that they weren't punishing the Clan or signaling their disapproval of kittypets by sending the apprentice away. He wasn't entirely convinced, but he was grateful to the Clan leader for her sympathy, and heartily relieved that she hadn't read any darker message into Cloudpaw's disappearance.

That night Fireheart dreamed again. The clear night sky stretched overhead as his dream swept him high above the forest to Fourtrees, holding him in its starry talons before dropping him down onto the Great Rock. Fireheart felt the ageless strength of the boulder beneath his paws and relished the coolness of the smooth stone on his pads, which still stung from chasing after Cloudpaw. He felt Spottedleaf coming, and with the feeling came a surge of relief that she had not abandoned him, like in his last dream.

"Fireheart." The familiar voice whispered in his ears, and Fireheart spun around, expecting to see the medicine cat's tortoiseshell coat glowing in the moonlight. But she was not there.

"Spottedleaf, where are you?" he called out, his heart aching with longing to see her.

"Fireheart," the voice murmured again. "Beware an enemy who seems to sleep."

"What do you mean?" asked Fireheart, his chest tightening. "What enemy?"

"Beware!"

Fireheart opened his eyes and jerked up his head. It was still dark inside the den and he could hear the steady breathing of the other ThunderClan warriors. He pushed himself up and weaved his way toward the entrance. As he slipped past Darkstripe, he noticed that the warrior's ears were pricked and alert, although his eyes were closed.

Beware an enemy who seems to sleep. The warning sounded again in Fireheart's head, but he shook the thought away. Spottedleaf didn't need to remind him to be wary of Darkstripe. Fireheart knew very well that Darkstripe's loyalty to ThunderClan did not necessarily mean loyalty to him. Spottedleaf's warning had been about something else, something she feared Fireheart could not see for himself.

The clearing brought pale, silvery moonlight and a cool breeze. Fireheart sat at the edge and stared up at the stars. What could it be that Spottedleaf feared on Fireheart's behalf? He searched his mind, going over everything that had happened to him recently—Bluestar's recovery, Cloudpaw's disappearance, his discovery of the sick

ShadowClan cats. *The ShadowClan cats!* Cinderpelt said she had cured their sickness, but perhaps she hadn't. Perhaps they only seemed better. Fireheart felt alarm pricking like fleabites at the base of his tail. Spottedleaf had been a medicine cat. She might know that the sickness was not really cured. Perhaps she was warning him that it had already spread into the ThunderClan camp. The more Fireheart thought about it, the more certain he felt that this was what his dream had meant.

Bats flitted between the trees overhead and their sound-less wings seemed to fan the flames of Fireheart's alarm. How could he have let the ShadowClan cats stay in ThunderClan territory? He had to ask Cinderpelt if she was sure she had cured their sickness. He leaped to his paws and raced silently across the clearing, through the tunnel of ferns, and into Yellowfang's den.

He skidded to a halt, panting. Yellowfang's rasping snores echoed from the dark crack in the rock ahead. Fireheart could hear Cinderpelt's gentler breathing from a nest among the ferns that walled the clearing. He thrust his head into the small hollow. "Cinderpelt!" he hissed urgently.

"Is that you, Fireheart?" she mewed sleepily.

"Cinderpelt," Fireheart hissed again, loud enough to make the gray cat open her eyes.

She squinted at him, then slowly rolled onto her belly and lifted her head. "What is it?" she asked, frowning.

"Are you certain that the ShadowClan cats are really cured?" Fireheart demanded. He kept his voice low, even though he knew Yellowfang would not be able to hear him from inside her den.

Cinderpelt blinked in confusion. "You woke me up to ask me that? I told you yesterday, they're getting better."

"But they're still sick?"

"Well, yes," Cinderpelt admitted. "But not nearly as sick as they were."

"And what about you? Do you have any signs of the sickness? Have any of our cats come to you with fever or pain?"

Cinderpelt yawned and stretched. "I'm fine," she mewed. "The ShadowClan cats are fine. ThunderClan is fine." She shook her head wearily. "Everybody's fine! What in StarClan is worrying you?"

"I had a dream," Fireheart explained uncomfortably. "Spottedleaf came and told me to beware an enemy who seems to sleep. I think she means the sickness."

Cinderpelt snorted. "The dream was probably warning you not to go waking poor old Cinderpelt, who's had a really long day, or you might get your whiskers pulled!"

Fireheart realized she looked exhausted. She must have been even busier than usual lately, carrying out her duties in the camp as well as caring for Littlecloud and Whitethroat. "I'm sorry," he meowed. "But I think the ShadowClan cats have to leave."

Cinderpelt opened her eyes fully for the first time. "You said they could stay till they were completely better," she reminded him. "Have you changed your mind because of this dream?"

"Spottedleaf has been right before," Fireheart answered. "I

can't take the risk of letting them stay."

Cinderpelt stared at him wordlessly for a moment, then mewed, "Let me speak to them."

Fireheart nodded. "But you must do it tomorrow," he insisted.

Cinderpelt rested her chin on her front paws. "I'll tell them," she promised. "But what if your dream was wrong? If ShadowClan is as riddled with the sickness as they say it is, you could be sending these cats to their deaths."

Fireheart felt his breath catch in his chest, but he knew he had to protect his own Clan. "You can show them how to make the healing mixture, can't you?" he suggested.

Cinderpelt nodded.

"Okay," Fireheart went on. "If you do that, they'll be able to take care of themselves, maybe even help their Clan-mates." The thought that he was not totally abandoning the desperate ShadowClan cats came as a relief, but he still felt the need to explain why he was turning them away. "Cinderpelt, I have to listen to Spottedleaf. . . ." A hard lump of sadness choked him into silence. The scent of ferns around him made the memory of the medicine cat even sharper, for this was where she had lived and worked.

"You talk about her as if she is still alive," murmured Cinderpelt, closing her eyes. "Why can't you let her rest with StarClan? I know she was special to you, but remember what Yellowfang said to me when I couldn't stop thinking about Silverstream: Put your energy into today. Stop worrying about the past."

"What's wrong with remembering Spottedleaf?" Fireheart protested.

"Because while you're dreaming about her, there's another cat—a living one—right under your nose whom you should be thinking about instead."

Fireheart stared at Cinderpelt, puzzled. "What are you talking about?"

"Haven't you noticed?"

"Noticed what?"

Cinderpelt opened her eyes and lifted her head. "Fireheart, every cat in the Clan can see that Sandstorm is very, very fond of you!"

Fireheart felt a hot flush spread through his fur and he started to protest, but Cinderpelt ignored him. "Now go away and let me rest," she muttered, resting her chin on her paws once more. "I'll tell Littlecloud and Whitethroat to leave tomorrow, I promise."

By the time Fireheart reached the fern tunnel he could hear Cinderpelt's gentle snoring mingling with the steady rasps of Yellowfang. His mind was still reeling as he padded into the clearing. He knew Sandstorm liked and respected him, far more than he would ever have expected when he first joined the Clan, but it had never occurred to him that she felt anything stronger than friendship for him. Suddenly he pictured the soft sparkle in her pale green eyes when she had licked his stinging paws, and his fur began to prickle with a sensation he had not felt before.

CHAPTER 14

Over the next few days, the streams in ThunderClan territory dwindled until the only freshwater to be found was near the RiverClan border, on the far side of Sunningrocks.

"There's never been a summer like it," grumbled One-Eye. "The forest is as dry as a kit's bedding."

Fireheart was searching the sky for clouds, sending a silent prayer to StarClan that rain would come soon. The drought was forcing the ThunderClan cats to fetch water nearer and nearer to the place where Cinderpelt had sheltered the sick ShadowClan cats, and he didn't want to risk any of the patrols coming into contact with lingering traces of disease. At the same time, he was almost grateful for the distraction of worrying about water, which left him less time to dwell on what had happened to Cloudpaw, and where his apprentice might be now.

The sunhigh patrol had just returned, and Frostfur was organizing a party of elders and queens to go to the river to drink. They gathered in the narrow shadows at the edge of the clearing.

"Why would StarClan send such a drought now?" Smallear

complained. Out of the corner of his eye Fireheart saw the old gray tom glance in his direction, and he remembered with a shiver the elder's warning about the broken rituals.

"It's not the dryness that bothers me," rasped One-Eye. "It's all the Twolegs out in the forest. I've never heard so many crashing around, scaring off the prey and ruining our scent markers with their stench. A bit of rain might drive them away."

"Well, I'm worried about Willowpelt," meowed Speckle-tail. "It's quite a journey to the stream and back, and she doesn't like to leave her kits for so long. But if she doesn't drink, her milk'll dry up and her kits will starve."

"Goldenflower too," Patchpelt put in. "Perhaps if we each carried back moss soaked in water, they could lick the moisture from that?" he suggested.

"That's a great idea," Fireheart meowed. He wondered why he hadn't thought of that himself. Perhaps he had been trying to put the nursery—and one kit in particular—out of his mind. "Can you bring some back today?"

The old black-and-white tom nodded.

"We'll all bring some," offered Speckletail.

"Thank you." Fireheart blinked gratefully at her. He couldn't help thinking with a pang of regret how eagerly Cloudpaw would have volunteered to help the elders. He'd always been particularly close to them, listening to their stories at night and sometimes even sharing their meals. It stung Fireheart, if he let himself think about it for too long, that the elders hardly seemed to notice Cloudpaw's absence. Was Fireheart the only cat in ThunderClan who thought Cloudpaw could have adjusted to life in the forest? He shook his ears irritably. Perhaps Bluestar was right, and the young cat had made the right decision to leave. But it didn't stop Fireheart from missing him with an unexpected intensity.

He called to Sandstorm and Brackenfur, who were resting in the shade of the nettle patch after the sunhigh patrol. They leaped up at once and trotted over to him.

"Would you escort Smallear and the others?" Fireheart meowed. "I don't know how close to the river they'll have to go, and they'll need some backup if they bump into a RiverClan patrol." He paused. "I know you're tired, but the other cats are out training, and I need to stay with Whitestorm to guard the camp."

"No problem," meowed Brackenfur easily.

"I'm not tired, Fireheart," insisted Sandstorm, fixing him with her leaf-green gaze.

Fireheart's paws tingled as he remembered what Cinderpelt had told him a few nights ago. "Er, great," he meowed, a little too loudly. He began washing his chest self-consciously, his licks becoming brisker as he noticed that Brackenfur's whiskers were twitching with amusement.

He was relieved when the group padded out of the gorse tunnel leaving him in the deserted clearing. Whitestorm was with Bluestar, in her den. Willowpelt and Goldenflower were in the nursery with their kits. Fireheart had noticed Tigerclaw's kit padding around the camp on unsteady legs these past few days, encouraged by Goldenflower. He'd found himself avoiding its eyes, and had looked on warily as, little by little, it joined in with Clan life.

Now, as he listened to it mewling with the other kits, Fireheart's main thought was how hungry it would be if its mother didn't get water soon. He hoped that the cats wouldn't have to travel all the way to the river, and he pictured the band of queens and elders moving slowly through the undergrowth with Sandstorm beside them, her orange fur glowing among the green fronds. With a jolt, he remembered the sick ShadowClan cats. What if Cinderpelt hadn't really sent them away and they were still hiding there?

Fireheart shuddered. He hurried toward Yellowfang's clearing and nearly bumped into Cinderpelt limping out of the tunnel entrance.

"What's the matter with you?" she mewed cheerily, and then she looked at the frown on Fireheart's face and her expression changed.

"Did you tell Littlecloud and Whitethroat they must leave?" Fireheart whispered urgently.

"We've been through all this already." Cinderpelt sighed impatiently.

"Are you sure they've gone?"

"They promised to leave that night." Her blue eyes challenged Fireheart to argue with her.

"And there's no stench of sickness left?" he persisted, his fur pricking with worry.

"Look!" she snapped. "I told them to leave and they said they would. I don't have time for this. There are berries to be collected, and the birds will get them if I don't. If you don't believe me about the ShadowClan cats, why don't you check for yourself?"

A low yowl came from the medicine cat's den. "I don't know who you're mewing at out there, but stop it now and go and fetch those berries!"

"Sorry, Yellowfang," Cinderpelt called over her shoulder. "I'm just talking to Fireheart." Her eyes flashed accusingly at him as Yellowfang's voice sounded again.

"Well, tell him to stop wasting your time, or he'll have me to answer to!"

Cinderpelt's shoulders relaxed and her whiskers twitched with amusement. Fireheart felt a pang of guilt. "I'm sorry to keep going on about it, Cinderpelt. It's not that I don't trust you. It's just that I—"

"You're just a fretful old badger," she told him, nudging him affectionately on his shoulder. "Go and check out the root cave for yourself, if you want to put your mind at rest." She brushed past him and limped toward the camp entrance.

Cinderpelt was right. Fireheart knew he would be satisfied only once he'd seen the ancient oak himself to make sure it was free of both ShadowClan cats and sickness. But he couldn't leave now. He and Whitestorm were the only warriors in the camp. His fur itching with frustration and worry, Fireheart began to pace the clearing. As he turned below the Highrock to retrace his steps yet again, he spotted Whitestorm padding toward him.

"Have you decided on the evening patrol yet?" called the white warrior.

"I thought Runningwind could take Thornpaw and Mousefur."

"Good idea," answered Whitestorm distractedly. He clearly had something on his mind. "Could Brightpaw go with the dawn patrol tomorrow?" he asked. "The experience will do her good. I . . . I haven't been keeping up with her training lately." Whitestorm's ear twitched and, with a twinge of unease, Fireheart realized that the white warrior had been spending more and more of his time with Bluestar. He couldn't help suspecting that Whitestorm was afraid of what the ThunderClan leader might do if he left her alone for too long. At the same time Fireheart felt guiltily relieved that there was another cat in the Clan—the most respected senior warrior, no less—who shared his concerns for their troubled leader.

"Of course," he agreed.

Whitestorm sat down beside Fireheart and looked around the clearing. "It's quiet this afternoon."

"Sandstorm and Brackenfur have taken the elders and queens to drink by the river. Patchpelt suggested bringing back moss soaked with water for Willowpelt and Goldenflower."

Whitestorm nodded. "Perhaps they could share some with Bluestar. She seems reluctant to leave the camp." The old warrior lowered his voice. "She's been licking the dew from the leaves each morning, but she needs more than that in this heat."

Fireheart felt a fresh wave of anxiety swell in his chest. "She seemed so much better the other day."

"She is getting better all the time," the white warrior assured him. "But still, she . . ." His deep mew trailed away and, although Fireheart felt shaken by the dark frown on the old warrior's face, there was no need to say any more.

"I understand," he murmured. "I'll ask Patchpelt to take her some when they return."

"Thank you." Whitestorm narrowed his eyes at Fireheart. "You're doing very well, you know," he remarked calmly.

Fireheart sat up. "What do you mean?"

"Being deputy. I know it hasn't been easy, with Bluestar . . . the way she is, and the drought. But I doubt there's a cat in the Clan who would deny that Bluestar made the right choice when she appointed you."

Apart from Darkstripe, Dustpelt, and half the elders, Fireheart responded silently. Then he realized he was being churlish, and he blinked gratefully at the white warrior. "Thank you, Whitestorm," he purred. He couldn't help feeling encouraged by such high praise from this wise cat, whose opinion he valued as much as Bluestar's.

"And I'm sorry about Cloudpaw," Whitestorm went on gently. "It must be very hard for you. After all, he was your kin, and I think it is too easy for Clanborn cats to take that bond for granted."

Fireheart was taken aback by the warrior's shrewdness. "Well, yes," he began hesitantly. "I do miss him. Not just because he was my kin. I truly believe he could have made a good warrior in the end." He glanced sideways at White-storm, half expecting the old cat to contradict him, but to his surprise the warrior was nodding.

"He was a good hunter, and a good friend to the other apprentices," Whitestorm agreed. "But perhaps StarClan has a different destiny for him. I am no medicine cat; I can-not read the stars like Yellowfang or Cinderpelt, but I have always been willing to trust our warrior ancestors, wherever they might lead our Clan."

And that is what makes you such a noble warrior, Fireheart thought, filled with admiration for Whitestorm's loyalty to the warrior code. If Cloudpaw had had one whisker's worth of such understanding, perhaps things would have been very different. . . .

The sound of pebbles clattering outside the camp wall made both cats jump. Fireheart dashed to the camp entrance. Speckletail and the others were crashing down the rocky slope, sending grit and dirt crumbling around them. Their fur was bristling and their eyes were filled with alarm.

"Twolegs!" Speckletail panted as she reached the foot of the ravine.

Fireheart looked up to where Brackenfur and Sandstorm were helping the eldest cats as they struggled down from boulder to boulder.

"It's okay," Sandstorm called down. "We lost them."

When they were all safely at the bottom, Brackenfur explained, his breath coming in frightened gasps: "There was a group of young ones. They chased us!"

Fireheart's fur bristled with alarm as a terrified mewing broke out among the other cats. "Are you all okay?" he meowed.

Sandstorm looked around the group and nodded.

"Good." Fireheart steadied himself with a deep breath. "Where were these Twolegs? Were they by the river?"

"We hadn't even reached Sunningrocks," answered Sandstorm. Her voice grew calmer as she got her breath back, and her eyes began to gleam with indignation. "They were loose in the woods, not on the usual Twoleg paths."

Fireheart tried not to betray his alarm. Twolegs rarely ventured this deep into the forest. "We shall have to wait till dark to fetch water," he decided out loud.

"Do you think they'll be gone by then?" asked One-Eye shakily.

"Why would they stay?" Fireheart tried to sound reassuring despite his private doubts. Who could predict what a Twoleg might do?

"But what about Willowpelt and Goldenflower?" fretted Speckletail. "They'll need water before then."

"I'll go and fetch some," offered Sandstorm.

"No," meowed Fireheart. "I'll go." Fetching water for Willowpelt would give him a perfect opportunity to take Cinderpelt's advice and check for himself that the ShadowClan cats and their sickness had gone from the cave beneath the old oak. He nodded to Sandstorm. "I need you to stay at the top of the ravine and look out for Twolegs." One-Eye let out an anxious mew. "I'm sure they'll have turned back by now," Fireheart soothed the elder. "But you'll be safe with Sandstorm on guard." He looked into the orange she-cat's sparkling emerald eyes and knew he spoke the truth.

"I'll come with you," meowed Brackenfur.

Fireheart shook his head. He had to make this journey alone to avoid any other cats finding out about Cinderpelt's foolish good deed. "You'll need to guard the camp with Whitestorm," he told the pale ginger warrior. "And I want you to report what you saw in the forest just now to Bluestar. I'll carry back as much moss as I can. The rest of you will have to wait till sunset."

Fireheart and Sandstorm climbed the ravine together, cautiously sniffing the air as they approached the top. There was no scent of Twolegs here.

"Be careful," whispered Sandstorm as Fireheart prepared to head into the forest.

He licked the top of her head. "I will," he promised softly.

Green eyes met green eyes for a long moment; then Fireheart turned and crept warily through the trees. He kept to the thickest undergrowth, his ears pricked and his mouth half-open as he strained his senses to pick up any signs of Twolegs. He smelled their unnatural stench as he approached Sunningrocks, but it was stale now.

Fireheart turned and cut through the woods to the slope above the river that marked the RiverClan border. As he checked for RiverClan patrols, he couldn't help looking out for the familiar gray head of his friend, Graystripe. But there was no sign of any cats in the airless forest. Fireheart would be able to fetch water from the stream without being challenged, but first he had to check the cave beneath the ancient oak.

He headed along the border, stopping at every other tree to leave his scent and freshen the boundary between the two Clans. Even this close to the river, the forest had lost its newleaf lushness and the leaves looked shriveled and worn. Fireheart soon spotted the gnarled oak, and as he drew near he saw the dusty cave where the ShadowClan cats had sheltered.

He breathed in deeply. The stench of sickness had gone. With a sigh of relief he decided to take a quick look inside and then fetch the water. He padded forward, his eyes fixed on the hole. He crouched low, then cautiously stretched his neck and peered into the makeshift den.

He let out a startled gasp as a weight dropped onto his back and claws grasped his sides. Fear and rage pulsed through him and he yowled, twisting violently in an attempt to throw off his attacker. But the cat who had ambushed him kept a firm hold. Fireheart braced himself for the pain of thorn-sharp claws in his flanks, but the paws that clutched him were wide and soft, their claws unsheathed. Then a familiar scent filled his nostrils—a scent overlaid now with the odors of RiverClan, but recognizable all the same.

"Graystripe!" he meowed joyfully.

"I thought you would never come to see me," purred Graystripe.

Fireheart felt his old friend slip from his back and realized that Graystripe was dripping wet with river water. His own orange pelt was soaked from their tussle. He shook himself and stared in amazement at the gray warrior. "You swam across the river?" he meowed in disbelief. Every cat in ThunderClan knew how much Graystripe hated getting his thick fur wet.

Graystripe gave himself a quick shake, and the water spattered easily from his pelt. His long fur, which used to soak up water like moss, looked sleek and glossy. "It's quicker than going down to the stepping-stones," he pointed out. "Besides, my fur doesn't seem to hold the water as much anymore. One of the advantages of eating fish, I suppose."

"About the only one, I should think," answered Fireheart, screwing up his face. He couldn't imagine how the strong flavor of fish could compare to the subtle, musky flavors of ThunderClan's forest prey.

"It's not so bad once you get used to it," meowed Graystripe. He blinked warmly at Fireheart. "You look well."

"You too," Fireheart purred back.

"How is everyone? Is Dustpelt still being a pain? How's Bluestar?"

"Dustpelt's fine," Fireheart began, and then hesitated. "Bluestar is . . ." He searched for words, unsure how much to tell his old friend about the ThunderClan leader.

"What's up?" asked Graystripe, his eyes narrowing.

Fireheart realized that the gray warrior knew him too well to miss his reaction. His ears flicked self-consciously.

"Bluestar's all right, isn't she?" Graystripe's voice was thick with concern.

"She's fine," Fireheart assured him quickly, relieved—it was his anxiety about the ThunderClan leader that Graystripe had detected, not his wariness of his old friend. "But she hasn't really been her old self lately. Not since Tigerclaw . . ." He trailed off uncertainly.

Graystripe frowned. "Have you seen that old poisonpaws since he left?"

Fireheart shook his head. "Not a sign of him. I don't know how Bluestar would react if she saw him again."

"She'd scratch his eyes out, if I know her," purred Graystripe. "I can't imagine anything keeping Bluestar down for long."

I wish that were true, Fireheart thought sadly. He looked into Graystripe's curious eyes, knowing with a pang of sadness that his desire to confide in his old friend had been an impossible dream. Graystripe was a member of RiverClan now, and Fireheart had to accept with a heavy heart that he couldn't share the details of his leader's weakness with a cat from another Clan. And he also realized that he wasn't prepared to tell Graystripe about Cloudpaw's disappearance—at least, not yet. Fireheart tried to tell himself this was because he didn't want to worry Graystripe when his friend was unable to help, anyway. But he suspected his silence might have more to do with pride. He didn't want Graystripe to know that he had failed as a mentor for a second time, so soon after Cinderpelt's accident.

"What's it like in RiverClan?" he meowed, deliberately

changing the subject.

Graystripe shrugged. "Not much different from ThunderClan. Some of them are friendly, some of them are grumpy, some of them are funny, some of them are . . . Well, they're just like normal Clan cats, I suppose."

Fireheart couldn't help envying the gray warrior for sounding so relaxed. Clearly Graystripe's new life didn't carry the burden of responsibility that Fireheart had to deal with now that he was deputy. And part of him still felt a small thorn of resentment that had mingled with his grief since Graystripe had left ThunderClan. Fireheart knew his friend could not have abandoned his kits; he just wished he'd fought harder to keep them in ThunderClan.

Fireheart pushed away these unfriendly thoughts. "How are your kits?" he asked.

Graystripe purred proudly. "They're wonderful!" he declared. "The she-kit is just like her mother, every bit as beautiful, and with the same temper! She gives her den mother quite a bit of trouble, but every cat loves her. Especially Crookedstar. The tom is more easygoing, happy whatever he's doing."

"Like his father," remarked Fireheart.

"And almost as handsome," boasted Graystripe, his eyes gleaming with amusement.

Fireheart felt a familiar rush of joy at being with his old friend. "I miss you," he meowed, suddenly overwhelmed with longing to have Graystripe back at the camp, to hunt and fight beside him again. "Why don't you come home?"

Graystripe shook his wide gray head. "I can't leave my kits," he meowed.

Fireheart couldn't help the look of disbelief that flashed in his eyes—after all, kits were raised by queens, not their fathers—and Graystripe went on quickly: "Oh, they are very well cared for in the nursery. They would be safe and happy with RiverClan. But I don't think I could bear to be away from them. They remind me too much of Silverstream."

"You miss her that much?"

"I loved her," Graystripe answered simply.

Fireheart felt a pang of jealousy until he remembered the sorrow he still felt whenever he awoke from a dream of Spottedleaf. He reached forward and touched Graystripe's cheek with his nose. Only StarClan knew if he might have done the same thing for Spottedleaf. *Or Sandstorm?* whispered a voice deep in Fireheart's mind.

Graystripe nudged him back, disturbing Fireheart's wandering thoughts and almost unbalancing him. "Enough soppy stuff!" he meowed, as if he could read his friend's mind. "You didn't really come here to see me, did you?"

Fireheart was caught off guard. "Well, not entirely . . ." he confessed.

"You were looking for those ShadowClan cats, right?"

"How did you know about them?" Fireheart demanded, stunned.

"How could I not know?" exclaimed Graystripe. "The

stench they were giving off. ShadowClan cats smell bad enough on their own, but sick ones . . . yuck!"

"Does the rest of RiverClan know about them?" Fireheart was alarmed to think that the other Clans could have found out ThunderClan was sheltering ShadowClan cats again—and ones tainted by sickness at that.

"Not as far as I know," Graystripe assured him. "I offered to do all the patrolling at this end of the river. The other cats just thought I was homesick and indulged me. I think they were secretly hoping I'd go back to ThunderClan if I got enough of the forest scents!"

"But why would you protect the ShadowClan cats like that?" Fireheart asked, puzzled.

"I came over and spoke to them soon after they arrived," Graystripe explained. "They told me that Cinderpelt had hidden them here. I reckoned that if Cinderpelt had something to do with it, then you must know. Sheltering a couple of sickly fleabags is just the sort of softhearted thing you'd do."

"Well, I wasn't exactly thrilled when I found out," Fireheart admitted.

"But I bet you let her off."

Fireheart shrugged. "Well, yes."

"She always could wrap you around her paw," meowed Graystripe affectionately. "Anyway, they've gone now."

"When did they leave?" Fireheart felt a wave of relief that Cinderpelt had kept her promise.

"I saw one hunting this side of the river a couple of days

ago, but not a whisker since."

"A couple of days ago?" Fireheart was alarmed to hear that the ShadowClan cats were still there so recently. Had Cinderpelt decided to nurse them until they were well enough to travel, after all? His fur prickled with irritation at the thought, but he trusted that she had not made the decision lightly. He was just grateful to StarClan that they hadn't bumped into a water-gathering patrol from ThunderClan. They were gone now, and with any luck so was the threat of sickness.

"Look," meowed Graystripe, "I have to go. I'm on hunting duty, and I promised I'd watch a couple of apprentices this afternoon."

"Have you got an apprentice of your own?" Fireheart asked.

Graystripe met his gaze steadily. "I don't think RiverClan is willing to trust me to train their warriors yet," he murmured. Fireheart couldn't tell if it was amusement or regret that made his old friend's whiskers twitch.

"I'll see you again sometime," Graystripe meowed, giving Fireheart a shove with his muzzle.

"Definitely." Fireheart felt a black hole of sadness yawn in his belly as the gray warrior turned to leave. Spottedleaf, Graystripe, Cloudpaw . . . Was Fireheart destined to lose every cat he grew close to? "Take care!" he called. He watched Graystripe pad through the ferns to the edge of the river and wade in confidently. The warrior's broad shoulders glided through the water, leaving a gentle wake as he swam with strongly churning paws. Fireheart shook his head, wishing he could scatter his troubled thoughts as easily as Graystripe's pelt had shed water after his swim. Then he turned away and headed into the trees.

CHAPTER 15

Fireheart carried the ball of wet moss gently between his teeth. Some of the moisture had dripped out on the journey home, soaking his chest and cooling his forepaws, but there would be enough to quench Goldenflower's and Willowpelt's thirst until a patrol could collect more after sunset.

The Clan lay in small groups around the clearing while the sun slowly slid toward the treetops. Most of them had eaten and were quietly sharing tongues in the customary grooming session, pausing briefly between licks to greet Fireheart as he emerged from the gorse tunnel. He nodded to Runningwind, Mousefur, and Thornpaw, who were about to go out on the evening patrol.

Brindleface was getting ready to lead another group of elders to fetch water. She was gathering them together at the fallen oak, and Fireheart heard Smallear's determined mew as he passed. "We'll need to keep our ears pricked and our eyes sharp while we're traveling." The old gray tom went on: "You see that nick in my ear? I got that when I was an apprentice. An owl swooped out of nowhere. But I'll bet my claws left a bigger scar than his!"

Fireheart felt his fur relax on his shoulders, soothed by the familiar murmurings of Clan life. The ShadowClan cats were gone, just as Cinderpelt had promised, and he had seen Graystripe. He slipped into the nursery and placed the moss gently beside Willowpelt and Goldenflower.

"Thanks, Fireheart," meowed Willowpelt.

"There'll be more after supper," Fireheart promised as the two queens began to lick the precious drops of water from the clump of moss. He tried to ignore the eyes of Tigerclaw's kit gleaming hungrily from the shadows as Goldenflower pressed the moss with her muzzle to squeeze out another mouthful.

"Brindleface is going to lead the other elders to the river once the sun has set and the woods are clear of Twolegs," Fireheart explained.

Goldenflower licked her lips. "It's been a while since some of them have been out in the forest after dark," she commented.

"I think Smallear is looking forward to it," purred Fireheart. "He was telling stories about the owl that used to hunt near Sunningrocks. Poor Halftail looked a bit nervous."

"A little excitement will do him good," Willowpelt remarked. "I wish I could go with them. A scrap with an owl would be just the thing to stretch my legs!"

"Do you miss being a warrior?" Fireheart asked, surprised. Willowpelt looked so comfortable lying in the nursery while her fast-growing kits scrambled over her. It hadn't occurred to him she might hanker after her old life.

"Wouldn't *you*?" Willowpelt challenged him.

"Well, yes," stammered Fireheart. "But you have your kits."

Willowpelt twisted her head to pick up a tiny tortoiseshell-and-white she-kit that had tumbled off her flank. She dropped it between her forepaws and gave it a lick. "Oh, yes, I have my kits," she agreed. "But I miss running through the forest, hunting for my own prey, and patrolling our borders." She licked the kit again and added, "I'm looking forward to taking these three out into the forest for the first time."

"They look like they'll make fine warriors," Fireheart meowed. The bittersweet memory of Cloudpaw's first expedition, when he went into the snowbound forest and came back with a vole, rose in Fireheart's mind, and he blinked. He dipped his head to the queens and turned to leave, glancing furtively at Tigerclaw's kit. He couldn't help wondering what sort of warrior it would be. "Bye," he mumbled as he squeezed out of the nursery.

He could smell the tempting scents of the fresh-kill pile wafting from nearby, but there was one more thing he had to do before he could settle down for his evening meal. He padded across the clearing to Yellowfang's den.

The elderly medicine cat was resting in the evening sun, her fur dull and unkempt as usual. She lifted her muzzle to greet him. "Hello, Fireheart," she rasped. "What are you doing here?"

"Looking for Cinderpelt," answered Fireheart.

"Why? What do you want now?" Cinderpelt's mew sounded from inside her fern nest, and her gray head popped out.

"Is that any way to greet your deputy?" Yellowfang scolded, her eyes glinting with amusement.

"It is when he disturbs my sleep," retorted Cinderpelt, clambering out. "He seems determined I shouldn't get any rest these days!"

Yellowfang narrowed her eyes at Fireheart. "Have you two been up to something I should know about?"

"Are you questioning your deputy?" Cinderpelt teased.

Yellowfang purred. "I know you've been up to something," she meowed. "But I won't pry. All I know is that my apprentice seems back to her old self again. Which is good, because she was no use to any cat while she was moping around like a damp mushroom!"

Fireheart was very relieved to see the two cats sparring with each other as they had done when Cinderpelt was first apprenticed to the medicine cat, before Silverstream had died. He shifted his paws awkwardly on the sun-baked ground. He had come to tell Cinderpelt that the ShadowClan cats had gone, but with Yellowfang here it was not easy.

"It's strange," Yellowfang growled, looking pointedly at Fireheart. "I suddenly feel like fetching another mouse from the fresh-kill pile." Fireheart blinked gratefully at the old medicine cat. "Anything you want, Cinderpelt?" she called over her shoulder as she padded toward the tunnel. Cinderpelt shook her head. "Okay, I'll be back in a moment," Yellowfang rasped. "Or maybe two."

When she had disappeared, Fireheart meowed quietly, "I checked on the ShadowClan cats. They've gone."

"I told you they would," replied Cinderpelt.

"But they didn't go until a couple of days ago," Fireheart added.

"It would haven't done them any good to travel any sooner," mewed Cinderpelt. "And I had to make sure they'd learned how to make the herb mixture before they went."

Fireheart twitched his tail at Cinderpelt's stubbornness, but he couldn't bring himself to argue with her. He knew she believed with all her heart that she had done the right thing in caring for them, and part of him agreed it had been worth the risk.

"I did tell them to leave, you know," she meowed, her tone losing some of its certainty.

"I believe you," Fireheart agreed gently. "It was my responsibility to make sure they left, not yours."

Cinderpelt looked up at him curiously. "How do you know when they left?"

"Graystripe told me."

"You spoke to Graystripe? Is he okay?"

"He's fine," Fireheart purred. "He swims like a fish now."

"You're kidding!" mewed Cinderpelt. "I'd never have expected that."

"Me neither," Fireheart agreed, then stopped, embarrassed, when his belly growled with hunger.

"Go and eat," Cinderpelt ordered. "You'd better hurry up before Yellowfang demolishes the entire pile."

Fireheart leaned down and licked Cinderpelt's ears. "See you later," he mewed.

Yellowfang had left him the choice of squirrel or a pigeon. Fireheart took the pigeon and looked around the clearing, wondering where to eat it. He sensed Sandstorm watching him, her slender body stretched out and her tail neatly curled over her hind legs.

Fireheart felt his heart begin to beat faster. Suddenly it didn't matter that she wasn't tortoiseshell, and that her eyes were pale green, not amber. Fireheart looked at the pale ginger warrior, the pigeon hanging limply from his jaws, and remembered what Cinderpelt had told him: live in the present, let go of the past. He knew Spottedleaf would always remain in his heart, but he couldn't deny the way the fur tingled along his spine at the sight of Sandstorm. He padded across the clearing to join her. As he laid his pigeon beside her and started to eat, he heard her begin to purr.

Suddenly a terrible caterwauling made Fireheart jerk up his head. Sandstorm scrambled to her paws as Mousefur and Thornpaw thundered into the clearing. Their fur was matted with blood, and Thornpaw was limping badly.

Fireheart swallowed his mouthful quickly and heaved himself up. "What happened? Where's Runningwind?"

The other cats gathered behind him, hissing with fear, their fur bristling as they prepared for trouble.

"I don't know. We were attacked," panted Mousefur.

"By who?" Fireheart demanded.

Mousefur shook her head. "We couldn't see. We were in the shadows."

"But what about their scent?"

"Too near the Thunderpath. Couldn't tell," answered Thornpaw, his breath coming in short gasps.

Fireheart looked at the apprentice, who was swaying unsteadily on his paws. "Go and see Yellowfang," he ordered. "Whitestorm!" he called to the white warrior who was already hurrying from Bluestar's den. "I want you to come with us." He turned to Mousefur. "Lead us to where this happened."

Sandstorm and Dustpelt looked expectantly at Fireheart, waiting to receive orders. "You two stay here and guard the camp," he meowed. "This might be a trap to lure our warriors away. It's happened before." With Bluestar on her last life, Fireheart knew he had to leave the camp well protected.

He charged out of the camp with Whitestorm at his side and Mousefur panting behind them. Together they scrambled up the ravine and raced into the forest.

Fireheart slowed his pace when he saw that Mousefur was struggling to keep up. "Quick as you can," he urged. He knew she must be in pain after the fight, but they had to find Runningwind. He had a horrible feeling that this attack must have something to do with ShadowClan. Littlecloud and Whitethroat had been in ThunderClan territory so recently. Had they tricked him into leading his Clan into danger after all? He headed instinctively toward the Thunderpath.

"No," called Mousefur. "It's this way." She brushed past him, quickening her pace, and veered toward Fourtrees. Fireheart and Whitestorm sped after her.

As they raced through the trees, Fireheart realized he had been this way before. This was the trail Littlecloud and Whitethroat had followed after Bluestar had sent them away the first time. Had a ShadowClan raiding party come through the stone tunnel under the Thunderpath?

Mousefur skidded to a halt between two towering ash trees. The Thunderpath droned in the distance, its foul stench drifting through the undergrowth. Ahead, Fireheart saw Runningwind's lean brown body lying on the ground, ominously still. A black-and-white tom was bending over the unmoving warrior. With a jolt, Fireheart realized that it was Whitethroat.

The ShadowClan warrior's eyes stretched wide as he saw the approaching cats. He began to back away from Runningwind, his legs stumbling with shock. "He's dead!" he wailed.

Fireheart's ears flattened as rage pulsed through him. Was this how ShadowClan warriors repaid another Clan's kindness? Without stopping to see what Whitestorm and Mousefur were doing, he let out a furious screech and flung himself at Whitethroat, who shrank away, hissing. Fireheart knocked the ShadowClan warrior backward, and Whitethroat landed limply on the ground, offering no resistance as Fireheart loomed over him.

Fireheart stared down, confused, as his enemy crouched helplessly beneath him, his eyes narrowed into terrified slits. While he hesitated, Whitethroat darted away and bolted into a tangle of brambles. Fireheart chased after him, ignoring the thorns that tore at his fur. The ShadowClan warrior must be heading for the stone tunnel. He pushed onward and caught a glimpse of the tip of Whitethroat's tail as the tom struggled out of the brambles onto the grass verge.

Fireheart emerged a moment later and saw Whitethroat poised on the edge of the Thunderpath. Fireheart hurtled toward him, expecting Whitethroat to flee to the tunnel, but Whitethroat took one look at the ThunderClan warrior and raced straight onto the Thunderpath.

Fireheart watched in horror as the terrified cat scrambled blindly across the hard gray surface. A deafening roar sounded in his ears. Fireheart shrank back, screwing up his face as the foul-smelling wind of a monster blasted his fur. When it had passed, he blinked open his eyes and shook the grit from his ear fur. A ragged shape was lying motionless on the Thunderpath. The monster had hit Whitethroat.

For a long heartbeat Fireheart froze, flooded by dreadful memories of Cinderpelt's accident. Then he saw Whitethroat stir. Fireheart couldn't leave any cat out there. Not even a ShadowClan enemy that had killed one of ThunderClan's bravest warriors. He peered up and down the Thunderpath. There were no monsters in sight. He scurried across to where Whitethroat lay. The tom looked smaller than ever, his white chest glistening with blood like fire in the rays of the slowly sinking sun.

Fireheart knew that moving the cat would only hasten his death. Trembling with shock, he looked down at the warrior Cinderpelt had taken such trouble to care for, in secret from the rest of her Clan. "Why did you attack our patrol?" he whispered.

He leaned down as Whitethroat opened his mouth to speak, but the warrior's gurgling mew was drowned as a monster roared past terrifyingly close, sending a wave of fumes and grit over the two cats. Fireheart sank his claws as well as he could into the unyielding surface and crouched closer to the ShadowClan warrior.

Whitethroat opened his mouth again, releasing a thin trickle of blood. He swallowed painfully, sending a juddering spasm the length of his body. But before he could speak, his eyes focused on a point over Fireheart's shoulder, back toward the woods of ThunderClan territory. Fireheart watched as Whitethroat's eyes glittered with fear before they glazed over for the last time.

He spun around to see what had filled Whitethroat's final moments with such terror. His heart lurched when he saw who stood at the edge of the Thunderpath—the dark warrior who had prowled through so many of his dreams.

Tigerclaw.

CHAPTER 16
✿

Fireheart's claws felt rooted to the Thunderpath as he stared at the cat that had cast a menacing shadow over his life for so long. There was no need for any pretense of shared Clan loyalty now. Tigerclaw was an outcast, the enemy of all cats who followed the warrior code.

The fiery evening sun bled through the tips of the trees, its orange rays glowing on the dark pelt of the massive tabby. Across the silence of the deserted Thunderpath, Tigerclaw sneered at Fireheart.

"Is chasing puny cats to their deaths the best you can do to defend your territory?"

Fireheart's mind cleared in a heartbeat, leaving his body pulsing with strength and cold fury. He stared straight into Tigerclaw's eyes as the thundering of another monster stirred his ear fur. He held his ground as it whipped by him, another roaring at its heels. But Fireheart felt no fear. In the fleeting gap between the two monsters he focused on Tigerclaw and sprang.

Tigerclaw's eyes widened with surprise as Fireheart crashed into him, claws unsheathed and hissing with rage.

They rolled together across the grass into the cover of the trees. Fireheart drew strength from the familiar scents of the forest—his territory now, not Tigerclaw's—and the pair struggled wildly, flattening the brittle undergrowth and gouging deep scars in the ground with their claws.

Fireheart had gotten a good grip on Tigerclaw in his first pounce. He could feel every one of the tabby's ribs. Tigerclaw had lost weight, but his muscles felt hard beneath his thick pelt, and Fireheart quickly realized that exile had not diminished the warrior's strength. Tigerclaw crouched and leaped upward, twisting in midair. Fireheart felt himself being flung from Tigerclaw's back, felt the impact of the parched ground as he landed on his side. He gasped for the air that had been knocked from his lungs and struggled to his paws. He wasn't fast enough. Tigerclaw pounced on him, pinning him to the ground with claws that seemed to pierce Fireheart to the bone.

Fireheart yowled in agony, but the massive tom held him down, and he smelled the stench of crowfood as Tigerclaw stretched his neck forward to hiss into Fireheart's ear, "Are you listening, kittypet? I will kill you, and all your warriors, one by one."

Even in the heat of battle, his words sent a chill through Fireheart. He knew Tigerclaw meant what he said. He suddenly became aware of new noises and smells around him—the rustle of unfamiliar paws and strange cat scents. They were surrounded. But by whom? Confused by the scents of the Thunderpath, Whitethroat's blood, and his own fear,

Fireheart wondered bleakly if these could be the remaining cats from Brokentail's band of outcasts, who not long ago had helped Tigerclaw attack the ThunderClan camp. Had Whitethroat chosen to join these rogues rather than return to his own disease-ridden Clan?

In desperation Fireheart pushed up with his hind legs, his claws raking for a hold on Tigerclaw's belly. His old enemy must have underestimated how strong Fireheart had grown, for his grip loosened and he slithered onto the ground. Fireheart scrabbled away from him, lifting his head in time to see Mousefur and Whitestorm hurl themselves from the undergrowth onto two of the cats that had surrounded them. He glanced back at Tigerclaw, who had sprung to his paws and was rearing onto his hind legs, towering over Fireheart with his teeth bared and his amber eyes gleaming with hatred. He ducked as Tigerclaw lunged, darting forward and turning to swipe the dark warrior on the nose. Beside him he could hear the yowls and hisses of Whitestorm and Mousefur as they battled with the courage of StarClan. But they were badly outnumbered. As Fireheart dodged Tigerclaw once more, he looked around desperately for any means of escape. Claws raked at his hind legs, and he turned to see one of Tigerclaw's rogues grasping him and snarling viciously. He was skinny and ungroomed like the others, his eyes glittering with spite.

Tigerclaw reared up again with a furious hiss. Fireheart was bracing himself for Tigerclaw's blow when he saw a blaze of gray. A broad pair of shoulders flashed past, and Fireheart recognized a warrior he had fought alongside many times before.

Graystripe!

The gray warrior lunged at Tigerclaw's exposed belly, knocking him backward. Fireheart whipped around and bit the shoulder of the cat that clung to his hind leg until he felt his teeth scrape against bone. He released the rogue when he squealed, and spat out the blood that had dripped into his mouth.

Astounded, Fireheart looked at the battle that raged around him. Graystripe must have brought a whole RiverClan patrol, for now it was the rogue cats who were outnumbered as they struggled against the sleek-furred warriors. He turned to see Graystripe twisting free of Tigerclaw's grasp and sprang to help his friend. Together they reared at Tigerclaw, swiping at him to drive him backward, matched step for step as they had practiced so many times in training. Then, without even exchanging a glance, they lunged as one and forced the massive tabby onto the ground. Tigerclaw let out a muffled hiss as Fireheart pressed his foe's muzzle into the dirt while Graystripe grasped the tabby's shoulders and pounded his flank with his hind legs.

Fireheart heard screeches fading into the woods and realized that the rogue cats were fleeing the battle. Tigerclaw took advantage of Fireheart's lapse of attention and wriggled free. He fled toward the brambles, spitting with fury, and disappeared among the barbed stems.

As the wails of the rogue cats faded away, the warriors

shook the dust from their pelts and licked their wounds. Fireheart realized for the first time that Bluestar's son, Stonefur, was among the RiverClan cats. "Is anyone badly hurt?" he gasped.

The cats shook their heads, even Mousefur, who was still bleeding from the first attack.

"We should return to our own territory," meowed Stonefur.

"ThunderClan thanks you for your help." Fireheart dipped his head respectfully.

"Rogue cats threaten all of us," Stonefur replied. "We couldn't leave you to fight them alone."

Whitestorm shook his muzzle, scattering drops of blood. He looked at Graystripe. "It's good to fight beside you again, friend. What brought you here?"

"He heard Fireheart's yowl from Fourtrees, where we were patrolling," Stonefur answered for Graystripe. "He persuaded us to come and help."

"Thanks," answered Fireheart warmly. "All of you."

Stonefur nodded and turned away into the trees. His patrol followed. Fireheart touched Graystripe with his muzzle as he passed, sorry to see him leave, and painfully aware that there was no time to say as much as he wanted. "See you, Graystripe," he meowed.

He felt Graystripe's purr rumbling through his thick coat. "See you," murmured the gray warrior.

Fireheart shivered as the sun finally disappeared from the forest. He could see Mousefur's eyes shining in the dark, tense with pain. Then he felt a fresh wave of sorrow as he remembered the price that had been paid for the rogue cats' attack. Runningwind's body would be growing cold by now. And this was not the only untimely death Tigerclaw had brought to the forest that day.

Fireheart looked at Whitestorm. "Can you and Mousefur get Runningwind back to camp without me?"

The white warrior narrowed his eyes curiously but said nothing and nodded.

Fireheart twitched his ear. "I'll follow you back soon. There's something I must do first."

CHAPTER 17

🍂

Fireheart padded heavily back to the Thunderpath. The smell of Tigerclaw and the rogue cats was still heavy in the air, but he could hear no noises other than birdsong and the whispering of the breeze through the leaves. In the calm after the battle, he noticed how strongly the scent of ShadowClan mingled with the other smells. Had there been other ShadowClan cats, as well as Whitethroat, among the rogues? He wondered if the sickness in the ShadowClan camp was so bad that its warriors were imposing their own exile and joining up with Tigerclaw's band of outcasts for protection. Or perhaps the scent had simply wafted from the territory on the other side of the Thunderpath.

Fireheart stared across the hard gray path at the body of the black-and-white warrior. If Whitethroat had joined the rogue cats because his Clan was too sick to support him, it didn't explain the look of horror on his face when he'd seen Tigerclaw. Why would Whitethroat have been so terrified if Tigerclaw were now his leader? With a flicker of guilt, Fireheart suddenly wondered if Whitethroat had stumbled on Runningwind's body by sheer accident, after Tigerclaw had led the attack on the ThunderClan patrol. But what was he doing in ThunderClan territory? And where was Littlecloud? There were too many questions, and none of the answers made sense.

One thing was certain: Fireheart could not leave Whitethroat's body to be battered by monsters on the Thunderpath. It was quiet now, and Fireheart crossed to the middle and grasped the warrior's scruff in his teeth. He dragged him gently across to the verge on the far side, hoping that his Clanmates would find him soon and give him an honorable burial. Whatever Whitethroat had or had not done, StarClan would judge him now.

When Fireheart entered the moonlit ThunderClan camp, Runningwind's body lay in the center of the clearing. He looked peaceful, stretched out as if he were asleep. Bluestar was pacing around the warrior's body, her broad gray head swinging from side to side.

The rest of the Clan hung back, keeping to the shadows at the edge of the clearing. The air was thick with distress. The cats weaved silently among one another, glancing anxiously at their leader as she padded back and forth, muttering under her breath. She didn't even try to control her grief, as she would have done once. Fireheart remembered how quietly she had mourned her old friend and deputy, Lionheart, many moons ago. She showed none of that silent dignity now.

Fireheart could feel the Clan watching him as he approached their leader. Bluestar looked up, and he felt a stab of alarm when he saw that her eyes were clouded with fear and shock.

"They say Tigerclaw did this," she rasped.

"It might have been one of his rogues."

"How many are there?"

"I don't know," Fireheart admitted. It had been impossible to count in the thick of battle. "Many."

Bluestar began to shake her head again, but Fireheart knew she had to be told everything, whether she wanted to know what was going on in the forest or not. "Tigerclaw wants vengeance against ThunderClan," he reported. "He told me he is going to kill our warriors one by one."

Behind him the Clan exploded into horrified yowls. Fireheart let them wail, keeping his eyes fixed on Bluestar. He felt his heart flutter like a trapped bird as he begged StarClan to give her the strength to cope with this openly declared threat. Gradually the Clan fell silent, and Fireheart waited with them for Bluestar to speak. An owl screeched in the distance as it dived through the trees.

Bluestar lifted her head. "It's only me he wants to kill," she murmured, so quietly that only Fireheart could hear her. "For the sake of the Clan—"

"No!" Fireheart spat, cutting her off. Did Bluestar really intend to give herself up to Tigerclaw? "He wants revenge on the whole Clan, not just you!"

She dropped her head. "Such vicious betrayal!" she hissed. "How could I not have seen his treachery when he lived among us? What a fool I've been!" She shook her head, her eyes closed. "What a mouse-brained fool."

Fireheart's paws trembled. Bluestar seemed determined to torture herself by claiming all responsibility for Tigerclaw's wickedness. With a sickening jolt he realized he would have to take charge.

"We must make sure the camp is guarded day and night from now on. Longtail." He looked over at the striped warrior. "You will sit guard till moonhigh." Then he swung his head toward Frostfur. "You will take over then." The two cats nodded, and Fireheart bent his head toward Runningwind's body. "Mousefur and Brackenfur can bury Runningwind at dawn. Bluestar will sit vigil with him until then." He glanced at his leader, who was staring blankly at the ground, and hoped that she'd heard him.

"I will join her," meowed Whitestorm. The white warrior shouldered his way through the crowd and sat beside Bluestar, pressing his pelt against hers.

One by one the Clan padded forward to pay their respects to their lost friend. Willowpelt slipped from the nursery and touched the dead warrior gently with her muzzle, whispering her sorrowful farewell. Goldenflower followed her, signaling to her kits to stay back. Fireheart felt a chilling sense of foreboding as he saw the dark tabby kit peering curiously around his mother. He couldn't help feeling that this kit, however innocent, kept Tigerclaw's menace alive inside the Clan. Fireheart shook away the thought as he watched Goldenflower gently lick Runningwind's cheek. He must have faith in her and the Clan to raise the kit to be a truer warrior than his father had been.

After Goldenflower had padded away, Fireheart stepped forward and leaned down to lick Runningwind's dull pelt. "I will avenge your death," he promised softly.

As he backed away, he saw a figure step forward from the shadow of the Highrock. It was Darkstripe. Fireheart watched his eyes flick from Runningwind to Bluestar and back, burning, not with fear or grief, but with a brooding thoughtfulness.

Unsettled, Fireheart headed for one place he knew he would find comfort. He padded through the ferns to Yellowfang's den, his bites and scratches beginning to sting as much as the thorn-sharp doubts that fretted in his mind.

Thornpaw sat in the well-trampled grass clearing. Cinderpelt and Yellowfang crouched beside him while he held up a paw for them to examine. Cinderpelt peeled a wad of cobwebs away from the pad, making Thornpaw grimace. "It's still bleeding," the apprentice medicine cat reported.

"It should have stopped by now," rasped Yellowfang. "We need to dry this wound before infection creeps in."

Cinderpelt's eyes narrowed. "We have those horsetail stems I gathered yesterday. What if we drip some sap onto the cobwebs before we bind them onto the paw? That might stop the bleeding."

Yellowfang let out a rumbling purr. "Good thinking." The old medicine cat turned at once and hurried toward her den while Cinderpelt pressed on Thornpaw's wound with her paw. Only then did she notice Fireheart standing in the tunnel entrance.

"Fireheart!" she mewed, her blue eyes showing her concern. "Are you okay?"

"Just a few scratches and a bite or two," Fireheart replied, padding forward to join them.

"I heard that it was rogue cats who attacked us," meowed Thornpaw, twisting his head to look up at Fireheart. "And that Tigerclaw was with them. Is it true?"

"It's true," Fireheart told him gravely.

Cinderpelt glanced at Fireheart, then shook the ginger apprentice's paw. "Here, press on this."

"Me?" mewed Thornpaw in surprise.

"It's your paw! Hurry up, or you'll have to change your name to Nopaw."

Thornpaw lifted his paw higher and clamped his jaws carefully around the wound.

"Bluestar should never have let Tigerclaw leave the Clan," Cinderpelt mewed quietly to Fireheart. "She should have killed him while she had the chance."

Fireheart shook his head. "She would never have killed him in cold blood. You know that."

Cinderpelt didn't argue. "Why has he come back now? And how could he kill a warrior he once fought beside?"

"He told me he is going to kill as many of us as he can," Fireheart meowed darkly.

Thornpaw let out a muffled mew, and Cinderpelt's whiskers quivered with shock. "But why?" asked the young medicine cat.

Fireheart felt his eyes cloud with anger. "Because

ThunderClan didn't give him what he wanted."

"What *did* he want?"

"To be leader," Fireheart answered simply.

"Well, he'll never get to be a leader this way. He's hardly going to make himself popular with the Clan if he starts attacking our patrols like this."

Doubt flickered through Fireheart at Cinderpelt's confident words. Bluestar was so weak. Who else had the strength to replace her if she . . . Fireheart winced. He knew the Clan's deep fear of the massive tom and his rogue cats. They might prefer to accept Tigerclaw as their leader rather than allow ThunderClan to be destroyed fighting him.

"Do you really believe that?" he pressed.

The noise of Yellowfang's pawsteps as she returned from her den startled them, and all three cats turned. A wad of cobwebs dangled from the old medicine cat's jaws. She dropped them beside Cinderpelt and meowed, "Believe what?"

"That Tigerclaw will never become Clan leader," Cinderpelt explained.

Yellowfang's eyes darkened and she didn't speak for several long heartbeats. "I think Tigerclaw has the strength of ambition to become whatever he wants to be," she meowed at last.

CHAPTER 18

❧

"*Not as long as Fireheart is* alive," Cinderpelt argued.

Fireheart felt warmed by her faith in him and was about to respond when Thornpaw complained, his words muffled, "It's still bleeding you know!"

"Not for long," answered Yellowfang briskly. "Here, Cinderpelt. You make use of these cobwebs while I see to Fireheart's wounds." She nudged the cobwebs closer to Cinderpelt and led Fireheart away to her den. "Wait here," she ordered, and disappeared inside. She emerged with a mouthful of well-chewed herbs. "Now, where does it hurt?"

"This one's the worst," answered Fireheart, twisting his head to point to a bite on his shoulder.

"Right," meowed Yellowfang. She began to rub in some of the herb mixture with a gentle paw. "Bluestar's very shaken," she murmured, not looking up from what she was doing.

"I know," Fireheart agreed. "I'm going to organize more patrols at once. That may calm her."

"It may help calm the rest of the Clan too," Yellowfang remarked. "They're really worried."

"They should be." Fireheart winced as Yellowfang pressed

the herbs deep into his wound.

"How are the new apprentices coming along?" she asked, her voice deceptively casual.

Fireheart knew the old medicine cat was offering advice in her wise and indirect fashion. "I'll speed up their training, starting at dawn," he told her. Sorrow caught in his throat as he thought of Cloudpaw. The Clan needed him now more than ever; no matter what the white apprentice had thought of the warrior code, no cat could deny that he was a brave and skillful fighter.

Yellowfang stopped massaging his shoulder.

"Have you finished?" he meowed.

"Nearly. I'll just put a little on those scratches; then you can go." The old cat blinked at him with wide yellow eyes. "Have courage, young Fireheart. These are dark times for ThunderClan, but no cat could do more than you have." As she spoke, there was a low rumble of thunder in the distance, a hint of menace that sent a chill through Fireheart's fur in spite of the medicine cat's encouragement.

When he returned to the main clearing, his wounds numbed by Yellowfang's healing herbs, Fireheart was surprised to find many of the cats still awake. Bluestar, Whitestorm, and Mousefur crouched silently beside Runningwind's body, their grief made plain in their lowered heads and tense shoulders. The other cats lay in small groups, their eyes blinking in the shadows and their ears twitching nervously as they listened to the noises of the forest.

Fireheart lay down at the edge of the clearing. The stifling air made his fur prickle. The whole forest seemed to be waiting for the storm to break. A shadow moved near the edge of the clearing. Fireheart swung his head around. It was Darkstripe.

Fireheart beckoned the striped warrior closer with his tail. Darkstripe slowly padded toward him. "I want you to take out a second patrol as soon as the dawn patrol returns tomorrow," Fireheart meowed. "From now on there will be three extra patrols every day, and all patrols will have three warriors."

Darkstripe looked coolly at Fireheart. "But I'm taking Fernpaw out training tomorrow morning."

Fireheart's fur prickled with irritation. "Then take her with you," he snapped. "It'll be good experience. We need to speed up apprentice training anyway."

Darkstripe's ears flicked, but his gaze remained steady. "Yes, deputy," he murmured, his eyes glittering.

Fireheart wearily pushed his way into Bluestar's den. Even though it was not yet sunhigh, he'd been out on patrol twice already that day. And he would be taking Whitestorm's apprentice, Brightpaw, out hunting this afternoon. The days since Runningwind's death had been busy. All the warriors and apprentices were exhausted trying to keep up with the new patrols. With Willowpelt and Goldenflower in the nursery, Whitestorm reluctant to leave his leader's side, Cloudpaw gone, and Runningwind dead, Fireheart barely had time to eat and sleep.

Bluestar crouched in her nest, her eyes half-closed, and for a moment Fireheart wondered if she had caught the ShadowClan sickness. Her fur was even more matted, and she sat with the stillness of a cat who could no longer care for itself, but waited silently for death.

"Bluestar," Fireheart quietly called her name.

The old she-cat turned her head slowly toward him.

"We've been patrolling the forest constantly," he reported. "There's been no sign of Tigerclaw and his rogues."

Bluestar looked away without answering. Fireheart paused, wondering whether to say more, but Bluestar had drawn her paws farther under her chest and closed her eyes. Disheartened, Fireheart dipped his head and backed out of the cave.

The sunlit clearing looked so peaceful that it was hard to believe the Clan faced any dangers. Brackenfur was playing with Willowpelt's kits outside the nursery, flicking his tail for them to chase, while Whitestorm rested in the shade beneath the Highrock. Only the fact that the white warrior's ears were pricked toward Bluestar's den betrayed the strain the Clan was under.

Fireheart stared unenthusiastically toward the growing pile of fresh-kill. His belly felt tight and hollow, but he couldn't imagine being able to swallow anything. He spotted Sandstorm eating a piece of fresh-kill. The sight of her sleek orange pelt was an unexpected pleasure, and Fireheart suddenly couldn't help thinking how much he'd enjoy her company while he was out hunting with Brightpaw. The thought restored Fireheart's appetite, and his belly growled with anticipation of the chase. He would leave the fresh-kill for the others to share.

At that moment Brightpaw trotted into the camp behind Mousefur, Frostfur, and Halftail. They were bringing water-soaked moss for the queens and elders. Brightpaw carried her dripping bundle toward Bluestar's den under Whitestorm's appreciative gaze.

Fireheart called across to Sandstorm. "You promised you'd catch us a rabbit whenever I asked. You up for coming hunting with Brightpaw and me?"

Sandstorm looked up. Her green eyes shone with an unspoken message that made Fireheart's pelt glow more warmly than the rays of the sun ever could. "Okay," she called back, and quickly gulped down her last mouthful of food. Still licking her lips, she trotted toward Fireheart.

They waited side by side for Brightpaw, and although their pelts barely touched, Fireheart could feel his fur tingle.

"Are you ready to go hunting?" Fireheart asked Brightpaw as soon as she emerged from Bluestar's den.

"Now?" mewed Brightpaw, surprised.

"I know it's not sunhigh yet, but we can leave now if you're not too tired."

Brightpaw shook her head and hurried after them as Fireheart and Sandstorm raced through the gorse tunnel, out into the forest.

With Brightpaw on his heels, Fireheart followed Sandstorm up the ravine and into the woods, impressed at the way her muscles flexed smoothly under her pale ginger coat. He knew she must be as tired as he was, but she kept up a quick pace through the undergrowth, her ears pricked and her mouth open.

"I think we've found one!" she hissed suddenly, dropping into a hunting crouch. Brightpaw opened her mouth to scent the air. Fireheart stood still while Sandstorm drew herself silently through the bushes. He could smell the rabbit and hear it snuffling in the undergrowth beyond a clump of ferns. Sandstorm suddenly shot forward, making the leaves rustle as she sped through them. Fireheart heard the rabbit's hind legs pound against the parched ground as it tried to escape. Leaving Brightpaw behind, he leaped instinctively, swerving around the ferns, and chasing it through the undergrowth and across the forest floor as it bolted away from Sandstorm's sharp claws. He took its life with one sharp bite, uttering a silent prayer of thanks to StarClan for filling the forest with prey, even if they hadn't sent rain for so long. The storm that had been promised by the rumbles of thunder a few evenings ago had not come, and the air was as brittle and stifling as ever.

Sandstorm skidded to a halt beside Fireheart as he crouched over the rabbit. He could hear her panting. His own breath was coming in gasps too.

"Thanks," she meowed. "I'm a bit slow today."

"Me too," Fireheart admitted.

"You need a rest," Sandstorm meowed gently.

"We all do." Fireheart felt the warmth of her soft green gaze.

"But you've been twice as busy as everyone else."

"There's a lot to do." Fireheart forced himself to add, "And I don't have to spend time training Cloudpaw anymore."

Cloudpaw's loss disturbed him more and more. He had been half hoping the young cat would turn up at the camp, having found his way back on his own, but there had been no sign of him since the monster had taken him away. As Fireheart began to give up hope of ever seeing his apprentice again, his awareness that he'd lost two apprentices— Cinderpelt as well as Cloudpaw—wreathed his mind in thorns. How could he take on the responsibilities of deputy when he couldn't handle his duties as a mentor? By giving himself more patrols and hunting missions than any other cat, Fireheart knew that he was trying to prove himself to the rest of the Clan, and to push away his own private doubts about his abilities as a warrior.

Sandstorm seemed to sense Fireheart's anxiety. "I know there's a lot to do. Perhaps I can help more." She glanced up at him, and Fireheart thought he detected a tiny hint of bitterness in her mew as she added, "After all, I don't have an apprentice either."

Seeing Dustpelt with Ashpaw must have pricked at her pride, and Fireheart felt a twinge of guilt. "I'm sorry . . ." he began. But tiredness had clouded his brain, and he realized too late that Sandstorm would have no idea that he had chosen the mentors. She would have assumed, along with the rest of the Clan, that Bluestar had made the decision.

Sandstorm stared at him, bewildered. "Sorry about what?"

"Bluestar asked me to choose the mentors for Fernpaw

and Ashpaw," Fireheart confessed. "And I chose Dustpelt instead of you." He anxiously searched Sandstorm's face for a trace of irritation, but she gazed steadily back at him.

"You'll make a great mentor one day," he went on, desperate to explain. "But I had to choose Dust—"

"It's okay." She shrugged. "I'm sure you had your reasons." Her tone was casual, but Fireheart couldn't help noticing the fur prickling along her spine. An awkward silence stretched between them until Brightpaw pushed her way out of the undergrowth behind them.

"Did you get it?" She panted.

Suddenly Fireheart realized how tired the apprentice looked, and remembered how hard it had been to keep up with the bigger, stronger warriors when he was training. He nudged the dead rabbit toward Brightpaw with his nose. "Here, you have first bite," he offered. "I should have given you time to eat before we left camp."

As Brightpaw gratefully began to eat, Sandstorm caught his eye. "Perhaps you could order fewer patrols?" she suggested doubtfully. "Everyone's so tired, and we haven't seen Tigerclaw since Runningwind died."

Fireheart felt a twinge of regret. He knew she couldn't really believe her hopeful words. The whole of ThunderClan knew that Tigerclaw would not give up so easily. Fireheart had seen the tension in the warriors' lean bodies as they patrolled with him, their ears always pricked, their mouths always open, tasting the air for danger. He had also sensed their growing frustration with their leader, who was needed more than ever to unite her Clan against this invisible threat. But Bluestar had hardly left her den since the vigil for Runningwind.

"We can't cut down our patrols," Fireheart told Sandstorm. "We need to be on our guard."

"Do you really think Tigerclaw will kill us?" Brightpaw mewed, looking up from her meal.

"I think he'll try."

"What does Bluestar think?" Sandstorm asked the question tentatively.

"She's worried, of course." Fireheart knew he was being evasive. Only he and Whitestorm understood how completely Tigerclaw's return had swept Bluestar back into the dark and tortured place she had been in after the treacherous warrior had tried to murder her.

"She's lucky she has such a good deputy," Sandstorm meowed. "Every cat in the Clan trusts you to lead us through this."

Fireheart couldn't help glancing away. He had been well aware of the way the other cats had been looking at him lately, with a mixture of hope and expectancy. He felt honored to have their respect, but he knew he was young and inexperienced, and he longed for Whitestorm's unshakable faith in his StarClan-led destiny. He hoped he was worthy of the Clan's trust. "I'll do my best," he promised.

"The Clan couldn't ask for more than that," Sandstorm murmured.

Fireheart looked down at the rabbit. "Let's finish this and

find something else to take home."

When the three cats had eaten, they moved on, heading toward Fourtrees. They traveled without speaking, wary of betraying their presence in the forest to any watching eyes. With Tigerclaw around, Fireheart felt as if the ThunderClan cats were the hunted as well as the hunters.

An unfamiliar cat-scent hit his nostrils as they neared the slope that led down to Fourtrees, and his fur bristled. Sandstorm had clearly smelled it too, for she froze, arching her back, her muscles tense.

"Quick," Fireheart hissed. "Up here!" He clawed his way up a sycamore tree. Sandstorm and Brightpaw followed, and the three cats crouched on the lowest branch and peered down at the forest floor.

Fireheart saw a shadow weaving through the ferns, dark and slender. Two black ears poked above the fronds. There was something about the shape of them that stirred a distant memory, not unpleasant. Was it a cat that they had helped from one of the other Clans? But with Tigerclaw's dark, plotting presence in the forest, there was no way of knowing which cats were to be trusted. All strangers were enemies.

Fireheart flexed his claws, preparing to pounce. Beside him Sandstorm quivered with anticipation, and Brightpaw stared down, her small shoulders tense. As the stranger padded under the ash tree, Fireheart let out a vicious yowl and dropped onto its back.

The black cat screeched with surprise and rolled over, knocking Fireheart to the ground. Fireheart leaped nimbly to his paws. He had felt the size and strength of this cat in his first pounce, and knew it would be easy to chase off. He faced the cat, arching his back, and gave a warning hiss. Sandstorm leaped down from the tree, Brightpaw right behind her, and Fireheart saw the black cat's eyes widen in panic as it realized it was outnumbered.

But Fireheart was already letting the fur lie flat on his shoulders. His first instinct had been right: he recognized this intruder. And from the look on the cat's face, which had turned from panic to relief in a single heartbeat, the intruder recognized Fireheart too.

CHAPTER 19

❧

"Ravenpaw!" Fireheart sprang forward to give his old friend a welcoming nuzzle.

"It's so good to see you, Fireheart!" Ravenpaw nudged him in return and turned his eyes to Sandstorm. "And can this really be Sandpaw?"

"Sand*storm!*" the ginger she-cat corrected him sharply.

"Of course. The last time I saw you, you were half the size!" The black tom's eyes narrowed. "How's Dustpaw?"

Fireheart understood Ravenpaw's wary tone. Sandstorm and Dustpelt had trained at the same time as him, and had viewed Ravenpaw more as a rival than a denmate. When Ravenpaw had fled from his mentor, Tigerclaw, and gone to live in the Twoleg territory beyond the uplands, Dustpaw and Sandpaw had not been sad to see him go. Fireheart doubted that Ravenpaw had missed them either.

"Dustpelt's fine." Sandstorm shrugged. "He has his own apprentice now."

"And is this one your apprentice?" Ravenpaw asked, looking at Brightpaw.

Fireheart felt his ears twitch as Sandstorm answered

curtly, "I don't have an apprentice yet. This is Whitestorm's. Her name is Brightpaw."

The warm breeze ruffled the leaves at the tops of the trees. Fireheart glanced up at the noise. This unexpected meeting had disarmed him, and he'd let his guard slip. He scanned the undergrowth warily as he remembered the threat of Tigerclaw and his band of rogues. "What are you doing here, Ravenpaw?" he asked urgently.

Ravenpaw, who had been studying Sandstorm with a curious expression in his amber eyes, turned his head. "Looking for you."

"Really? Why?" Fireheart knew it had to be important for Ravenpaw to come back to the forest. The young black cat had lived in constant fear after he had accidentally witnessed Tigerclaw killing Redtail, the ThunderClan deputy. When Tigerclaw had tried to kill Ravenpaw too, to keep him quiet, Fireheart and Graystripe had helped their friend escape. Ravenpaw now lived on a Twoleg farm with Barley, another loner—a cat who wasn't a kittypet, nor part of a forest Clan. Ravenpaw must have a very good reason for returning to his old enemy's territory now. After all, he had no way of knowing that Tigerclaw's treachery had been revealed and he had been driven out of ThunderClan. As far as Ravenpaw knew, Tigerclaw was still the deputy.

Ravenpaw flicked his tail uneasily. "A cat has come to live on the edge of my territory," he began.

Fireheart stared at him, confused, and Ravenpaw tried to explain. "I found him while I was out hunting. He was scared and lost. He didn't say much, but he smelled of Thunder-Clan."

"ThunderClan?" Fireheart echoed.

"I asked him if he had come over the uplands, but he didn't seem to have any idea where he was. So I took him back to the Twoleg nest where he said he was living."

"So he was a kittypet?" Sandstorm was staring intently at the black cat. "Are you sure it was ThunderClan you smelled on him?"

"I wouldn't forget the scent I was born to," Ravenpaw retorted. "And he didn't seem like the usual sort of kittypet. In fact he didn't seem at all pleased to be back with his Twolegs."

A glimmer of excitement sparked in Fireheart's belly, but he forced himself to stay silent until Ravenpaw had finished his story.

"I couldn't get his scent out of my mind. I went back to the Twoleg nest to speak to him again, but he was shut in. I tried to talk to him through a window, but the Twoleg chased me away."

"What color was this cat?" Fireheart felt Sandstorm glance sharply at him.

"White," replied Ravenpaw. "He had a fluffy white pelt."

"But . . . that sounds like Cloudpaw!" It was Brightpaw who spoke.

"Then you know him?" Ravenpaw meowed. "Was I right? Is he a ThunderClan cat?"

Fireheart hardly heard Ravenpaw's words. Cloudpaw was

safe! He began to circle his old friend, his paws tingling with joy and relief. "Was he okay? What did he say?"

"W-well," stammered Ravenpaw, turning his head to follow Fireheart as he padded around him. "Like I said, the first time I met him he seemed utterly lost."

"That's not surprising. He's never been outside ThunderClan territory before." Fireheart weaved impatiently around Sandstorm and Brightpaw. "He hasn't made his journey to Highstones yet. There's no way he'd know he was so close to home."

Sandstorm nodded, and Ravenpaw remarked, "That would explain why he was so upset. He must have thought—"

"Upset?" Fireheart stopped pacing. "Why? Was he hurt?"

"No, no," Ravenpaw mewed quickly. "He just seemed really miserable. I thought he'd cheer up when I showed him the way back to his Twoleg nest, but he still seemed unhappy. That's why I came to find you."

Fireheart looked down at his paws, hardly knowing what to think. He realized that he had been hoping that Cloudpaw would be happy in his new life, even if Fireheart never saw him again.

Ravenpaw blinked uncertainly. "Did I do the right thing in coming here?" he meowed. "Has this . . . er . . . Cloudpaw been banished from the Clan?"

Fireheart gravely met Ravenpaw's gaze. The black cat had risked his life coming here; he deserved an explanation. "Cloudpaw was stolen from the forest by Twolegs," Fireheart began. "He was my apprentice, and my sister's son. He's been missing for a quarter moon. I . . . I was beginning to think I'd never see him again."

Sandstorm glanced quizzically at Fireheart. "What makes you think you *are* going to see him again? He's living in Ravenpaw's territory with *Twolegs.*"

"I'm going to go and get him!" Fireheart declared.

"Go and get him? Why?"

"You heard Ravenpaw. He's not happy!"

"Are you sure he wants rescuing?"

"Wouldn't you?" Fireheart countered.

"I wouldn't *need* rescuing. I wouldn't have been taking food from Twolegs in the first place," Sandstorm pointed out sharply.

There was a startled grunt from Ravenpaw, but the black cat said nothing.

"It would be good to have him back in the den," Brightpaw put in, but Fireheart hardly heard her. He stared back at Sandstorm, the fur on his neck bristling with anger.

"You think Cloudpaw deserves to be left there, unhappy and alone?" he spat. "Just because he made a stupid mistake?"

Sandstorm snorted impatiently. "That's not what I'm saying. You don't even know for sure if he wants to come back."

"Ravenpaw said he looked miserable," Fireheart insisted. But even as he spoke, doubt flickered through his mind. What if Cloudpaw had gotten used to kittypet life by now?

"Ravenpaw only spoke to him once." Sandstorm turned to Ravenpaw. "Did he look upset when you saw him through the Twoleg window?"

Ravenpaw's whiskers twitched uncomfortably. "It's hard to say. He was eating."

Sandstorm whipped her head back to Fireheart. "He's got a home, he's got food, and you still think he needs rescuing. What about the Clan? They need you. Cloudpaw sounds like he's safe. I say leave him there."

Fireheart stared at Sandstorm. The fur across her shoulders was bristling, and her eyes glittered with determination. With a sinking feeling, Fireheart realized that she was right. How could he leave the Clan now, even for a short while, with Bluestar so weak and Tigerclaw and his band of rogues threatening them? All for the sake of a cat who had already proved to be a lazy, greedy apprentice.

But still, his heart told him he had to try. He couldn't give up on his belief that Cloudpaw would make a great warrior one day, and the Clan needed all the warriors it could get right now.

"I have to go," he meowed simply.

"And what if you do manage to bring him back?" Sandstorm argued. "Will he be safe in the forest?"

Fireheart felt a cold shiver run along his spine. Could he bear to bring Cloudpaw home, only to see him slaughtered by Tigerclaw? But even as uncertainty prickled in his paws, he knew what he was going to do. "I'll be back by sunhigh tomorrow," he meowed. "Tell Whitestorm where I've gone."

Alarm stretched Sandstorm's eyes wide. "You're going right now?"

"I'll need Ravenpaw to show me where he is, and I can't

expect him to hang around in the forest," he explained. "Not with Tigerclaw on the loose."

Ravenpaw's tail fluffed up with sudden fear. "What do you mean? On the loose?"

Sandstorm shot Fireheart a wry look.

"Come on," Fireheart meowed to the black cat. "I'll explain as we go. The sooner we get moving, the better."

"You're not going without me," Sandstorm told him. "It's a mouse-brained journey, but you'll need all the help you can get if you bump into Tigerclaw or a WindClan patrol!"

Fireheart felt a surge of joy at Sandstorm's words. He glanced gratefully at her and turned to face Brightpaw. "Will you go back to the camp and tell Whitestorm where we've gone?" he asked the apprentice. "He knows Ravenpaw."

Brightpaw's eyes flashed with alarm, but she blinked it away and dipped her head. "Of course."

"Go straight back home, and keep your ears low," Fireheart ordered her, feeling a twinge of worry at leaving the young cat to travel alone.

"I'll take care," Brightpaw promised him earnestly. She turned and vanished into the undergrowth.

Fireheart pushed away his anxiety about the apprentice and began to trek through the ferns. Sandstorm and Ravenpaw fell into step beside him, and he was reminded of all the times he had hunted in the forest with Ravenpaw and Graystripe. But as the stifling forest air pressed down on him and his fur prickled with anticipation of the journey ahead, he couldn't help wondering if he was leading them all into disaster.

❈   ❈   ❈

The three cats raced through Fourtrees and climbed into WindClan territory. Fireheart remembered the last time he had been here, with Bluestar. They would be following the same route, straight across the uplands to the Twoleg farmland that lay between WindClan territory and Highstones. At least there was no breeze this time to carry their scents across the moor. The air on the uplands was unnaturally still, and so dry that Fireheart felt his fur crackle as it brushed through the heather.

He chose a trail that kept them as far as possible from the camp that lay at the heart of WindClan's territory. The ground up here was usually peaty and wet, but now it had dried to a hard crust and the heather was browning in places, shriveled by the sun.

"So what's happened to Tigerclaw?" Ravenpaw broke the silence without slowing his pace.

Fireheart had often looked forward to telling Ravenpaw that his old tormentor had been exposed at last. But now it seemed there was only darkness in the news about Tigerclaw's treachery and banishment, and, since he had killed Runningwind, Fireheart stumbled over the story with a heart that ached with bitterness and regret.

Ravenpaw stopped dead in his tracks. "He killed Runningwind?"

Fireheart stopped too and nodded heavily. "Tigerclaw leads a band of rogues now, and he's sworn to kill us all."

"But who would follow such a leader?"

"Some of them are Brokentail's old friends, who were exiled with him when we drove him out of ShadowClan." Fireheart paused, forcing himself to revisit the scene of the recent battle in his mind. "But there were other cats that I hadn't seen before. I don't know where they've come from."

"So Tigerclaw is more powerful than ever," Ravenpaw mewed darkly.

"No!" Fireheart spat. "He's an outcast now, not a warrior. He has no Clan. StarClan *must* oppose him as long as he breaks the warrior code. Without a Clan or the warrior code to support him, there's no way Tigerclaw can defeat ThunderClan." Fireheart fell silent, realizing that he had spoken with a conviction he had hardly been aware of until now. Sandstorm was staring proudly at him.

"I hope you're right," Ravenpaw meowed.

Me too, thought Fireheart. He began to pad onward once more, narrowing his eyes against the glaring sun.

"Of course he's right," Sandstorm insisted, following.

Ravenpaw fell into step beside Sandstorm. "Well, I'm just glad I'm out of it."

She glanced at him accusingly. "Don't you miss Clan life at all?"

"I did in the beginning," Ravenpaw admitted. "But now I have a new home, and I like it there. I've got Barley for company if I want, and that's plenty for me. I'd rather have that than Tigerclaw any day."

Sandstorm's eyes glittered. "How do you know he won't come looking for you?"

Ravenpaw's ears twitched.

"Tigerclaw has no idea where you are," Fireheart told him quickly. He flashed a warning glance at Sandstorm. "Come on; let's get out of WindClan's territory."

He quickened the pace until they were racing through the heather too fast to speak. He avoided the swathe of gorse where he and Bluestar had met Mudclaw, and instead led them in a broad circle across the open moor. The barren hillside offered no protection from the sun, and Fireheart felt as if his pelt were on fire by the time they reached the slope that led down to Twoleg territory. The valley stretched out below them, patched with meadows and paths and Twoleg nests like the dappled coat of a tortoiseshell.

"The WindClan cats must have been keeping out of the heat in their camp," he meowed, puffing as they ran down the hillside. "Let's hope the rest of the journey is this easy."

They reached a copse of trees, and Fireheart welcomed the cool shade and the familiar woodland smells. High above them two buzzards circled with high-pitched calls, and he could hear the rumbling of a Twoleg monster in the distance. His aching legs tempted him to lie down and rest for a while, but his longing to find Cloudpaw drove him on.

As they padded through the trees, Sandstorm stared around with her whiskers trembling. Fireheart realized that she had traveled this far from ThunderClan territory only once before, when she had accompanied Bluestar to the Moonstone as an apprentice. It was a journey all cats had to make before they became warriors. Fireheart had been here several times, not just to visit Highstones, but to see Ravenpaw and to lead WindClan out of exile. But it was Ravenpaw who was most at home in these woods.

"We can't hang around here," the black cat warned. "Especially not this time of day. Twolegs like to walk their dogs here."

Fireheart could smell the scent of dog nearby. He flattened his ears and followed Ravenpaw in silence as the black tom led them out of the copse.

Ravenpaw squeezed through the hedge first. Fireheart waited for Sandstorm to go next, then pushed his way through the thickly tangled leaves. He recognized the red dirt track on the other side. He had crossed it with Graystripe on their journey to find the exiled WindClan. Ravenpaw looked both ways before racing across and disappearing into the far hedgerow at the other side. Sandstorm glanced at Fireheart, and he nodded encouragingly. She darted forward, and Fireheart followed at her heels.

The barley in the field beyond the hedge stretched high above their heads. Instead of skirting the edge, Ravenpaw headed straight into the forest of crackling stems. Fireheart and Sandstorm weaved after him, hurrying so they didn't lose sight of the black cat's tail flicking ahead of them. Fireheart felt a ripple of unease as he realized he could never find his way out alone. He had lost all sense of direction, with nothing to see but the endless golden stems and a strip of clear blue sky above. He was very relieved when they finally emerged and sat down to rest under the hedge on the far side of the field. They were making good progress. The sun was only halfway down the sky and the uplands were already far behind them.

Fireheart smelled a familiar scent on the hedge beside him. "Your marker," he commented to Ravenpaw.

"This is where my territory begins." Ravenpaw swung his head around, signaling that the wide sweep of fields ahead of them was where he lived and hunted.

"Then Cloudpaw is near here?" asked Sandstorm, sniffing warily.

"There's a dip on the other side of that rise," Ravenpaw told her, pointing with his nose. "The Twoleg nest is there."

Fireheart suddenly felt the fur on his spine tingle. What was that smell? He froze and opened his mouth to let the scent reach the glands inside.

Beside him Ravenpaw had lifted his nose, his black ears pricked and his tail flicking nervously. His eyes widened in alarm. "Dogs!" he hissed.

CHAPTER 20

❧

Fireheart heard grass swishing behind the hedge and tensed his shoulders as the strong odor filled the air. A loud bark made his tail fluff out, and a heartbeat later he saw the quivering nose of a dog thrusting through the hedge.

"Run!" he yowled, spinning around. Another rustle and a yelp of excitement told him that a second dog was following the first.

Fireheart fled. Sandstorm raced beside him, her fur brushing his as they pelted along the hedgerow with the dogs at their heels. The drumming of the dogs' paws made the ground tremble, and Fireheart could feel their breath hot on his neck. He glanced over his shoulder. Two massive dogs loomed behind them, their soft flesh rippling, their eyes glaring, and their tongues lolling. With a jolt, Fireheart realized that Ravenpaw was nowhere to be seen.

"Keep running," he hissed to Sandstorm. "They won't be able to keep this pace up for long." Sandstorm managed to nod, her paws pounding faster.

He was right. When he turned his head again, he saw that the dogs had begun to fall behind. Fireheart sized up an ash tree in the hedgerow ahead of them. It was some way off, but if they could put enough distance between themselves and the dogs, they might be able to scramble up it to safety.

"See that ash?" he meowed to Sandstorm, panting. "Climb it as quickly as you can. I'll follow."

Sandstorm grunted in agreement, her breath coming in ragged gasps. They raced on toward the tree. Fireheart yowled to Sandstorm and she shot up the trunk, clawing her way to safety.

Before he leaped for the tree, Fireheart looked over his shoulder once more to see how far away the dogs were. His fur shot up when he saw huge teeth barely a rabbitlength from his face. With a vicious snarl the dog lunged at him. Fireheart whipped around and lashed out with his forepaws, his claws sharp as blackthorns. He felt the flesh rip on the dog's swaying jowls and heard it yelp in pain. He slashed once more, then turned and scrambled up the tree, as fast as a squirrel. He stopped on the lowest branch and looked down. Below him the dog yowled in frustration while the other joined it, throwing its huge head back and bellowing angrily.

"I . . . I thought he'd gotten you!" Sandstorm stammered. She crawled along the branch and pressed her flank against Fireheart's ruffled fur until they both stopped trembling.

The dogs fell silent, but they stayed at the bottom of the tree, pacing back and forth.

"Where's Ravenpaw?" Sandstorm asked suddenly.

Fireheart shook his head, trying to clear away the terror he had felt when the dogs were chasing him. "He must have run the other way. He should be okay. I think there were only two dogs."

"I thought this was his territory. Didn't he know there were dogs on this side of the field too?"

Fireheart couldn't answer. He saw Sandstorm's expression darken. "You don't suppose he led us here on purpose?" she growled, narrowing her eyes.

"Of course not," snapped Fireheart, a flash of uncertainty making him sound defensive. "Why would he?"

"It's just strange he should turn up out of nowhere and lead us here, that's all."

A high-pitched mew made Fireheart and Sandstorm peer down through the leaves. Was that Ravenpaw? The dogs swung their heads around as they tried to locate the sound. Fireheart spotted a sleek black shape disappearing into the barley. Ravenpaw yowled again, and the dogs pricked up their ears. With barks of excitement they hurtled toward the swaying stems that gave away Ravenpaw's hiding place.

Fireheart stared down from the tree. Could Ravenpaw outrun the dogs? He watched the barley tremble as Ravenpaw zigzagged invisibly through the field. The brown backs of the dogs crashed after him like ungainly fish, flattening the stalks with their clumsy paws and barking with frustration.

Suddenly Fireheart heard the sharp yap of a Twoleg. The dogs stopped in their tracks and lifted their heads above the barley stalks, their tongues lolling out. Fireheart peered along the field. A Twoleg was climbing over a wooden fence set in the hedge. Two lengths of something like twine dangled from its hand. Reluctantly the dogs began to push their way through the barley toward the Twoleg, who grabbed the collars around their necks and attached them to the twine. With a sigh of relief Fireheart watched the dogs being dragged away, their tails down and their ears drooping.

"I see you're as fast as ever!"

Fireheart whipped around in surprise. Ravenpaw was clawing his way from the trunk onto their branch. The black cat nodded at Sandstorm. "Not sure why they bothered chasing her, though. She wouldn't have made much of a meal."

Sandstorm stood up and brushed past Ravenpaw. "Don't we have an apprentice to rescue?" she inquired icily.

"I see she's still a bit prickly," Ravenpaw remarked.

"I wouldn't tease her if I were you," Fireheart murmured as he followed Sandstorm down the tree. He decided not to tell his old friend that Sandstorm had suspected him of leading them into a trap. Ravenpaw was no fool—he'd probably worked that out for himself, but it was a sign of his newfound confidence that he wouldn't let her hostility bother him. And with the dogs safely out of the way, the only thing Fireheart wanted to think about was finding Cloudpaw.

Ravenpaw led them to the top of the rise and stopped. A Twoleg dwelling lay in the shallow valley ahead of them, just as he had promised.

"That's where you took Cloudpaw?" Fireheart asked.

When the black cat nodded, Fireheart's belly began to churn with nervous excitement. Even if they did find Cloudpaw, what if he didn't want to come back with them?

And if he did, would the Clan ever be able to trust a cat who had been lured into the softness of kittypet life?

"I can't smell him," Sandstorm remarked, and Fireheart didn't miss the suspicious edge to her tone.

"His scent was already stale when I came to see him last time," Ravenpaw explained patiently. "I think the Twolegs are keeping him locked in."

"Then how exactly are we supposed to rescue him?"

"Come on," Fireheart meowed, determined not to give the two cats a chance to start arguing. He began to head down the slope toward the dwelling. "Let's take a closer look."

The Twoleg dwelling was surrounded by a neatly clipped hedge. Fireheart pushed his way through it and stared across the browning grass to the Twoleg nest silhouetted against the dusky sky. He flattened his body to the ground and crept toward the nearest bush, his ears pricked. His nose was no good here. The evening air was filled with cloying flower scents that drowned out more useful smells. He heard paw-steps on the grass behind him and turned to see Ravenpaw and Sandstorm following, their quarrel apparently put aside for now. He nodded to them, grateful for their company, and carried on across the lawn.

By the time they reached the Twoleg nest, Fireheart could feel the blood pulsing through his ears. Suddenly the hedge, and the safety that lay beyond it, seemed very far away.

"Here's the window where I saw him," whispered Ravenpaw, leading the way around the corner of the nest.

"And probably where the Twoleg saw you," muttered

Sandstorm. Fireheart could smell her fear-scent, and knew her irritation was due as much to barely suppressed tension as to old rivalries.

A light glared from the window above their heads, and Sandstorm dropped into a crouch. Fireheart could hear the clatter of Twoleg feet inside. He craned his neck to look up the wall of the Twoleg nest. The window was too high to reach in one leap. He crept to the patch of earth directly below it, where a gnarled and twisted tree climbed the side of the nest. Fireheart studied the curving branches. He considered clambering up it, but he could still hear the Twoleg crashing around inside.

"Cloudpaw must be half-deaf, living with that racket!" hissed Sandstorm, her ears flat against her head.

Curiosity gnawed at Fireheart like a hungry rat until he couldn't bear it any longer. "I'm going to have a look," he meowed, and began to claw his way up the winding stem, ignoring Sandstorm's warning to be careful.

With his heart pounding, Fireheart reached the window and cautiously pulled himself up onto the ledge.

Inside, a Twoleg was standing over something that spat out clouds of steam. Fireheart winced at the harsh unnatural light, but he felt old memories of his kithood stirring inside him, and he knew he was looking into a kitchen, where Twolegs prepared food. His mind flooded with long-buried memories of eating dry, tasteless food and drinking water with a sharp, metallic taste. Blinking the images away, he began to look for any sign of Cloudpaw.

In the corner of the Twoleg den, he spotted a nest of what looked like dried branches woven tightly together. His paws began to tremble with excitement. A small white shape was curled inside. Fireheart held his breath as the shape stretched and leaped from its box. It ran to the Twoleg's feet and began yapping noisily. It was a dog! Fireheart shrank back, disappointment making his head spin and almost causing him to lose his grip on the window ledge. Where was Cloudpaw?

The Twoleg reached down and patted the noisy creature. Fireheart hissed under his breath, then sat up in surprise as Cloudpaw strolled through a doorway into the room. To Fireheart's alarm the dog rushed toward Cloudpaw, still yapping. He waited for Cloudpaw to arch his back and spit, but instead the white cat coolly ignored it.

Fireheart ducked as Cloudpaw suddenly jumped onto the ledge at the far end of the window. The dog carried on yapping from the floor, out of sight. "He's here," Fireheart hissed down to Ravenpaw and Sandstorm.

"Has he seen you?" called back Sandstorm.

Fireheart cautiously raised his eyes, but kept his body flattened against the hard stone. Cloudpaw was gazing blindly out over Fireheart's head. His eyes were shadowed with unhappiness, and he looked thinner. With a prickle of guilt, Fireheart couldn't help feeling relieved. This was proof enough for him that Cloudpaw wasn't suited to kittypet life.

He sat up and pressed his forepaws against the window that separated them. With a quiver of frustration he scrabbled at the glass, keeping his claws sheathed so that his soft pads made no sound that might alert the Twoleg or the dog. He held his breath as Cloudpaw's ears twitched. Then the white apprentice turned and spotted him, and his mouth opened wide in a delighted yowl that Fireheart couldn't hear.

Inside, the noise made the Twoleg swing around in surprise. Fireheart leaped down from the ledge, landing beside his friends.

"What's the matter?" asked Sandstorm.

"Cloudpaw saw me, but I think the Twoleg did too!"

"We should go," Ravenpaw meowed urgently.

"No," hissed Fireheart. "You two can go. I'm staying here till Cloudpaw gets out."

Sandstorm glared at him. "What are you going to do? What if they let that dog loose?"

"I can't leave now that Cloudpaw's seen me," Fireheart insisted. "I'm staying here."

As he spoke, a creaking noise sounded behind them. Fireheart snapped his head around. Light flooded from a door in the wall and spilled out into the garden, illuminating the grass all the way to the hedge. The bright pool darkened suddenly as the shadow of a Twoleg fell across it.

Fireheart froze. There was no time to hide. He knew they had been spotted. The Twoleg called, its cries hard and questioning, and then it stepped out and began to walk slowly toward them. The three cats huddled together as the Twoleg came nearer and nearer. Fireheart heard Sandstorm draw in a trembling breath. He looked up and his belly tightened with terror. The Twoleg was looming over them. They were trapped.

CHAPTER 21

"Quick! This way!"

Cloudpaw's urgent mew made Fireheart jump. He saw a white shape tear out of the doorway and flee across the lawn, yowling loudly. The Twoleg turned, distracted, and in that moment Fireheart felt Sandstorm and Ravenpaw shoot away from his side. He chased after them, following Cloudpaw across the grass. Behind them the Twoleg called into the night, the dog yapping at its side, but Fireheart kept running, through the hedge and out into the field beyond, tracking the scents that Cloudpaw, Sandstorm, and Ravenpaw had left until he caught up with them, huddled in a clump of nettles.

Sandstorm pressed herself against him, her whole body trembling. Fireheart looked over her head and saw Cloudpaw staring at him, his blue eyes wide. Fireheart's relief at finding his apprentice was suddenly tempered by all his old doubts about Cloudpaw's place in ThunderClan, and he didn't know what to say.

Cloudpaw looked down at his paws. "Thanks for coming."

"Well? Do you want to come back to the Clan?" Confusion

made Fireheart blunt. He had assured himself that Cloudpaw was safe; now the interests of the Clan began to crowd into his mind.

The young cat lifted his chin, his eyes clouded. "Of course! I know I should never have gone near Twolegs," he admitted. "I've learned my lesson. I promise I'll never do it again."

"Why should we believe you?" asked Sandstorm. Fireheart glanced at her, but her tone was mild, not challenging. Ravenpaw stayed silent, sitting with his tail curled neatly over his front paws, his amber eyes missing nothing.

"You came to find me," Cloudpaw mewed uncertainly. "You must want me back."

"I need to be able to trust you." Fireheart wanted Cloudpaw to understand that there were more cats to consider than just him. "I need to know you understand the warrior code, and that you can learn to follow it."

"You can trust me!" Cloudpaw insisted.

"Even if you can convince me, do you think the rest of the Clan will believe you?" meowed Fireheart gravely. "All they will see is that you left with Twolegs. What makes you think they'll trust a cat who chose kittypet life over the Clan?"

"But I didn't choose it!" objected Cloudpaw. "I belong with the Clan. I didn't want to go with the Twolegs!"

"Don't be too tough on him," murmured Sandstorm.

Fireheart was taken aback by her unexpected sympathy for the young apprentice. Perhaps she had been convinced by the seriousness that darkened Cloudpaw's eyes. He hoped the rest of the Clan would be, too. Fireheart couldn't keep his anger burning any longer. He leaned forward and gave Cloudpaw a rough lick on the head. "Just make sure you listen to me in the future!" he warned, speaking close to the apprentice's ear so that he could be heard over the rumbling purr that rose from the young cat's chest.

"The moon is rising," Ravenpaw meowed quietly from the shadows. "If you want to be back by sunhigh, we don't have much time."

Fireheart nodded and turned to Sandstorm. "Are you ready?"

"Yes," Sandstorm answered, stretching her forelegs in front of her.

"Good," meowed Fireheart. "Then we'd better get going."

Ravenpaw led the Clan cats as far as the uplands and left them at the bottom of the dew-covered slope that led to WindClan's territory. Dawn was not far off, but it was the height of greenleaf and the sun rose early. They had made good progress.

"Thanks, Ravenpaw," Fireheart meowed, touching the black cat's nose with his own. "You did the right thing, coming to get me. I know it must have been hard, coming back to the forest."

Ravenpaw dipped his head. "Even if we aren't Clanmates anymore, you will always have my friendship and loyalty."

Fireheart blinked away the emotion that clouded his eyes. "Be careful," he warned the black cat. "Tigerclaw may not know where you live, but we have learned not to underestimate him. Be on your guard."

Ravenpaw nodded soberly and turned away.

Fireheart watched his old denmate trot across the sparkling grass and disappear into the copse. "If we hurry, we can get to Fourtrees before the WindClan dawn patrol sets out," he meowed. He set off up the slope, flanked by Cloudpaw and Sandstorm. It was a relief to travel through the uplands before the sun had risen. As they reached the highest part of the uplands, where deserted badger sets lay, the sun lifted its head above the horizon and sent a wave of golden light across the heather. Fireheart saw Cloudpaw watching it in wonder, his blue eyes wide. Hope rose in his heart that the young cat would keep his promise and stay in the forest.

"I smell home," murmured the white apprentice.

"Really?" meowed Sandstorm doubtfully. "All I smell is old badger dirt!"

"And I smell ThunderClan intruders!"

The three ThunderClan cats spun around, their fur bristling. Deadfoot, the WindClan deputy, stepped out of the heather and jumped on top of the sandy badger set. He was small and skinny, and he moved with the distinctive lopsided gait that gave him his name, but Fireheart knew that, like the rest of WindClan, his size concealed an agility and speed that other Clans found hard to match.

There was a rustle and Mudclaw stalked from the heather. Fireheart eyed him tensely as the brown warrior circled the group and stopped behind them.

"Webpaw!" called Mudclaw. The tabby apprentice who had been with Mudclaw before padded out into the open. Fireheart waited, his heart pounding, to see if there were any more warriors with this patrol.

"You seem to be making WindClan territory your second home," hissed Deadfoot.

Fireheart sniffed the air before answering. No more WindClan cats. They were evenly matched. "There's no other way from the forest to the lands beyond," he answered, keeping his voice calm. He didn't want to provoke a fight, but he couldn't forget the way he and Bluestar had been treated by Mudclaw before.

"Are you trying to travel to Highstones *again*?" Deadfoot narrowed his eyes. "Where's Bluestar? Is she dead?"

Sandstorm arched her back and hissed furiously. "Bluestar is fine!"

"So what are you doing here?" snarled Mudclaw.

"Just passing through." Cloudpaw's fearless mew sounded puny next to the full-grown warriors, and Fireheart felt his muscles tense.

"I see it's not just Fireheart who needs a lesson in respect!" growled Deadfoot.

Out of the corner of his eye Fireheart saw the black tom flick his tail. It was a signal to his Clanmates to attack. With a sinking heart, Fireheart realized they were going to have to fight. When Deadfoot leaped from the badger set onto his back, he rolled with him, falling to the ground and throwing the WindClan deputy off.

Deadfoot landed on his paws and turned back to Fireheart, hissing, "Neat move. But you're slow, like all forest cats." He lunged and Fireheart felt the deputy's claws rake his ears as he ducked away.

"I'm fast enough," he spat. He pushed down with his hind legs and flung himself at Deadfoot. The WindClan tom gasped as Fireheart knocked the breath from him, but he still managed to spin and land on his paws. Quick as an adder he struck back at Fireheart, and Fireheart hissed as the warrior slashed his nose. He retaliated, swinging a forepaw at Deadfoot and feeling a wave of satisfaction as his claws dug into the deputy's fur. Now he had a firm hold on Deadfoot's shoulder. Fireheart tightened his grip and swung himself up onto the black cat's back, forcing his muzzle onto the hard ground.

As he held down the struggling deputy, Fireheart realized that Webpaw, the WindClan apprentice, had already fled. Sandstorm and Cloudpaw were fighting side by side to drive Mudclaw back into the heather, Sandstorm striking with her forepaws while Cloudpaw nipped at the warrior's hind legs. With a final screech of fury Mudclaw turned and ran away.

"I'll start showing respect when you've earned it," Fireheart hissed into Deadfoot's ear. He gave the WindClan deputy a sharp nip on the shoulder before releasing him. Deadfoot yowled with rage and raced into the heather.

"Come on, you two," Fireheart called. "We'd better get going before they come back with more warriors."

Sandstorm nodded, her face grim, but Cloudpaw was

bouncing from paw to paw with excitement. "Did you see them run away?" he boasted. "Looks like I haven't forgotten my training after all!"

"Shh!" growled Fireheart. "Let's get out of here." Cloudpaw fell silent, although his eyes still shone. The three cats raced side by side to the slope that led down into Fourtrees, out of WindClan territory.

"Did you see Cloudpaw fight?" Sandstorm whispered to Fireheart as they jumped from rock to rock.

"Just at the end, when he helped you drive off Mudclaw."

"But before that?" meowed Sandstorm. Her voice, though quiet, was warm. "He saw that WindClan apprentice off in about three rabbit hops. The poor tabby was terrified."

"Webpaw has probably just started training," Fireheart suggested generously, feeling a glow of pride in his apprentice all the same.

"But Cloudpaw's spent the last moon shut up in a Twoleg nest!" Sandstorm pointed out. "He's completely out of shape, but still . . ." She paused. "I really think, once he's been trained, that Cloudpaw will make a great warrior."

Cloudpaw's mew piped up from behind them. "Hey! Come on; admit it! I was pretty good, wasn't I?"

"And once he's learned a little humility!" Sandstorm added, her whiskers twitching with amusement.

Fireheart said nothing. Sandstorm's faith in Cloudpaw pleased him more than he could say, but he couldn't get rid of the niggling doubt that his nephew would ever truly understand the warrior code.

❊   ❊   ❊

They traveled swiftly through the forest, which was ringing with birdsong and thick with tempting smells of prey. But there was no time to stop and hunt. Fireheart wanted to be back at camp. Anxiety pricked at his paws, a sense of foreboding that was heightened by the stifling heat. The storm was closing in like a giant cat, preparing to pounce and crush the forest between its mighty paws. Fireheart picked up speed as they neared the camp and crashed down the ravine at full pelt, praying that Tigerclaw had stayed away. He raced through the gorse entrance, leaving Sandstorm and Cloudpaw to follow wearily behind, and emerged, panting, in the clearing. With a rush of relief that left him weak, Fireheart saw that the camp looked just as he had left it.

A few early waking cats were sunning themselves at the edge of the clearing. They looked up, and Fireheart saw their tails flick as they exchanged anxious glances.

Whitestorm padded up to Fireheart. "I'm glad you're back safely."

Fireheart dipped his head apologetically. "I'm sorry if I worried you. Ravenpaw came to find me because he said he'd found Cloudpaw."

"Yes, Brightpaw told me what happened," meowed Whitestorm.

As he spoke, Sandstorm and Cloudpaw padded from the gorse tunnel, and all the cats turned to stare in surprise at the white apprentice.

Sandstorm padded up to Fireheart and nodded a greeting

to Whitestorm. Cloudpaw sat down next to her, curling his tail over his paws and respectfully lowering his eyes.

Whitestorm's gaze flickered over the apprentice. "We thought you'd gone to live with Twolegs."

"Yes," Darkstripe's mew sounded lazily across the clearing. The striped warrior lay outside his den. "We understood you decided to return to *kittypet* life." He pushed himself to his paws and padded to Whitestorm's side. The other cats watched silently with curious, unblinking eyes as they waited for Cloudpaw's answer. Fireheart felt his paws prickle with anxiety.

Cloudpaw raised his chin. "I was stolen by the Twolegs!" he announced dramatically.

A murmur of surprise rippled through the Clan; then Ashpaw dashed forward and touched noses with Cloudpaw. "I told them you wouldn't have wanted to leave!" he mewed.

Cloudpaw nodded. "I hissed and spat and fought, but the Twolegs took me anyway!"

"Typical Twolegs!" Speckletail called from outside the nursery.

Fireheart stared in amazement. Was Cloudpaw going to win the sympathy of the Clan with his one-sided tale?

"I was lucky Ravenpaw found me," the apprentice went on, letting a desperate edge enter his voice. "He came to get Fireheart to rescue me. If it weren't for Fireheart and Sand-storm, I'd still be trapped in the Twoleg nest with that dog!"

"Dog?" Patchpelt's horrified yowl sounded from the fallen oak.

"Did he say dog?" rasped One-Eye, who lay next to him.

"I did," answered Cloudpaw. "It was loose in the nest with me!"

Fireheart watched as the elders' eyes filled with alarm.

Ashpaw's tail flicked in outrage. "Did it attack you?" he meowed.

"Not exactly," Cloudpaw admitted. "But it did bark a lot."

"You can tell your denmates all the details later," Fireheart interrupted him. "You need to rest. All the Clan needs to know for now is that you've learned from your experience and that from now on you will follow the warrior code."

"But I haven't got to the bit about meeting the WindClan patrol!" objected Cloudpaw.

"A WindClan patrol?" Darkstripe lifted his cold gaze from Cloudpaw to Fireheart. "That explains that scratch on your nose, Fireheart. Did they chase you off?"

Sandstorm glared at the striped warrior. "We chased them off, actually! And Cloudpaw fought like a warrior."

"Did he?" Whitestorm eyed Cloudpaw with surprise.

"He beat a WindClan apprentice by himself and then helped Sandstorm send Mudclaw running for home," Fireheart put in.

"Well done." Mousefur dipped her head to Cloudpaw. Cloudpaw nodded back graciously.

"Is that it?" asked Darkstripe. "Do we just take him back?"

"Well," began Whitestorm slowly, "that will be for Blue-star to decide, of course. But ThunderClan needs warriors more than ever before. I think we would be foolish to send Cloudpaw away now."

Darkstripe snorted. "How can we trust this kittypet not to run off again when things get tough?"

"I'm no kittypet. And I didn't run away," hissed Cloudpaw. "I was stolen!"

Fireheart saw Darkstripe flex his claws angrily. "Darkstripe's point is a fair one," he conceded, reluctantly accepting that the tabby warrior's misgivings might be shared by the rest of the Clan. It would take more than fine words to persuade the Clan that they should trust this apprentice again. "I'll go and speak with Bluestar," he meowed. "Whitestorm is right. It's up to her to decide."

CHAPTER 22

❧

"Fireheart?" Bluestar looked up as he pushed his way through the lichen. She was still huddled in her nest, her fur ruffled and her eyes anxious. Fireheart couldn't help wondering if she'd moved at all since he'd seen her last.

"Cloudpaw is back," he announced. He had no idea how Bluestar would react to any news nowadays, so he might as well tell her straight out. "He was in the Twoleg territory beyond the uplands."

"And he found his way back from there?" asked Bluestar in surprise.

Fireheart shook his head. "Ravenpaw saw him and came to tell me where he was."

"Ravenpaw?" Confusion flickered in the old cat's eyes.

"Er . . . Tigerclaw's old apprentice," Fireheart reminded her awkwardly.

"I know who Ravenpaw is!" snapped Bluestar. "What was he doing in ThunderClan territory?"

"He came to tell me about Cloudpaw," Fireheart repeated.

"Cloudpaw," echoed Bluestar, tipping her head slightly to one side. "He's back? Why did he come back?"

"He wanted to rejoin the Clan. The Twolegs took him against his will."

"So StarClan led him home," murmured Bluestar.

"Ravenpaw helped," Fireheart added.

Bluestar stared at the sandy floor of the den. "I thought StarClan wanted Cloudpaw to find a life outside the Clan." Her voice was thoughtful. "Perhaps I was wrong." She turned to Fireheart. "Ravenpaw helped you?"

"Yes. He led us to where Cloudpaw was shut in. He even saved us from dogs."

"What did Ravenpaw say when you told him about Tigerclaw's treachery?" Bluestar demanded suddenly.

Fireheart was caught off guard by the question. "Well, he . . . he was shocked, of course," he stammered.

"But he tried to warn us about him, didn't he?" Bluestar's voice sounded full of regret. "I remember now. Why didn't I listen to him?"

Fireheart struggled to find a way to comfort his leader. "Ravenpaw was just an apprentice then. Every cat admired Tigerclaw. He hid his treachery well."

Bluestar sighed. "I misjudged Tigerclaw and I misjudged Ravenpaw. I owe him an apology." She looked up at Fireheart with heavy eyes. "Should I invite him back into the Clan?"

Fireheart shook his head. "Ravenpaw wouldn't want to come back, Bluestar. We left him in Twoleg territory, where Barley lives," he explained. "He's happy there. You were right when you told me he would find a life that suited him better outside the Clan."

"But I was wrong about Cloudpaw," Bluestar fretted.

Fireheart felt as if the conversation were getting out of control. "I think Clan life will suit him in the end," he meowed, hoping he sounded more confident than he felt. "But only you can decide whether we should take him back."

"Why shouldn't we?"

"Darkstripe thinks Cloudpaw will be drawn back to his kittypet roots," Fireheart admitted.

"And what do you think?"

Fireheart took a deep breath. "I think Cloudpaw's time with the Twolegs has taught him that his heart lies in the forest, just as mine does."

He was relieved to see Bluestar's eyes brighten. "Very well. He can stay," she agreed.

"Thanks, Bluestar." Fireheart knew he should feel more joyful that Cloudpaw had been accepted back into ThunderClan, but his relief was still tinged with doubt. Cloudpaw had fought well against the WindClan patrol, and seemed genuinely pleased to be back in the camp, but how long would this last? Until he got bored with training? Or fed up with catching his own food?

Bluestar went on thoughtfully, "And we should also tell the Clan that if they see Ravenpaw in our territory, they should welcome him as they would a denmate."

Fireheart dipped his head gratefully. Ravenpaw had made few friends as an apprentice, mainly due to his paralyzing fear of Tigerclaw, but there was no cause for any cat in ThunderClan to hold a grudge against him. "When will you make the announcement about Cloudpaw?" he asked. It would be good for the Clan to see their leader on the High-rock once more.

"You tell them," Bluestar ordered. A thorn of disappointment pricked at him. Had Bluestar reached the point where she felt unable to address her own Clan? And even though he itched to tell the other cats that Cloudpaw could stay, Fireheart needed the Clan to be certain it was Bluestar's decision. She had kept to her den for so long and left so much of the daily running of the camp to Fireheart, how could the cats be sure that she had ordered this? If she made the announcement herself, not even Darkstripe could complain.

Fireheart stood in silence, his mind whirling.

"Is something wrong?" Bluestar narrowed her eyes quizzically.

"Perhaps Darkstripe should tell the others," Fireheart ventured slowly. "After all, he was the one to object."

The breath caught in Fireheart's throat as a glimmer of suspicion momentarily clouded Bluestar's gaze. "You're becoming shrewd, Fireheart. You're right. Darkstripe should be the one to spread the news. Send him to me."

Fireheart searched her expression, wondering if Bluestar had been unnerved by his cunning or the thought of seeing Darkstripe. But her eyes betrayed nothing as he meowed his farewell and backed out of the den.

Darkstripe had not moved. He sat, waiting for Bluestar's judgment, while the other cats carried on with their duties as usual. The few who remained around the clearing looked up inquisitively as Fireheart walked away from the Highrock.

Fireheart stared into Darkstripe's amber eyes, trying not to betray his sense of triumph, and nodded toward Bluestar's den, signaling with a flick of his tail that the ThunderClan leader wanted to see him. As the striped warrior strode past him, Fireheart padded to the pile of fresh-kill, which was already well stocked even though the sun was still climbing in the sky. The patrols were hunting well, he thought with satisfaction. Tired and hungry, he picked up a squirrel in his jaws. If there was a storm coming, Fireheart thought, he hoped it would break soon.

On the way to the nettle clump, Fireheart made a detour to the apprentices' den where Cloudpaw sat alone, hungrily gulping down a sparrow.

The white cat looked up and swallowed hastily as Fireheart approached. "What did she say?" For once there was an anxious edge to his mew.

Fireheart dropped his squirrel. "You can stay."

Cloudpaw broke into a loud purr. "Great," he mewed. "When are we going out training?"

Fireheart's weary paws ached at the thought, and he answered, "Not today. I have to rest."

Cloudpaw looked disappointed.

"Tomorrow," Fireheart promised with a glimmer of amusement. He couldn't help feeling cheered by his apprentice's enthusiasm to get back into the old routines. "By the way," he went on, "you tell a fine story. You made your little escapade sound like quite an adventure." Cloudpaw looked awkwardly down at his paws as Fireheart continued, "But as long as you start living by the warrior code, I'll let the Clan go on believing you were 'stolen' by the Twolegs. . . ."

"But I was," muttered Cloudpaw.

Fireheart stared sternly back at him. "We both know that's not entirely true. And if I catch you even looking over a Twoleg fence again, I'll chase you out of the Clan myself!"

"Yes, Fireheart," mewed Cloudpaw. "I understand."

Fireheart curled up in his nest the following evening feeling pleased. His training session with Cloudpaw had gone well. For once his apprentice had listened carefully to every instruction, and there was no denying that his fighting techniques were getting better and better. *I just hope it lasts*, he thought as he drifted into slumber.

The forest weaved its way into his dreams. Tree trunks loomed toward him through the mist, disappearing into clouds as they soared upward. Fireheart called out, but his voice was sucked into the eerie silence. Panic rose in his chest as he searched for familiar landmarks, but the mist was too thick. The trees seemed to crowd in on him, growing closer together than he remembered, their blackened trunks scraping against his fur. He sniffed the air, his fur bristling in alarm at an acrid scent that he recognized but could not name.

Suddenly he felt the softness of another pelt pressing against his own. An achingly familiar scent enveloped him, soothing his fretful mind like a drink of cool water. It was Spottedleaf.

"What's happening?" Fireheart meowed, but Spottedleaf didn't reply. Fireheart spun around to face her, but he could barely see her through the mist. He could just make out her amber eyes filled with fear before the sound of Twoleg howling exploded into the silence.

A pair of young Twolegs came running out of the mist, their faces twisted in fear. Fireheart felt Spottedleaf dive away and turned to see her disappear into the fog. Terrified, Fireheart was left alone with the Twolegs rushing toward him, their feet thundering on the forest floor.

He woke with a start. His eyes flashed open and he stared fearfully around the den. Something was wrong. The world of his dreams had invaded his waking world; the acrid scent still filled the air, and a strange, choking mist seeped through the branches. Fireheart leaped to his paws and scrambled out of the den. An orange light shone dimly through the trees. Could it be dawn already?

The smell grew stronger, and with a sense of horror Fireheart knew what it was.

Fire!

CHAPTER 23

❧

"Fire! Wake up!" Fireheart yowled.

Frostfur stumbled out of the warriors' den, her eyes wide with fear.

"We must leave the camp at once!" Fireheart ordered. "Tell Bluestar the forest is on fire!"

He ran to the elders' den and called through the branches of the fallen oak, "Fire! Get out!" Then he raced to where the apprentices were clambering drowsily from their nests. "Leave the camp! Head for the river," he called. Cloudpaw's bewildered face stared at him, still dazed by sleep. "Head for the river!" Fireheart repeated urgently.

Frostfur was already helping Bluestar across the shadowy clearing. The leader's face was a grotesque mask of fear as Frostfur nudged her forward with her nose.

"This way!" Fireheart yowled, beckoning with his tail before rushing to help the white she-cat guide Bluestar toward the entrance. Cats were streaming past on either side of them, their fur bristling.

The forest seemed to roar around them, and above the noise came a hideous two-tone wailing and the frantic barking of Twolegs as they crashed through the forest. Smoke was billowing thickly into the clearing now, and behind it the light of the fire grew ever brighter as it bore down on the camp.

Not till she was outside did Bluestar begin to run, caught in the jostling stream of cats surging up and out of the ravine. "Head for the river," Fireheart ordered. "Keep an eye on your denmates. Don't lose sight of one another." He felt an eerie calm within him, like a pool of icy water, while noise and heat and panic raged outside.

Fireheart darted back to round up Willowpelt's kits as they struggled after their mother. She was carrying the smallest one in her mouth, her eyes stricken with fear above the bundle that bumped against her forelegs.

"Where's Goldenflower?" Fireheart demanded.

Willowpelt signaled with her nose, pointing up the ravine. Fireheart nodded, relieved that at least one queen and her kits were safely out of the camp. He called to Longtail, who was already halfway up the rocky slope. As the warrior scrambled back down, Fireheart scooped up another of Willowpelt's kits and passed it to Mousefur, who had raced up behind him. He picked up the third, and when Longtail reached his side he gave the kit to him. "Stay near Willowpelt!" he ordered, knowing that the queen would keep running only if she knew her kits were safe.

Fireheart stood at the bottom of the ravine and watched the cats scrambling upward. Clouds of smoke swirled across the sky, hiding Silverpelt from view. Was StarClan watching this? he wondered briefly. He lowered his eyes and saw

Bluestar's thick gray pelt reach the top, bundled along by the other cats. Finally he followed, glancing over his shoulder as he scrambled upward to see fire stretching greedy orange tongues into the ravine, ripping through the bone-dry bracken toward the camp.

Fireheart scrambled onto the ridge. "Wait!" he called to the fleeing cats. They stopped and turned to face him. Smoke stung Fireheart's eyes as he peered at his Clanmates through the choking clouds. "Is any cat missing?" he demanded, scanning the faces.

"Where are Halftail and Patchpelt?" Cloudpaw's voice rose in a terrified mew.

Fireheart saw heads turning to look questioningly at one another, and Smallear answered, "They're not with me."

"They must still be in camp!" meowed Whitestorm.

"Where's Bramblekit?" Goldenflower's desperate wail rose through the trees above the noise of the fire. "He was behind me when I was climbing the ravine!"

Fireheart's mind reeled. This meant three of the Clan were missing. "I'll find them," he promised. "It's too dangerous for you to stay here any longer. Whitestorm and Darkstripe, make sure the rest of the Clan make it to the river."

"You can't go back down there!" Sandstorm protested, forcing her way through the cats to stand beside him. Her green eyes searched his desperately.

"I have to," Fireheart replied.

"I'm coming too," Sandstorm told him.

"No!" called Whitestorm. "We are short of warriors already.

1111

We need you to help get the Clan to the river." Fireheart nodded in agreement.

"Then I'll come!"

Fireheart stared in horror as Cinderpelt limped forward. "I'm no warrior," she mewed. "I'd be no use anyway if we met an enemy patrol."

"No way!" Fireheart spat. He could not let Cinderpelt risk her life. Then he saw the matted pelt of Yellowfang as she shouldered her way through the crowd.

"I may be old, but I'm steadier on my paws than you," the old medicine cat told Cinderpelt. "The Clan will need your healing skills. I'll go with Fireheart. You stay with the Clan."

Cinderpelt opened her mouth, but Fireheart snapped, "There's no time to argue. Yellowfang, come with me. The rest of you, head for the river."

He turned before Cinderpelt could argue and began to pick his way back down the ravine into the smoke and heat below.

Fireheart was terrified, but he forced himself to keep running when he reached the bottom of the ravine. He could hear Yellowfang gasping behind him. The smoke made every breath painful, even for his young lungs. Bright flames flickered just beyond the wall of the camp, tearing greedily at the carefully woven ferns, but they hadn't reached the clearing yet. The elders' den was nearest, and Fireheart struggled half-blind toward it. He could hear the crackling of flames as they licked at the far side of the fallen oak. The heat here was so intense, it felt as though the fire would burst into the camp at any moment.

Fireheart saw the shape of Halftail slumped below a branch. Patchpelt lay beside him, his jaws buried in Halftail's scruff as if he'd been trying to drag his friend to safety when he collapsed.

Fireheart stopped in dismay, but Yellowfang had already rushed past him and began dragging Halftail's body toward the camp entrance.

"Don't just stand there," she growled through a mouthful of fur. "Help me get them out of here."

Fireheart grasped Patchpelt in his jaws and pulled him across the smoke-filled clearing and into the tunnel. He struggled not to cough as he tugged Patchpelt through the gorse, its sharp spines clutching at the old cat's matted fur. Fireheart reached the bottom of the ravine and started to scramble upward. Patchpelt twitched in his jaws, and Fireheart felt his body convulse as he retched in a series of violent spasms. Fireheart pushed on up the steep slope, his neck aching from the weight of the unconscious cat.

At the top he dragged Patchpelt onto the flat rocks, and the old tom lay there, wheezing and helpless. Then Fireheart turned to look for Yellowfang. The medicine cat was just struggling out of the gorse tunnel, her flanks heaving as she fought against the deadly smoke. The trees that had sheltered the Clan were being swallowed up by fire, their trunks enveloped in flames. Fireheart saw Yellowfang stare up at him with Halftail clutched in her jaws, her orange eyes huge. He flexed his hind legs, ready to jump down the rocks toward her, but a terrified mewling made him look up. Peering through the billowing smoke, he saw Goldenflower's kit clinging to the branches of a small tree that sprouted from the side of the ravine. The bark of the tree was already smoldering, and as Bramblekit cried desperately, the trunk burst into flame.

Without stopping to think, Fireheart sprang at the blazing tree. He dug his claws into the trunk above the flames and hauled himself up to the kit. The fire raced up the trunk behind him, licking at the bark as Fireheart reached forward, wobbling, and lunged for the kit. The tiny tom was clinging to a branch, his eyes tightly shut and his mouth open wide in a silent scream. Fireheart grabbed him in his jaws and almost lost his balance as Bramblekit let go immediately and swung down into thin air. With his teeth still embedded in Bramblekit's scruff, Fireheart managed to keep a grip on the rough bark. There was no way he could climb back down the trunk now. The flames had taken too strong a hold. He would have to go as far along the branch as he could, then jump down to the ground. Clenching his jaws, and blocking out Bramblekit's screams, Fireheart crept away from the trunk.

The branch dipped and swayed under his weight, but Fireheart forced himself to keep going. One more pawstep and he tensed, ready to jump. Behind him flames scorched his pelt, filling his nostrils with the bitter smell of burning fur. The branch dipped again, this time with an ominous splintering sound. *StarClan help me!* Fireheart prayed silently.

Shutting his eyes, he flexed his hind legs and leaped toward the ground.

Behind him a loud crack split the air. Fireheart landed with a thud that almost knocked the breath out of him. Scrambling to find a clawhold on the side of the ravine, he twisted his head around. To his horror he saw that the fire had burned right through the trunk, sending the whole tree toppling into the ravine. Alive with flame, the tree crashed away from the terrified cat, hiding the entrance to the camp behind a wall of burning branches. There was no way Fireheart could reach Yellowfang now.

CHAPTER 24

"Yellowfang!"

Fireheart dropped Bramblekit and yowled the medicine cat's name. The blood pounded in his ears as he listened for her reply, but he heard nothing except the dreadful crackling of the flames.

Bramblekit crouched at his paws, pressing his small body against Fireheart's legs. Pulsing with fear and frustration, and dimly aware of the pain from his singed flanks, Fireheart grabbed him and raced up the slope back to Patchpelt.

The old tom hadn't moved. Fireheart saw his chest weakly rising and falling and knew that Patchpelt would not be able to run to safety. He lowered Bramblekit onto the ground. "Follow me!" he yowled before clamping his tired jaws onto Patchpelt's scruff. With a final glance down the burning slope, Fireheart dragged the black-and-white tom away from the ravine into the trees. Bramblekit stumbled after them, too shocked to mew, his eyes huge and unfocused. Fireheart wished he were somehow able to carry both of them, but he couldn't leave Patchpelt to die where he lay. Somehow Bramblekit would have to find the strength to survive the terrifying journey on his own paws.

Fireheart followed the trail of the other cats blindly, hardly aware of the forest around him, even though he turned back every few moments to check that Bramblekit was still keeping up. His last sight of the ravine filled his mind, a terrifying trough of flame and smoke that engulfed the camp, his home. And of Yellowfang and Halftail, there had been no sign at all.

They caught up with the rest of ThunderClan at Sunningrocks. Fireheart laid Patchpelt gently on the flat surface of the stone. Bramblekit raced straight to Goldenflower, who grasped him by his scruff and gave him a sharp, angry shake, choked by the purring that rose from her chest. Then she dropped him and began washing his smoke-stained fur with furious laps that softened to gentle strokes. The pale ginger queen glanced up at Fireheart, her eyes glistening with a gratitude she could not begin to put into words.

Fireheart blinked and looked away. It was beginning to dawn on him that Yellowfang might be lost because he stopped to save Tigerclaw's son. He shook his head violently. He couldn't think about that. His Clan needed him. He gazed around at the horror-struck cats that crouched on the smooth stones. Did they think they were safe here? They should have kept going to the river. Fireheart narrowed his eyes, trying to spot Sandstorm among the huddled shapes, but an infinite weariness made his legs feel heavier than stone, and he couldn't find the strength to get up and look for her.

He felt Patchpelt stir beside him. The old tom lifted his head, gasping for air, before collapsing into a coughing fit that brought Cinderpelt hobbling stiffly out from the throng of cats. Fireheart watched as she pressed her paws heavily on Patchpelt's chest, desperately trying to clear his lungs.

Patchpelt stopped coughing. He lay still, strangely silent now that he was not even wheezing, and Cinderpelt looked up, her eyes brimming with sorrow. "He's dead," she murmured.

Shocked mews rippled back across the rock. Fireheart stared at Cinderpelt in disbelief. How could he have brought Patchpelt this far, only for him to die? And on almost the exact spot where Silverstream had passed into the paws of StarClan. He looked anxiously at Cinderpelt, knowing she must be sharing the same thought. Her eyes were shadowed with grief and her whiskers quivered as she leaned down to close the old tom's eyes gently. Fireheart feared the pain would be more than she could bear, but as the other elders padded forward to share tongues with Patchpelt, the gray medicine cat sat up and raised her eyes to Fireheart. "We've lost another cat," she whispered, her voice ringing hollow with disbelief. "But my grief won't help the Clan."

"You're beginning to sound as strong as Yellowfang," Fireheart told her softly.

Cinderpelt opened her eyes wide. "Yellowfang! Where is she?"

Fireheart felt a pain in his chest, so sharp it was as if a splinter from the burning tree had lodged in his heart. "I don't know," he admitted. "I lost her in the smoke while she was rescuing Halftail. I was going to go back, but the kit . . ." His voice trailed away and he could only stare at the gray medicine cat as her eyes clouded with unimaginable pain. What was happening to their Clan? Did StarClan truly want to kill them all?

Bramblekit began coughing, and Cinderpelt roused herself, shaking her head as if emerging from icy water. Fireheart watched her hobble to the kit's side and bend her head, vigorously licking his chest to stimulate his breathing. The coughing died away into a rhythmic wheezing that in turn eased as Cinderpelt worked.

Fireheart sat still and listened to the forest. He could feel his fur prickling in the sultry air. A breeze rustled through the trees, blowing from the direction of the camp. Fireheart opened his mouth, trying to distinguish fresh smoke from the stench of his singed fur. Was the fire still burning? Then he realized he could see the sky filling with clouds of smoke as the breeze drove the flames steadily toward Sunningrocks. His ears flattened as he heard the roaring of the fire rise above the soft murmuring of the leaves.

"It's coming this way," he yowled, his voice sore and harsh after breathing in the smoke. "We must keep going to the river. We'll only be safe if we cross to the other side. The fire won't reach us there."

The cats looked up, startled, their eyes gleaming dimly through the night. The light from the fire was already shining through the trees. Clouds of smoke began to billow down onto Sunningrocks, and the sound of the flames grew louder, fanned by the rising wind.

Without warning the rocks and the forest were illuminated

by a blinding flash. A thunderous crack exploded over the heads of the cats, making them flatten themselves against the rock. Fireheart lifted his eyes toward the sky. Behind the billowing smoke, he could see rain clouds rolling in overhead. Age-old terror mingled with relief as he realized that the storm had broken at last.

"Rain is coming!" he yowled, encouraging his cowering Clanmates. "It will put out the fire! But we must go now or we won't outrun the flames!"

Brackenfur pushed himself up from the rock first. As understanding rippled through the rest of the Clan, the other cats stood up too. Their horror of the fire outweighed their instinctive fear of the raging skies. They shifted restlessly across the rock face, not sure which way to run, and to Fireheart's relief he saw Sandstorm among them, her tail fluffed up and her ears flat back. The cats started to move farther apart, revealing Bluestar sitting motionless halfway up the rock, her face tilted to the stars. A brilliant fork of lightning split the sky, but Bluestar remained still. Was she praying to StarClan? Fireheart wondered in disbelief.

"This way!" he ordered. He signaled with his tail as another crash of thunder drowned out his voice.

The Clan began to stream down the rock toward the trail that led to the river. Fireheart could see the flames flickering between the trees now. A rabbit pelted past him, terrified. It didn't even seem to notice the cats, weaving through them as it hurtled from the fire and the storm and slipped under the rock, instinctively seeking out the sanctuary of the ancient stone. But Fireheart knew that the flames would soon engulf this part of the forest, and he didn't want to risk losing any more cats to such a terrible death.

"Hurry!" he called, and the cats broke into a run. Mousefur and Longtail were carrying Willowpelt's kits once more, while Cloudpaw and Dustpelt dragged Patchpelt's body between them, the limp black-and-white shape jerking awkwardly over the ground. Whitestorm and Brindleface flanked Bluestar, encouraging the ThunderClan leader onward with gentle nudges.

Fireheart was turning to look for Sandstorm when he saw Speckletail struggling with her kit grasped in her jaws. The kit was well grown and Speckletail was not as young as the other queens. Fireheart raced over and took the kit from her. Speckletail flashed him a grateful look and started running.

The fire was beside them now that they had turned toward the river. Fireheart kept one eye on the advancing wall of flames as he urged the Clan onward. Around them the trees began to sway as the storm winds swelled and began to stir the burning forest, fanning the flames toward them. The river was in sight, but they still had to cross it, and few of the ThunderClan cats had done much swimming. There was no time to go farther downstream to the stepping-stones.

As they hurtled across the RiverClan scentline, Fireheart felt the heat of the fire against his flank and a cruel roaring that was even louder than the Thunderpath. He raced forward to lead the way down to the riverbank and skidded to a halt where the forest floor gave way to the pebbly shore. The smooth stones glowed silver as lightning flashed once more, but the thunder that followed was hardly audible above the roaring of the fire. The Clan stumbled after Fireheart, their eyes filled with a new terror as they stared at the fast-flowing river. Fireheart felt his spirit quail at the thought of persuading his water-shy Clanmates to enter the river. But behind them the fire tore through the trees in relentless pursuit, and he knew there was no choice.

CHAPTER 25

Fireheart dropped Speckletail's kit at Whitestorm's paws and turned to
face the Clan. "It's shallow enough to wade most of the way,"
he yowled. "Much shallower than usual. There's a place in the
middle where you'll have to swim, but you'll make it." The
cats looked at him with horrified eyes. "You have to trust
me!" he urged.

Whitestorm met Fireheart's gaze for a long heartbeat,
then nodded calmly. He picked up Speckletail's kit and waded
into the river until he stood up to his belly in the dark water.
Then he turned and flicked his tail for the others to follow.

Fireheart felt a familiar scent in his nostrils, and a soft ginger pelt brushed against his shoulder. He looked down into
Sandstorm's bright green gaze.

"You think it's safe?" she murmured, pointing with her
nose to the fast-flowing river.

"Yes, I promise," Fireheart replied, wishing with all his
heart that they were somewhere else, far from this flame-
threatened shore. He blinked slowly at the steadfast warrior beside him, trying to comfort her with his gaze when
really he wanted to bury his muzzle in her fur and hide

until this nightmare was over.

Sandstorm nodded as if she could read his mind. Then she raced through the shallows and plunged into the deep central channel just as lightning lit up the rippling water. Fireheart's chest tightened as the she-cat lost her footing on the pebbles and disappeared under the surface. He felt his heart stop beating and his ears roar like thunder as he waited for her to reappear.

Then Sandstorm bobbed up, coughing and thrashing with her paws, but swimming steadily toward the far shore. She struggled out on the other side, her coat dark with water and clinging to her body, and called to her Clanmates, "Just keep your paws moving and you'll be okay!"

Fireheart's chest ached with pride. He stared at the lithe shape, silhouetted against the trees on the other shore, and could hardly stop himself from leaping into the water and swimming to her side. But he had to see the rest of the Clan across first, and he forced himself to watch his Clanmates as they began to plunge headlong into the river.

Dustpelt and Cloudpaw dragged Patchpelt's body to the water's edge. Dustpelt looked down at it, then gazed across the river, his expression bleak at the impossibility of carrying the dead cat to the other side when it would be difficult enough to swim alone.

Fireheart padded to the warrior's side. "Leave him here," he murmured, even though the prospect of leaving another cat behind tore at his heart. "We can come back and bury him when the fire has passed."

Dustpelt nodded and waded into the river with Cloudpaw. The apprentice was almost unrecognizable under the smoke stains, and Fireheart touched his nose to the young cat's flank as he passed, hoping Cloudpaw could sense how proud his mentor was of his quiet courage.

When Fireheart lifted his head he saw Smallear hesitating at the river's edge. On the far side, Sandstorm was standing belly-deep in water, helping the cats as they struggled to the shore. She called encouragingly to the old gray tom, but Smallear backed away as another bolt of lightning lit up the sky. Fireheart dashed toward the trembling elder, grabbed him by the scruff, and plunged into the river. Smallear wailed and floundered as Fireheart struggled to keep his head above the surface. The water felt icy after the heat of the flames, and Fireheart found himself gasping for breath, but he plowed on, trying to remember how easily Graystripe had swum this same channel.

Suddenly a swift current dragged him and Smallear off course. Fireheart flailed with his paws, feeling panic rise in his chest as he saw the gently sloping bank slip past and a steep wall of mud loom in its place. How would he climb out here, especially with Smallear? The elderly tom had stopped struggling now, and hung like a deadweight in Fireheart's jaws. Only his rasping breaths in Fireheart's ears showed that he was still alive, and might yet survive the crossing. Fireheart floundered in the water, trying to fight the current and keep Smallear's muzzle above the water.

Without warning, a mottled head reached down from the

bank and grabbed Smallear from him. It was Leopardfur, the RiverClan deputy! Scrabbling in the mud for a pawhold, she dragged Smallear out, dropped him on the ground, and reached down again for Fireheart. He felt her teeth sharp in his scruff as she hauled him up the slippery bank. He felt a wave of relief as his paws sank into dry ground.

"Is that everyone?" Leopardfur demanded.

Fireheart looked around him. RiverClan cats were weaving among the ThunderClan cats as they crouched, drenched and shocked on the pebbles. Graystripe was one of them.

"I—I think so," Fireheart stammered. He could see Bluestar lying under some trailing willow branches. She looked small and frail with her soaked fur flattened against her scrawny flanks.

"What about that one?" Leopardfur pointed with her nose to the unmoving black-and-white shape on the far shore.

Fireheart turned to look. The ferns on the other side were burning now, sending sparks flying into the river and illuminating the trees with flickering light. "He's dead," Fireheart whispered.

Without a word Leopardfur slipped into the river and swam to the other side. With her golden fur flickering in the light from the flames, she snatched up Patchpelt's body and paddled strongly back, her front paws churning through the black water. A clap of thunder exploded overhead, making Fireheart flinch, but the RiverClan deputy didn't stop swimming.

"Fireheart!" Graystripe raced over to Fireheart and

pressed himself against his friend, his flank warm and soft against Fireheart's drenched body. "Are you okay?"

Fireheart nodded, dazed, as Leopardfur hauled Patchpelt's body onto the shore. She laid it at Fireheart's paws and meowed, "Come on. We'll bury him back at camp."

"The . . . the RiverClan camp?"

"Unless you prefer to return to your own," answered Leopardfur coldly. She turned and led the way up the slope, away from the river and the flames. As the ThunderClan cats heaved themselves to their paws and began to follow, heavy drops of rain began to fall through the canopy above. Fireheart twitched his ear. Had the rain come soon enough for the burning forest? More exhausted than he could ever remember being, he watched Graystripe lift Patchpelt's drenched body easily in his strong jaws. The rain began to fall more heavily, pounding the forest as Fireheart fell in behind the other cats, his paws stumbling over the smooth pebbles.

The RiverClan deputy led the blackened, bedraggled group through the reed beds beside the bank, until an island appeared ahead. In any other season it would have been surrounded by water; now the path merely glistened in the fresh rainfall.

Fireheart recognized this place. It had been ringed by ice the first time he had been here. Reeds had poked sharply through the frozen water then; now they swayed in great swathes, and silvery willow trees grew among the rustling stems. The rain cascaded down their delicate, trailing branches onto the sandy ground below.

Leopardfur followed a narrow passage through the rushes and onto the island. There was a lingering smell of smoke here, but the roar of the flames had faded, and Fireheart could hear the merciful sound of raindrops splashing down into the water beyond the reeds.

Crookedstar stood in a clearing in the center of the island, his fur bristling on his shoulders. Fireheart noticed the RiverClan leader glance suspiciously at Graystripe as the ThunderClan cats limped into the camp, but Leopardfur padded over to the light brown tabby and explained, "They were fleeing the fire."

"Is RiverClan safe?" asked Crookedstar at once.

"The fire won't cross the river," replied Leopardfur. "Especially now that the wind has changed."

Fireheart sniffed the air. Leopardfur was right; the wind had changed. The storm had been carried in on a wind much fresher than any he had smelled for a while. It rippled through his sodden fur, and Fireheart felt his mind begin to clear. Water dripped from his whiskers as he swung his head around to see where Bluestar was. He knew she should greet Crookedstar formally, but she was huddled among her Clan, her head low and her eyes half-closed.

Fireheart felt his belly clench with anxiety. ThunderClan could not afford to let RiverClan know how weak their leader was. He quickly stepped forward in her place. "Leopardfur and her patrol showed great kindness and courage in helping us flee the fire," he meowed to Crookedstar, dipping his head low. Above him lightning still flickered across the cloudy sky and thunder rumbled in the distance, rolling away from the forest.

"Leopardfur was right to help you. All the Clans fear fire," replied the RiverClan leader.

"Our camp was burned and our territory is still on fire," Fireheart went on, blinking away the rain that streamed into his eyes. "We have nowhere to go." He knew he had no choice but to throw himself on the mercy of the RiverClan leader.

Crookedstar narrowed his eyes and paused. Fireheart felt his paws grow hot with frustration. Surely the RiverClan leader didn't think this wretched group of cats posed any threat? Then Crookedstar spoke. "You may stay until it is safe for you to return."

Relief flowed through Fireheart. "Thank you," he meowed, blinking gratefully.

"Would you like us to bury your elder?" offered Leopardfur.

"You are very generous, but Patchpelt should be buried by his own Clan," Fireheart answered. It was sad enough that the old warrior would not be laid to rest in his own territory, and Fireheart knew that his denmates would want to send him on his final journey to StarClan.

"Very well," meowed Leopardfur. "I'll have his body moved outside the camp so that your elders may sit vigil with him in peace." Fireheart nodded his thanks as Leopardfur went on: "I'll ask Mudfur to help your medicine cat." The mottled she-cat scanned the drenched and shivering cats. Her eyes narrowed as her gaze fell on the huddled shape of the ThunderClan leader. "Is Bluestar injured?"

"The smoke was very bad," Fireheart replied carefully. "She was among the last to leave the camp. Excuse me, I must see to my Clan." He stood up and padded over to where Cloudpaw and Smallear sat, side by side. "Are you fit enough to bury Patchpelt?" he asked.

"I am," meowed Cloudpaw. "But I think Smallear is—"

"I'm well enough to bury an old denmate," rasped Smallear, his voice scratched by smoke.

"I'll ask Dustpelt to help you," Fireheart told them.

A brown tom was following Cinderpelt among the ThunderClan cats. He carried a bundle of herbs in his mouth, which he placed on the damp ground when Cinderpelt paused beside Willowpelt and her kits. The tiny cats were wailing pitifully, but refused to drink when Willowpelt pressed them to her belly.

Fireheart hurried over. "Are they okay?"

Cinderpelt nodded. "Mudfur suggested we give them honey to soothe their throats. They'll be fine, but it's done them no good to breathe in the smoke."

The brown cat at her side meowed to Willowpelt, "Do you think they could manage a little honey?" The gray queen nodded and watched gratefully as the RiverClan medicine cat held out a wad of moss dripping with sticky, golden liquid. She purred as her tiny kits licked at it, first tentatively, then greedily as the soothing sweetness entered their mouths.

Fireheart padded away. Cinderpelt had everything under control. He found a sheltered corner at the edge of the clearing and sat down to wash. His singed pelt tasted foul as he brushed his tongue along it. His body ached with tiredness but he carried on licking. He wanted to wash away all trace of the smoke before he rested.

When he had finished, he glanced around the camp. The RiverClan cats had fled the rain into their dens, leaving the ThunderClan cats to huddle in groups at the edge of the clearing beneath the whispering wall of reeds, seeking any protection from the pounding rain. Fireheart was aware of the dark shape of Graystripe moving among his former Clanmates, soothing them with his gentle mew. Cinderpelt had finished tending to the cats and was curled up, exhausted, beside Ashpaw. Fireheart could just make out Sandstorm's pale ginger flank, rising and falling steadily next to Longtail's silver tabby back. Bluestar was asleep beside Whitestorm.

Fireheart rested his muzzle on his forepaws, listening to the beating of the rain on the muddy clearing. As his eyes closed, the unbearable image of Yellowfang's terrified face burst into his mind. His heart began to pound, but exhaustion took over and he finally retreated into the refuge of sleep.

CHAPTER 26

Fireheart felt as if he had slept for only a moment when he woke. A cool breeze was ruffling his fur. The rain had stopped. Above, the sky was filled with billowing white clouds. For a moment he felt confused by the unfamiliar surroundings. Then he became aware of the sound of voices meowing nearby and recognized Smallear's trembling mew.

"I told you StarClan would show its anger!" rasped the old tom. "Our home has gone; the forest is no more."

"Bluestar should have appointed the deputy before moon-high," fretted Speckletail. "It's the custom!"

Fireheart leaped to his paws, his ears burning, but before he could say anything, Cinderpelt's mew rose into the air.

"How can you be so ungrateful? Fireheart carried you across the river, Smallear!"

"He nearly *drowned* me," complained Smallear.

"You'd be dead if he'd left you behind," spat Cinderpelt. "If Fireheart hadn't smelled the smoke in the first place, we might *all* be dead!"

"I'm sure Patchpelt, Halftail, and Yellowfang are deeply grateful to him."

Fireheart's fur rippled with anger as he heard Darkstripe's sarcastic yowl.

"Yellowfang will thank him herself when we find her!" hissed Cinderpelt.

"*Find* her?" echoed Darkstripe. "There's no way she'll have escaped that fire. Fireheart should never have allowed her to go back to the camp."

Cinderpelt growled deep in her throat. Darkstripe had gone too far. Fireheart padded quickly from the shadows and saw Fernpaw sitting beside Darkstripe, staring up at her mentor with horror in her eyes.

Fireheart opened his mouth, but it was Dustpelt who spoke first. "Darkstripe! You should show more respect for your lost Clanmates, and"—he glanced sympathetically at the frightened Fernpaw—"be more careful with what you say. Our Clanmates have suffered enough already!"

Fireheart was taken aback to hear the young warrior challenge his former mentor.

Darkstripe eyed Dustpelt with equal surprise, than narrowed his eyes dangerously.

"Dustpelt's right," Fireheart meowed quietly, stepping forward. "We shouldn't be arguing."

Darkstripe, Smallear, and the others whipped around to stare at Fireheart, their ears and tails flicking awkwardly as they realized he had heard their conversation.

"Fireheart!" Graystripe's mew interrupted them, and Fireheart saw his friend crossing the clearing, his fur damp from the river.

"Have you been on patrol?" Fireheart asked, turning away from the ThunderClan cats and padding over to meet Graystripe.

"Yes. And hunting," meowed Graystripe. "We can't all sleep the morning away, you know." He nudged Fireheart on the shoulder and went on: "You must be hungry. Come with me." He led Fireheart toward a pile of fresh-kill at the edge of the clearing. "Leopardfur says this is for your Clan," Graystripe told him.

Fireheart's belly growled with hunger. "Thanks," he meowed. "I'd better let the Clan know." He went over to where the ThunderClan cats were gathered. "Graystripe says that pile of food is for us," he announced.

"Thank StarClan," Goldenflower meowed gratefully.

"We don't need other Clans to feed us," sneered Darkstripe.

"I suppose you can go hunting if you want," Fireheart meowed, narrowing his eyes at the tabby warrior. "But you'll need to ask Crookedstar's permission first. After all, this is his territory."

Darkstripe snorted impatiently and padded toward the fresh-kill pile. Fireheart looked at Bluestar. She hadn't reacted to the news of food at all.

Whitestorm twitched his ears. "I'll make sure everyone gets a share," he promised, glancing at Bluestar.

"Thanks," Fireheart answered.

Graystripe padded up and dropped a mouse on the ground at his paws. "Here, you can eat this at the nursery," he meowed. "There are some kits I want you to see."

Fireheart picked up the mouse and followed his friend toward a tangle of reeds. As they approached, two silver bundles hurtled through a tiny gap in the thickly woven stems and rushed toward Graystripe. They flung themselves at him, and Graystripe rolled over happily, batting with gentle sheathed paws as the kits climbed over him. Fireheart knew at once whose kits they were.

Graystripe purred loudly. "How did you know I was coming?" he rumbled.

"We smelled you!" answered the larger kit.

"Very good!" Graystripe praised him.

As Fireheart finished the last mouthful of mouse, the gray warrior sat up and the kits tumbled off him. "Now it's time you met an old friend of mine," he told them. "We trained together."

The kits turned their amber eyes on Fireheart, staring up at him in awe.

"Is this Fireheart?" mewed the smallest one. Graystripe nodded, and Fireheart felt a glow of pleasure that his friend had spoken about him already to his kits.

"Come back here, you two!" A tortoiseshell face appeared in the entrance of the nursery. "It's going to rain again." Fireheart saw the eyes of the kits narrow crossly, but they turned and padded obediently toward the den.

"They're great," he purred.

"Yeah," Graystripe agreed, his eyes soft. "More thanks to Mosspelt than me, I have to say. She's the one who looks after them." Fireheart heard a note of wistfulness in his friend's voice, and wondered just how much Graystripe missed his old home.

Neither cat spoke as the gray warrior got to his paws and led Fireheart out of the camp. They sat down on a small patch of bare earth among the reeds. A willow tree arched above their heads, its branches quivering in the fresh breeze. Fireheart felt the wind tug at his fur as he stared through the willow curtain toward the distant woods. It looked as if StarClan was going to send more rain to the forest.

"Where's Yellowfang?" asked Graystripe.

Fresh grief welled up in Fireheart's chest. "Yellowfang came back to the ThunderClan camp with me to look for Patchpelt and Halftail. I lost her in the smoke. A . . . a tree fell into the ravine as she was coming out." Was there any way she could have survived the flames? He couldn't help a flare of hope bursting in his chest, like a trapped pigeon frantically stretching its wings. "I don't suppose you found any scent of her on your patrol?"

Graystripe shook his head. "I'm sorry."

"Do you think the fire's still burning after that storm?" meowed Fireheart.

"I'm not sure. We saw a few plumes of smoke while we were out."

Fireheart sighed. "Do you think any of the camp will be left?"

"You'll find out soon enough," answered Graystripe. He lifted his head and stared through the leaves at the darkening skies. "Mosspelt was right—more rain's coming." As he spoke, a large drop landed on the ground beside them. "That should put out the last of the flames."

Fireheart felt his head spin with grief as more drops spattered through the trees and splashed on the brittle reeds. Before long, the rain was pouring down for the second time, and it seemed that StarClan was weeping for all that had been lost.

CHAPTER 27

By late afternoon the lingering smell of smoke had been replaced by the stench of wet ash, but Fireheart relished its bitter odor.

"The fire must be out by now," he meowed to Graystripe, who was sheltering beside him beneath a clump of reeds. "We could go back and see if it's safe for the Clan to return."

"And look for Yellowfang and Halftail," Graystripe murmured.

Fireheart had known that his old friend would guess why he really wanted to go back to the camp. He blinked at the gray warrior, grateful for his understanding.

"I'll have to ask Crookedstar if I can come," Graystripe added. The words came as a shock to Fireheart. He had almost forgotten that Graystripe belonged to another Clan now.

"I'll be back soon," called the gray warrior, already bounding away.

Fireheart gazed across the clearing to where Bluestar was huddled next to Whitestorm, as if the white warrior were the only barrier between her troubled mind and the horrific fate that had befallen her Clan. Fireheart wondered if he should tell her where he was going. He decided not to. For the moment he would act alone and rely on his Clan to shield their leader's weakened state from the curious RiverClan cats.

"Fireheart." Cloudpaw was heading toward him. "Do you think the fire is out?"

"Graystripe and I are going to check," Fireheart told him.

"Can I come?"

Fireheart shook his head. He didn't know what they would find at the ThunderClan camp. Uncomfortably he also realized that he was afraid Cloudpaw would take one look at his ruined forest home and be tempted back into the cozy life of a kittypet.

"I'd do everything you told me," Cloudpaw promised earnestly.

"Then stay and help take care of your Clan," Fireheart meowed. "Whitestorm needs you here."

Cloudpaw hid his disappointment by lowering his head. "Yes, Fireheart," he mewed.

"Tell Whitestorm where I'm going," Fireheart added. "I'll be back by moonrise."

"Okay."

Fireheart watched the white apprentice pad back toward the other cats, praying that Cloudpaw would follow his orders for once and stay in the RiverClan camp.

Graystripe returned with Crookedstar at his side. The pale tabby's amber eyes were narrowed inquiringly. "Graystripe tells me that he wants to travel with you to your camp," he meowed. "Can't you take one of your own warriors?"

"We lost two Clanmates in the fire," Fireheart explained,

getting to his paws. "I don't want to find them by myself."

The RiverClan leader seemed to understand. "If they have not survived, you'll need the comfort of an old friend," he meowed gently. "Graystripe may go with you."

"Thank you, Crookedstar," replied Fireheart, dipping his head.

Graystripe led the way to the river. On the other side of the swiftly flowing water, the forest was blackened and charred. The tallest trees had managed to retain a few of their leaves, which fluttered bravely at the tips of their highest branches. But it was a small victory when the rest of their branches were black and stripped bare. StarClan may have sent the storm to put out the fire, but it had come too late to save the forest.

Graystripe slipped into the river without speaking and swam across. Fireheart followed him, struggling to keep up with his strongly paddling friend. As they climbed onto the bank at the other side, the two cats could only stare in horror at the remains of their beloved woodland.

"Seeing this place from across the river was the only comfort I had," murmured Graystripe.

Fireheart glanced at his friend with a pang of sympathy. It sounded as if Graystripe were even more homesick than he had thought. But he didn't have a chance to ask any questions before Graystripe charged up the shore toward the ThunderClan border. The gray warrior crossed it eagerly, pausing to add his own scent mark. Fireheart couldn't help wondering if his old friend was thinking of RiverClan boundaries—or ThunderClan.

Despite the devastation Graystripe seemed to relish being back in his old territory. As Fireheart pushed on to the camp, Graystripe wove back and forth behind him, sniffing intently before catching up with his friend. Fireheart was amazed that he could recognize anything. The forest was changed beyond belief, the undergrowth burned away, the air empty of the scent or sound of prey. The ground felt sticky underpaw where rain and ash had mingled to make black, acrid-smelling mud that clung to their fur. Fireheart shivered as raindrops splashed onto his wet pelt. The sound of a single, brave bird singing in the distance made his heart ache for everything that had been lost.

At last they reached the top of the ravine. The camp was clearly visible, stripped of its protective canopy, the hard earth gleaming like black stone in the rain. Only the Highrock was unchanged by the fire, apart from a slick of sticky black ash.

Fireheart rushed down the slope, sending grit and ash crumbling ahead of him. The tree where he had saved Goldenflower's kit was nothing but a heap of charred sticks now, and he leaped over them easily. He searched for the gorse tunnel that had once led to the clearing, but only a tangle of blackened stems remained. He picked his way through and hurried into the smoke-stained clearing.

As he stared around, his heart pounding, he felt Graystripe nudge him. He followed the gray warrior's gaze to where

Halftail's scorched body lay at what used to be the entrance to Yellowfang's fern tunnel. The medicine cat must have tried to get the unconscious elder back into the safety of the camp, hoping perhaps that the cracked rock where she had made her den would protect them from the flames.

Fireheart started toward the burned shape, but Graystripe meowed, "I'll bury Halftail. You look for Yellowfang." He picked up the limp brown body and started to drag it out of the camp toward the burial place.

Fireheart watched him go, his heart frozen with dread. He knew this was why he had come back to the camp, but his legs suddenly felt too weak to move. He forced himself to walk over to the burned stumps that lined the path to Yellowfang's clearing. There was no sheltering green tunnel now. The medicine cat's home was open to the sky, and the only sound was the relentless patter of raindrops on the slimy ground.

"Yellowfang!" he called, his voice hoarse, as he padded into the clearing.

The rock where the medicine cat had made her den was black with soot, but, mingled with the smell of ash, Fireheart detected the familiar scent of the old medicine cat. "Yellowfang?" he called again.

A low, rasping mew answered him from inside the rock. She was alive! Shaking with relief, Fireheart squeezed into the shadowy cave.

There was barely light enough to see. Fireheart had never been in here before, and he paused for a moment, blinking as his eyes adjusted to the gloom. At the foot of one wall was a row of herbs and berries, stained by smoke but unburned. Then he glimpsed a pair of eyes shining at him from the far end of the narrow cavern.

"Yellowfang!" Fireheart rushed to the medicine cat's side. She lay with her legs crumpled beneath her, soot-covered and wheezing, too weak to move. She could barely hold his gaze, and when she spoke her voice was breathless and feeble.

"Fireheart," she croaked. "I'm glad it's you who came."

"I shouldn't have left you here." Fireheart pressed his muzzle against her matted fur. "I'm so sorry."

"Did you save Patchpelt?"

Fireheart shook his head hopelessly. "He had breathed in too much smoke."

"Halftail too," rasped Yellowfang.

Fireheart saw her eyelids quiver and begin to close, and he meowed desperately, "But we saved Goldenflower's kit!"

"Which one was it?" Yellowfang murmured.

"Bramblekit." He watched as Yellowfang closed her eyes briefly, and his blood ran cold. Now Yellowfang knew that he had risked her life to save Tigerclaw's. Had StarClan shared something with her, something she feared enough to wish the kit had not survived?

"You're a brave warrior, Fireheart." Yellowfang suddenly opened her eyes wide and stared fiercely at him. "I could not be prouder of you if you were my own son. And StarClan knows how many times I have wished that you were, instead of"—she drew a shallow, grating breath, and Fireheart knew every word stuck thorn-sharp in her throat—"Brokentail."

Fireheart flinched as the old medicine cat revealed her terrible secret: that ShadowClan's brutal leader had been her son, given up at birth because medicine cats were not allowed to have children. Who knew what agonies Yellowfang had endured as she watched her son kill his own father to become leader, and then destroy her Clan with his bloodthirsty ambitions?

And how could Fireheart tell her that he already knew this? That he had understood that the reason she had wanted to give Brokentail sanctuary in her adopted Clan was because she wanted one last chance to take care of the son she had given up? He leaned forward and licked her ears, hoping to soothe her, but she went on.

"I killed him. I poisoned him. I wanted him to die." Her rasping admission collapsed into painful coughing.

"Hush. Save your strength," Fireheart urged. He knew this, too. He had watched, hidden, as she fed Brokentail the poisonous berries after the traitorous cat helped Tigerclaw's rogues attack ThunderClan. He had witnessed the cruel warrior die at his mother's paws, and he had heard Yellowfang give away her real relationship with the heartless tom. "Let me fetch you some water," he offered.

But Yellowfang shook her head slowly. "Water's no use to me now," she croaked. "I want to tell you everything before I—"

"You're not going to die!" Fireheart gasped, feeling a shard of ice pierce his heart. "Tell me what I can do to help you."

"Don't waste your time." Yellowfang coughed angrily.

"I'm going to die whatever you do, but I'm not afraid. Just listen to me."

Fireheart wanted to beg her to be silent, to save her breath so that she could live a few moments longer, but he respected her enough to obey her even now.

"I wish you'd been my son, but I could not have borne a cat like you. StarClan gave me Brokentail to teach me a lesson."

"What did you need to learn?" Fireheart protested. "You are as wise as Bluestar herself."

"I killed my own son."

"He deserved it!"

"But I was his mother," whispered Yellowfang. "StarClan may judge me how they will. I am ready."

Unable to answer, Fireheart dipped his head and began frantically licking her fur, as if his love for this old she-cat were enough to hold her in the forest for a while longer.

"Fireheart," Yellowfang murmured.

Fireheart paused. "Yes?"

"Thank you for bringing me to ThunderClan. Tell Bluestar I have always been grateful for the home she gave me. This is a good place to die. I only regret that I will miss watching you become what StarClan has destined you to be." The old medicine cat's voice trailed away, and her flanks heaved with the effort of sucking air into her smoke-scorched lungs.

"Yellowfang," Fireheart pleaded. "Don't die!"

Her painful breathing clawed at his heart, and he realized there was nothing he could do. "Don't be afraid of StarClan.

They will understand about Brokentail," he promised wretchedly. "You will be honored by our warrior ancestors for your loyalty to your Clanmates and for your endless courage. So many cats owe their lives to you. Cinderpelt would have died after her accident if you had not tended to her. And when there was greencough, you fought day and night. . . ."

Fireheart could not stop the words from tumbling out even though he knew the old medicine cat's breathing had faded into everlasting silence. Yellowfang was dead.

CHAPTER 28

❧

With a tender lick, Fireheart closed the medicine cat's eyes for the last time. Then he lowered his head onto her shoulder and felt the warmth fade from her body.

He didn't know how long he lay there, listening to his heart beating alone in the shadowy cavern. He thought for a moment he caught the familiar scent of Spottedleaf, drifting into the den on the rain-chilled breeze. Had she come to guide Yellowfang to StarClan? Fireheart let the soothing thought flow through him and felt sleep swell like clouds at the edges of his mind.

"She will be safe with us." Spottedleaf's gentle mew ruffled his ear fur, and Fireheart lifted his head and looked around.

"Fireheart?" Graystripe called from the entrance. Fireheart struggled to sit up.

"I've buried Halftail," the gray warrior meowed.

"Yellowfang's dead," Fireheart whispered. His hollow mew echoed off the stone walls. "She was alive when I found her, but she died."

"Did she say anything?"

Fireheart closed his eyes. He would never share Yellowfang's tragic secret with any cat, not even his oldest friend. "Just that . . . she was thankful Bluestar let her live in ThunderClan."

Graystripe padded into the cave and bent his head to lick the old medicine cat's cheek. "When I left, I never thought I wouldn't speak to her again," he murmured, his voice thick with sorrow. "Shall we bury her?"

"No," Fireheart meowed firmly, his mind suddenly clear. Spottedleaf's words echoed in his mind: *She'll be safe with us.* "She was a warrior as well as a medicine cat. She will have her vigil and we can bury her at dawn."

"But we must get back to the RiverClan camp and tell the others what has happened," Graystripe reminded him.

"Then I'll come back tonight and sit vigil with her," Fireheart replied.

The two friends trekked back through the devastated forest in silence. The gray afternoon light was fading by the time they padded into the RiverClan camp. Groups of cats lay at the edge of the clearing, sharing tongues after their evening meal. The ThunderClan cats crouched in an isolated huddle at one side. As soon as Fireheart and Graystripe appeared, Cinderpelt struggled to her paws and limped toward them.

Bluestar rose too from where she lay beside Whitestorm. She brushed past Cinderpelt and reached the returning warriors first, her eyes filled with desperate hope. "Did you find Yellowfang and Halftail?"

Fireheart saw Cinderpelt hanging back, her ears pricked, as desperate for news as her Clan leader. "They're both dead," he told them. Fresh pain filled his heart when he saw Cinderpelt sway on her paws. The little cat backed away unsteadily, her eyes clouded. Fireheart wanted to go to her but Bluestar stood in his way. The ThunderClan leader's blue eyes showed no pain. Instead they grew hard and cold, and a shiver ran down Fireheart's spine.

"Spottedleaf told me that fire would *save* the Clan!" she hissed. "But it has destroyed us."

"No," Fireheart began, but he could not find the words to comfort his leader. His gaze followed Cinderpelt as she stumbled back to the others. To Fireheart's relief, Sandstorm hurried forward to meet her, pressing her flank against Cinderpelt to support the medicine cat's thin gray body. He looked back at Bluestar, his heart sinking at her stony expression.

"ThunderClan will return home tonight," she decided in a voice like ice.

"But the woods are empty. The camp is ruined!" protested Graystripe.

"It doesn't matter. We are strangers here. We should be back in our own territory," spat Bluestar.

"Then I'll escort you," Graystripe offered.

Fireheart glanced at his friend and suddenly understood the longing in his eyes. Graystripe wanted to go home. The realization flooded Fireheart's mind like a shooting star illuminating the night sky. Fireheart looked expectantly at Bluestar. Surely she could see Graystripe's desire to return to ThunderClan?

"Why would we need an escort?" demanded Bluestar, her eyes narrowing.

"Well, perhaps I could help you rebuild the camp," Graystripe suggested uncertainly. "Maybe stay for a while . . ." He faltered as Bluestar's eyes flashed angrily.

"Are you trying to say that you want to come back to ThunderClan?" she spat. "Well, you can't!"

Fireheart stared at her in stunned silence.

"You chose to be loyal to your kits rather than your Clan," the leader snarled. "Now you must live with your decision."

Graystripe flinched. Fireheart gazed at the old leader in disbelief as she turned and called to her Clan, "Get ready to leave. We are returning home!"

The ThunderClan cats leaped to their paws at once, but Fireheart felt nothing but disappointment and anger as he watched Bluestar gather her Clan around her.

The leader's gaze was fixed on a point beyond the cats at the edge of the clearing. Mistyfoot and Stonefur stood there, watching the ThunderClan cats. Fireheart saw sorrow pass through Bluestar's eyes as she stared at her grown kits. Bluestar knew better than any cat what it was like to be torn between Clan and kin. She had once chosen to be loyal to her Clan rather than her kits, and it had caused her more pain than she would have wished on an enemy.

With a flash of insight, Fireheart thought he understood her reaction to Graystripe's request. It was not the gray warrior she was angry at, but herself. She still regretted leaving her kits all those years ago. Part of her was trying to make sure that Graystripe didn't make the same mistake.

The ThunderClan cats circled impatiently in the growing darkness, and Bluestar padded toward Crookedstar.

Fireheart turned and licked Graystripe's shoulder. "Bluestar has her reasons for saying those things," he murmured. "She's suffering at the moment, but she'll recover. And maybe then you can come home."

Graystripe lifted his eyes and stared hopefully at Fireheart. "You think so?"

"Yes," answered Fireheart, praying to StarClan that it was true.

He hurried after Bluestar and caught up in time to hear the ThunderClan leader thank Crookedstar formally for RiverClan's generosity. Leopardfur stood beside them, gazing coolly at the ThunderClan cats.

"ThunderClan is in your debt," Bluestar meowed, dipping her head.

Fireheart saw Leopardfur narrow her eyes at Bluestar's words, her emerald eyes glittering. His paws prickled warily. What payment would RiverClan demand for this kindness? he wondered. He knew Leopardfur well enough to suspect that she would ask for something in return.

He followed Bluestar as she stalked to the head of her Clan and led them out of the RiverClan camp. Fireheart glanced backward and saw Graystripe standing alone in the shadows, his eyes filled with pain as he watched his former Clanmates walk away.

❈   ❈   ❈

Fireheart sighed inwardly as Smallear hesitated again at the edge of the river. It was swollen from the rain, but Darkstripe and Whitestorm had already crossed and were waiting in the shallows at the other side. Dustpelt swam beside Fernpaw as the apprentice struggled to keep her little gray head above water. Sandstorm had crossed with Cinderpelt. The pale orange warrior had not left the medicine cat's side since Fireheart had returned with the news about Yellowfang.

"Hurry up!" ordered Bluestar, snapping impatiently at Smallear.

The gray tom glanced over his shoulder in surprise at her harsh tone, and then hurled himself into the dark water. Fireheart tensed his muscles, ready to spring to the rescue, but there was no need. Longtail and Mousefur appeared on either side of the frantically splashing elder, buoying him up with their strong shoulders.

Bluestar leaped into the river and swam easily to the other side, all frailty gone from her body as if fire had purged the weakness from her and burned her strong again. Fireheart slipped into the water after her. The clouds above the trees were beginning to thin, and he felt a chill through his wet fur from the fresher wind as he waded from the river. He padded over to Cinderpelt, leaning down to lick her head. Sandstorm glanced at him, her eyes reflecting his sorrow, while the rest of the Clan paused on the shore and stared in silent horror at the forest. Even in the faint moonlight, the devastation was obvious, the trees stripped bare, the musty fragrances of the leaves and ferns replaced by the bitter stench of burned wood and scorched earth.

Bluestar seemed blind to it all. She strode past the other cats without pausing and headed up the slope toward Sunningrocks and the trail home. Her Clan could do nothing but follow.

"It's like being somewhere else," whispered Sandstorm. Fireheart nodded in agreement.

"Cloudpaw." Fireheart slipped through the cats ahead of him and fell in step beside his apprentice. "Thank you for staying in the RiverClan camp as I asked."

"No problem." Cloudpaw shrugged.

"How are the elders?"

"They're going to take a while to get over Halftail's and Patchpelt's deaths." Cloudpaw's voice was subdued. "But I managed to get them to eat some fresh-kill while you were away. They need to keep their strength up, however much they are grieving."

"Well done. That was the right thing to do," Fireheart told him, proud of his apprentice's unexpectedly wise compassion.

The ravine lay like an open wound in the landscape. Sandstorm stopped and peered over the edge, and Fireheart could see her trembling. He was shivering too, even though his fur had already dried from the river crossing. The Clan filed slowly down the steep slope and followed Bluestar into the camp. Inside the clearing the cats gazed silently around the stripped, blackened space that had once been their home.

"Take me to Yellowfang's body!" Bluestar meowed sharply at Fireheart, cracking the silence.

Fireheart's fur bristled. This wasn't the weak shell of a leader he had struggled to protect in recent moons; but nor was it the wise and gentle leader who had welcomed him to the Clan and been his mentor. He began to pad toward Yellowfang's clearing, and Bluestar followed. Fireheart glanced over his shoulder and saw Cinderpelt limping behind the ThunderClan leader.

"She's in her den," he meowed, standing at the entrance. Bluestar slipped into the shadows inside the rock.

Cinderpelt sat down and waited.

"Aren't you going in?" Fireheart asked.

"I'll grieve later," Cinderpelt told him. "I think Bluestar needs us now."

Surprised at the composure in Cinderpelt's voice, Fireheart looked into her eyes. They were unnaturally bright with sadness, but seemed calm as she blinked gently at him. He returned the gesture, grateful for her strength of spirit in the middle of such endless tragedy.

A chilling wail echoed from Yellowfang's den. Bluestar staggered out, twisting her head wildly and glaring around at the blackened trees. "How could StarClan do this? Have they no pity?" she spat. "I will never go to the Moonstone again! From now on, my dreams are my own. StarClan has declared war on my Clan, and I shall never forgive them."

Fireheart stared at his leader, frozen with horror. He noticed Cinderpelt creep quietly to Yellowfang's den and wondered if she'd gone to grieve for her old friend, but she reappeared a moment later holding something in her jaws, which she dropped beside Bluestar.

"Eat these, Bluestar," she urged. "They will ease your pain."

"Is she injured?" asked Fireheart.

Cinderpelt turned to look at him and lowered her voice. "In a way. But her injuries cannot be seen." She blinked. "These poppy seeds will calm her and give her mind time to heal." She turned back to Bluestar and whispered again, "Eat them, please."

Bluestar bent her head and obediently licked up the small black seeds.

"Come," Cinderpelt meowed gently, and led the ThunderClan leader away.

Fireheart felt his paws tremble as he watched Cinderpelt's quiet skill. Yellowfang would be so proud of her apprentice. He padded into the den and grasped Yellowfang's crumpled, smoke-stained body by its scruff. He heaved it into the moonlit clearing, and arranged it so that Yellowfang rested with the same dignity with which she had lived. When he had finished he bent down to give his old friend one final lick. "You shall sleep beneath the stars for the last time tonight," he whispered, and settled down beside her to sit in vigil as he had promised.

Cinderpelt joined him as the three-quarter moon began to slide away and the horizon glowed cream and pink above the blackened treetops. Fireheart stood and stretched his tired legs. He gazed around the devastated clearing.

"Don't grieve too much for the forest," murmured the gray

cat beside him. "It will grow back quickly, stronger because of the injuries it has suffered, like a broken bone that heals twice as well."

Fireheart let her words soothe him. He dipped his head gratefully to her and went to find the rest of the Clan.

Mousefur was sitting on guard outside Bluestar's den.

"Cinderpelt ordered it," Whitestorm explained, padding out of the shadows. The warrior's pelt was still stained with smoke and his eyes were red-rimmed from the fire and exhaustion. "She said Bluestar was sick, and needed to be watched over."

"Good," Fireheart meowed. "How are the rest of the Clan?"

"Most of them slept a little, once they'd found places dry enough to lie down."

"We should send out a dawn patrol," Fireheart thought out loud. "Tigerclaw might take advantage of what has happened."

"Who will you send?" asked Whitestorm.

"Darkstripe seems the fittest of the warriors, but we'll need his strength to start rebuilding the camp." Even as he spoke, Fireheart knew he wasn't telling the whole truth. He wanted to keep the dark tabby warrior where he could see him. "I'd like you to stay here as well, if that's okay." Whitestorm dipped his head in agreement as Fireheart continued, "We need to tell the other cats what's happening."

"Bluestar is sleeping. Do you think we should disturb her?" A worried frown crossed Whitestorm's face as he spoke.

Fireheart shook his head. "No. We'll let her rest. I'll speak to the Clan."

He bounded onto the Highrock in a single leap and called the familiar summons. Below him, the Clan cats padded drowsily from the wreckage of their dens, their tails and ears flicking in surprise when they saw Fireheart waiting where their leader usually stood to address them.

"We must rebuild the camp," he began once they had settled in front of him. "I know it looks a mess now, but it is the height of greenleaf. The forest will grow back quickly, stronger because of the injuries it has suffered." He blinked as he repeated Cinderpelt's words.

"Why isn't Bluestar telling us this?" Fireheart stiffened as Darkstripe challenged him from the back of the group.

"Bluestar is exhausted," Fireheart told him. "Cinderpelt has given her poppy seeds so that she can rest and recover." Anxious murmurs rippled through the cats below.

"The more she rests, the quicker she'll recover," Fireheart reassured them. "Just like the forest."

"The forest is empty," fretted Brindleface. "The prey has run away or died in the fire. What will we eat?" She glanced anxiously at Ashpaw and Fernpaw, her face shadowed with a mother's concern even though her kits had left the nursery.

"The prey will come back," Fireheart assured her. "We must hunt as usual, and if we need to go a little farther to find fresh-kill, then we will." Murmurs of agreement rose from the clearing, and Fireheart began to feel a surge of confidence.

"Longtail, Mousefur, Thornpaw, and Dustpelt—you'll take

the dawn patrol." The four cats looked up at Fireheart and nodded, unquestioning. "Swiftpaw, you can replace Mousefur on guard duty and make sure Bluestar is not disturbed. The rest of us will start work on the camp. Whitestorm will organize parties to gather materials. Darkstripe, you can supervise the rebuilding of the camp wall."

"And how am I supposed to do that?" demanded Darkstripe. "The ferns are all burned away."

"Use whatever you can," answered Fireheart. "But make sure it is strong. We mustn't forget Tigerclaw's threat. We need to stay alert. All kits shall remain in camp. Apprentices will travel only with warriors." Fireheart gazed down on the silent Clan. "Are we agreed?"

Loud mews rose from the crowd. "We are!" they called.

"Right," Fireheart meowed. "Let's start work!"

The cats began to move away from the Highrock, weaving among one another swiftly to gather around Whitestorm and Darkstripe for their instructions.

Fireheart jumped down from the Highrock and padded to Sandstorm. "We need to organize a burial party for Yellowfang."

"You didn't mention her death," Sandstorm pointed out, her green eyes puzzled.

"Or Halftail's!" Fireheart glanced down as Cloudpaw's mew sounded beside him. The young apprentice sounded reproachful.

"The Clan knows they are dead," Fireheart told them, feeling his fur prickle uncomfortably. "It is for Bluestar to honor them with the proper words. She can do it when she's better."

"And what if she doesn't recover?" ventured Sandstorm.

"She will!" Fireheart snapped. Sandstorm winced visibly, and he cursed himself. She was only voicing the fears of all the Clan. If Bluestar had really turned her back on the rituals of StarClan, Yellowfang and Halftail would never hear the proper words to send them on their journey to Silverpelt.

Fireheart felt his confidence slide away. What if the forest didn't recover before leaf-bare? What if they couldn't find enough fresh-kill to feed the Clan? What if Tigerclaw attacked? "If Bluestar doesn't get better, I don't know what will happen," he murmured.

Fire flared in Sandstorm's eyes. "Bluestar made you her deputy. She'd expect you to know what to do!"

Her words hit Fireheart like stinging hail. "Put your claws away, Sandstorm!" he spat. "Can't you see that I'm doing the best I can? Instead of criticizing me, go and organize the apprentices to bury Yellowfang." He glared at Cloudpaw. "You can go too. And try to keep out of trouble for once," he added.

He turned away from the pair of startled-looking cats and marched across the clearing. He knew he had been unfair, but they had asked a question he wasn't ready to answer, a question so frightening that he couldn't begin to think what it might mean.

What if Bluestar never recovered?

CHAPTER 29

The sky stayed gray and cloudy over the next few days, but the showers didn't hamper the rebuilding of the camp. In fact Fireheart welcomed the cleansing rain that would wash the ash into the soil and help the forest to recover.

But this morning the sun shone high overhead, the clouds billowing away over the horizon. *The sky will be clear for tonight's Gathering,* Fireheart thought ruefully, wishing for once that the moon could be hidden so that the Gathering could not be held. Bluestar was still a long way from being her former self, emerging from her den only when Whitestorm persuaded her to come and see how the repairs were coming along. The ThunderClan leader had nodded blankly at the cats as they worked before limping back to the security of her nest. Fireheart wondered if she even remembered that the Gathering was tonight. Perhaps he should go and find out.

He padded around the edge of the clearing, feeling a ripple of pride at the work the Clan had done so far. The camp was already regaining some of its former shape. The trunk of the elders' oak was blackened but still in one piece, although its maze of branches had burned away to nothing.

The bramble nursery, which had been stripped of its protective leaves down to a tangle of stems, had been carefully patched with leafy twigs fetched from less damaged parts of the forest. And the camp wall had been shored up with the strongest branches the cats could find, although there was little they could do to replace the thick barrier of ferns that used to surround the camp. For that they would have to wait for the forest to grow again.

Fireheart heard a scratching behind the nursery. Through the patchy walls, he saw a familiar pelt of white fur. "Cloudpaw!" he called.

The apprentice emerged from behind the bramble bush, his jaws crammed with twigs that he'd been weaving through the nursery walls. Fireheart blinked in welcome. He hadn't been the only cat to notice how hard Cloudpaw had worked these past few days to fix the camp. There had been no more questions about the white apprentice's commitment to the Clan. Fireheart wondered if it had taken something as severe as a fire for Cloudpaw to discover the true meaning of loyalty. The young cat stood in front of him now without speaking, his fur flattened and blotchy with soot and mud, his eyes strained and exhausted.

"Go and rest," Fireheart ordered gently. "You've earned it."

Cloudpaw dropped his bundle of twigs. "Let me finish these first."

"You can finish them later."

"But I've only got a few left to do," Cloudpaw argued.

"You look dead on your paws," Fireheart insisted. "Go on."

"Yes, Fireheart." He turned to leave and glanced forlornly at the fallen oak where Smallear sat with Dappletail and One-Eye. "The elders' den seems so empty," he mewed.

"Patchpelt and Halftail are with StarClan now," Fireheart reminded him. "They'll be watching you tonight from Silverpelt." A wave of regret tugged at his belly as he remembered that Bluestar had refused to conduct the proper ceremony for her dead Clanmates.

"I will not place them in the paws of StarClan," she had told him bitterly. "Our warrior ancestors do not deserve the company of ThunderClan cats." And so Whitestorm had soothed the anxious Clan by speaking the words that would send Yellowfang and Halftail safely to their old friends in Silverpelt, just as he had done for Patchpelt at the RiverClan camp.

Cloudpaw nodded, but he looked unconvinced. Fireheart knew that the apprentice still found it hard to believe that the lights of Silverpelt were the spirits of their warrior ancestors, watching over their old hunting grounds. "Go and rest," he repeated.

The young cat dragged his paws toward the charred stump where the apprentices gathered to eat and share tongues. Brightpaw hurried across the clearing to greet her friend, and Cloudpaw met her with a friendly nuzzle. But the white apprentice's eyelids were already drooping, and his greeting was interrupted by a huge yawn. He lay down where he was, resting his head on the ground and closing his sore eyes. Brightpaw crouched at his side and gently began to wash Cloudpaw's grubby pelt. Watching them, Fireheart felt a pang of loneliness as he remembered the same companionship he had once shared with Graystripe.

He turned his paws once more toward Bluestar's den. Longtail was sitting outside, and he nodded as Fireheart passed. Fireheart paused at the entrance. The lichen had been burned away and the stone was black with soot. He mewed a quiet greeting and stepped inside. Without the lichen, the wind as well as daylight flooded in, and Bluestar had dragged her bedding into the shadows at the back of the drafty cave.

Cinderpelt sat beside the huddled shape of the leader, pushing a pile of herbs toward her. "They'll make you feel better," she urged.

"I feel fine," snapped Bluestar, keeping her eyes fixed on the sandy floor.

"I'll leave them here, then. Perhaps you'll manage them later." Cinderpelt stood and walked unevenly toward the den entrance.

"How is she?" Fireheart whispered.

"Stubborn," replied Cinderpelt, brushing past him out of the den.

Fireheart cautiously approached the old leader. Bluestar was even more of a stranger to him now, locked in a world of fear and suspicion directed not just against Tigerclaw, but at all their warrior ancestors in StarClan. "Bluestar," he began tentatively, dipping his head. "The Gathering is tonight. Have you decided who will go?"

"The Gathering?" Bluestar spat with disgust. "You decide who to take. I won't be going. There is no longer any reason for me to honor StarClan." As she spoke, a cloud of ash blew through the open doorway, cutting off her words with a bout of coughing.

Fireheart stared in dismay as spasms racked her frail body. Bluestar was the leader of the Clan! It was she who'd taught him about StarClan and the way the warrior spirits watched over the forest. Fireheart couldn't believe she would reject the beliefs she had based her whole life upon.

"Y-you don't have to honor StarClan," he stammered at last. "Just be there to represent your own Clan. They need your strength now."

Bluestar looked at him for a long moment. "My kits needed me once, but I gave them to another Clan to raise," she whispered. "And why? Because StarClan told me I had a different destiny. Is this it? To be attacked by traitors? To watch my Clan die around me? StarClan was wrong. It was not worth it."

Fireheart felt his blood turn to ice. He turned and padded blindly out of the den. Sandstorm had replaced Longtail outside. Fireheart looked hopefully at the pale orange warrior, but she clearly hadn't forgiven his harsh words, because she fixed her eyes on her paws and let him pass without speaking.

Feeling unsettled, Fireheart spotted Whitestorm trotting back into camp with the sunhigh patrol. He signaled to the white warrior with his tail, and Whitestorm headed toward him while the rest of the patrol split up in search of food and a place to rest.

"Bluestar isn't well enough to attend the Gathering," Fireheart meowed when Whitestorm reached him.

The elderly warrior shook his head as if the news came as no surprise. "There was a time when nothing would have kept Bluestar from a Gathering," he observed quietly.

"We should take a party anyway," Fireheart told him. "The other Clans must be warned about Tigerclaw. His group of rogues is a threat to all the Clans."

Whitestorm nodded. "We could tell them Bluestar is ill, I suppose," he suggested. "But we might be inviting trouble if we let it be known that our leader is weak."

"It would be worse not to go at all," Fireheart pointed out. "The other Clans will know about the fire. We must appear to be as strong as we can."

"WindClan is clearly still hostile," Whitestorm agreed.

"The fact that Sandstorm, Cloudpaw, and I fought them and won in their own territory won't have helped," Fireheart admitted. "And there's RiverClan to consider."

Whitestorm curiously looked at him. "But they gave us shelter after the fire."

"I know," Fireheart replied. "But I can't help wondering if Leopardfur might demand something in return."

"We have nothing to give."

"We have Sunningrocks," Fireheart answered. "RiverClan made no secret of their interest in that part of the forest, and right now we need every bit of our territory for hunting."

"At least ShadowClan is weakened by sickness," meowed Whitestorm. "That's one Clan that won't be attacking us for a while."

"Yes," agreed Fireheart, feeling guilty that they should be helped by another Clan's suffering. "Actually, the news about Tigerclaw might work in our favor." Whitestorm stared at him, puzzled, and Fireheart went on: "If I can persuade the other Clans that he's a threat to them as well as us, they might put all their energy into protecting their own borders."

Whitestorm nodded slowly. "It might be our best hope of keeping them away from our territory while we recover our strength. You're right, Fireheart. We must go to the Gathering, even if Bluestar is unable to come with us." His blue gaze met Fireheart's, and he knew that they were thinking the same thing. Bluestar was able to go if she wanted—but she chose not to.

As the sun set, the cats began to take fresh-kill from the meager pile they had collected. Fireheart helped himself to a tiny shrew, which he carried to the nettle clump and gulped down in a few hungry mouthfuls. The Clan's bellies hadn't been full for days. The prey was returning, but slowly, and Fireheart knew they had to be careful about how much they caught. The forest must have a chance to replenish itself before they could eat their fill once more.

Once the cats had finished their paltry meal, Fireheart got to his paws and padded across the clearing. He felt the eyes of the Clan follow him as he leaped onto the Highrock. There was no need to call them—they gathered below with questioning eyes in the fading evening light.

"Bluestar will not be coming to this Gathering," he announced.

Mews of alarm ripped through the cats, and Fireheart saw Whitestorm weaving among them, calming and reassuring them. How much had the Clan guessed about their leader's state of mind? In the RiverClan camp they had united to protect Bluestar from prying eyes. But here in their own camp, her weakness left them vulnerable and afraid.

Tigerclaw's tabby kit sat outside the nursery, staring up at the Highrock with round, curious eyes. For a moment Fireheart let himself be mesmerized by its yellow gaze, and images of Tigerclaw began to prowl around the edges of his mind.

"Does this mean ThunderClan won't attend?" He was roused by Darkstripe's voice as the striped warrior shouldered his way to the front. "After all, what is a Clan without a leader?"

Was Fireheart imagining the ominous glint in Darkstripe's eye? "ThunderClan will go to Fourtrees tonight," he meowed, addressing the whole Clan. "We must show the other Clans that we are strong, despite the fire." He saw nods of agreement. The apprentices shuffled their paws and looked eagerly at one another, too young to understand the seriousness of attending a Gathering without a leader, and distracted by the hope that they might be chosen to go themselves.

"We mustn't betray any weakness, for Bluestar's sake and for the sake of the whole Clan," Fireheart went on. "Remember, we are ThunderClan!" He yowled the final words, surprised by the fiery conviction that welled up from his heart, and the Clan responded by straightening their backs, licking at their ash-covered fur, and smoothing their singed whiskers.

"I shall take Darkstripe, Mousefur, Sandstorm, White-storm, Ashpaw, and Cloudpaw."

"Will the others be enough to protect the camp?" Dark-stripe demanded.

"Tigerclaw will know there is a Gathering," added Long-tail. "What if he uses the opportunity to attack?"

"We can't afford to leave more cats behind than usual. If we appear weak at the Gathering, we risk inviting attack from all the Clans," Fireheart insisted.

"He's right," agreed Mousefur. "We can't let the others see our weakness!"

"RiverClan already knows the fire destroyed our camp," added Willowpelt. "We must show them we are as strong as ever."

"Then we are agreed?" asked Fireheart. "Longtail, Dust-pelt, Frostfur, Brindleface, and Brackenfur will guard the camp. Elders, queens, you will be safe with them, and we shall return as soon as we can."

He listened to the murmurs and searched the eyes looking up at him. With a wave of relief, he saw heads begin to nod. "Good," he meowed, and leaped down from the rock.

The warriors and apprentices he had chosen to come with him were already circling at the camp entrance, impatiently flicking their tails. A familiar long-furred white pelt was among them. This would be Cloudpaw's first Gathering. Fireheart had been looking forward to this moment since the kit had first come to the Clan. He still remembered his own first Gathering, racing down the slope to Fourtrees surrounded by mighty warriors, and he couldn't help feeling a stab of disappointment as he looked around at the smoke-stained and hungry cats Cloudpaw would have to follow. And yet Fireheart could feel their excitement and pent-up energy as strong as ever. Sandstorm was kneading the ground with her forepaws, and Mousefur's eyes shone brightly in the growing darkness as Fireheart hurried across to them.

"Longtail," he meowed, pausing briefly beside the brown warrior. "You will be senior warrior here. Guard the Clan well."

Longtail dipped his head to Fireheart. "They'll be safe, I promise."

Fireheart's glow of satisfaction at Longtail's respectful gesture was soured by the mocking glance Darkstripe threw him from the camp entrance. It was as if the warrior could see through his outer confidence to the uncertainty that lay beneath. Fireheart caught Sandstorm's eye as he passed her. She was staring at him intently. *Bluestar made you her deputy. She'd expect you to know what to do!* Her challenging words, which had stung like an adder's bite before, suddenly strengthened him, and he flashed Darkstripe a look of defiance as he led the way out of the camp.

The cats charged silently through the forest, the burned trees reaching into the darkening sky like twisted claws. Fireheart felt his paws sink into the ash, damp and sticky, but there was a hopeful scent in the air of fresh green shoots sprouting from the cinders.

He glanced backward. Cloudpaw was keeping up well, and Sandstorm was pushing ahead, drawing closer until she ran at his side, matching his pace.

"You spoke well on the Highrock," she meowed, panting.

"Thanks," answered Fireheart. He pulled away as they scrambled up a steep mound, but Sandstorm caught up as they reached the top.

"I . . . I'm sorry about what I said about Bluestar," she meowed quietly. "I was just worried. The camp is looking great, considering . . ."

"Considering I'm deputy?" Fireheart suggested sourly.

"Considering it was so badly damaged," Sandstorm finished. Fireheart's ears twitched. "Bluestar must be proud of you," she went on, and Fireheart winced—he doubted if Bluestar had even noticed, but he was grateful for Sandstorm's words.

"Thanks," he meowed again. He turned his head as they ran down the other side of the mound and looked into the warrior's soft emerald eyes. "I missed you, Sandstorm—" he began.

He was interrupted by the sound of powerful paws drumming behind them, and the voice of Darkstripe growled, "So what are you going to tell the other Clans, then?"

Before Fireheart could answer, a fallen tree loomed ahead. He sprang into the air, but a branch caught his paw and he landed clumsily, stumbling. The other cats raced past him, but they slowed instinctively as Fireheart fell behind.

"Are you okay?" Darkstripe asked as Fireheart caught up to him. The striped warrior's eyes glinted in the moonlight.

"Yes, fine," Fireheart answered curtly, trying not to betray the pain in his paw.

It was still throbbing when the cats reached the top of the slope that led down to Fourtrees. Fireheart halted to catch his breath and gather his thoughts before they joined the other Clans. The valley below had been untouched by the fire, and the four oaks towered unscathed into the starry sky.

Fireheart glanced at the cats that waited beside him, tails twitching and ears pricked expectantly. They obviously trusted him to take Bluestar's place at the Gathering and convince the other Clans that ThunderClan had not been weakened by their recent tragedy. He had to prove himself worthy of that trust. He flicked his tail, signaling to them as he had seen Bluestar signal so many times before, and plunged down toward the Great Rock.

CHAPTER 30

The air in the clearing was heavy with the scent of WindClan and RiverClan. Fireheart felt a tremor of anxiety. In just a few moments he was going to have to stand on the Great Rock and address these cats. There was no sign of ShadowClan. Had the sickness taken such a firm hold that they couldn't make it to the Gathering? A pang of pity for Whitethroat reminded Fireheart of Tigerclaw, and of the terror in the young warrior's eyes as the massive cat loomed at the edge of the Thunderpath. Suddenly his paws itched to mount the Great Rock and warn the other Clans about the dark warrior's presence in the forest.

"Fireheart!" Onewhisker bounded up to Fireheart's side. He felt a flicker of surprise at Onewhisker's friendly purr. The last time he had seen a WindClan cat it had been Mudclaw screeching angrily away into the heather. But Onewhisker clearly hadn't forgotten how Fireheart had brought his Clan back from exile. The two warriors had grown close on that journey, and both cats still valued the bond they had forged.

"Hi, Onewhisker," Fireheart greeted the brown tabby.

"You'd better not let Mudclaw see you talking to me, truce or no truce. We didn't part on very good terms last time we met."

"Mudclaw takes pride in defending his territory," replied Onewhisker, shifting uncomfortably from paw to paw. He'd obviously heard about the two attacks on ThunderClan cats in WindClan territory.

"Maybe," Fireheart admitted. "But that's no excuse for turning Bluestar away from Highstones." He found himself wishing Bluestar had been able to share with StarClan at the Moonstone that day. Things might be very different now if she had received some assurance that her warrior ancestors had not turned against her.

"Tallstar wasn't happy when he heard about that. Even if you were sheltering Brokentail, it was no excuse—"

"Brokentail was *dead* by then," Fireheart interrupted him, regretting his tone when he saw Onewhisker's ears flicking uncomfortably. "I'm sorry, Onewhisker," he meowed more gently. "It's good to see you again. How are you?"

"Fine," answered Onewhisker, looking relieved. "I'm sorry to hear about the fire. I know how bad it is for a Clan to be driven from its home." His eyes met Fireheart's sympathetically.

"We've returned to our camp and we've rebuilt it the best we can. It won't be long before the forest recovers." Fireheart tried to sound confident.

"I'm glad to hear it," Onewhisker meowed. "You know, it's as if we've never been away from our camp now. There have been plenty of kits this greenleaf, and Morningflower's kit is here as an apprentice—it's his first Gathering." Fireheart remembered the tiny wet bundle of fur he had helped to carry through the rain, out of Twoleg territory and back to WindClan's home. He followed Onewhisker's gaze across the clearing to a young brown tom. Although small like the rest of his Clan, the apprentice's muscles were already lean and well developed beneath his short, thick fur.

Fireheart noticed Onewhisker suddenly dip his head. He turned to see Tallstar approaching them. The WindClan leader looked at Fireheart with narrowed eyes. "We've been seeing a lot of you lately, Fireheart," he remarked. "Just because you once led us home doesn't give you the freedom to wander around our territory."

"So I've been warned," replied Fireheart. He forced himself to stay calm, keeping his resentment at Bluestar's treatment out of his voice—after all, the Gathering was held under a truce, and this was a warrior he had learned to respect on their journey together through Twoleg territory. But Fireheart held the black-and-white leader's gaze and meowed firmly, "However, I must put the needs of my Clan first."

Tallstar's eyes glittered back at him; then he gave a tiny nod. "Spoken like a true warrior. Having traveled with you, I wasn't surprised when Bluestar made you her deputy." The WindClan leader glanced around the clearing and added, "There are those who thought such a young cat would never carry off such a great responsibility. I was not among them."

Fireheart was taken aback. He hadn't expected such a

compliment from the leader of WindClan. He stifled a delighted purr, and nodded his thanks.

"Where is Bluestar?" asked Tallstar. "I can't see her among your cats." His voice was casual but his eyes betrayed a keen interest.

"She's not feeling well enough to travel yet," Fireheart answered lightly.

"Was she injured in the fire?"

"Nothing she won't recover from," Fireheart meowed, hoping with all his heart that he was telling the truth.

Beside him, Onewhisker looked up sharply. Fireheart followed his gaze to the slope on the other side of the valley. Three ShadowClan cats were charging into the clearing, Runningnose at the head. Fireheart felt a glimmer of relief as he recognized one of the two warriors behind the gray-and-white medicine cat. It was Littlecloud, clearly recovered from the sickness—thanks to Cinderpelt.

The other Clan cats backed away from the ShadowClan warriors as they skidded to a halt in front of the Great Rock. News of their disease had obviously spread through the forest.

"It's all right," Runningnose meowed, panting, as if he could read their minds. "ShadowClan is free of the sickness. I have been sent ahead to tell you to wait before you begin the meeting. ShadowClan's leader is on his way."

"What makes Nightstar so late?" called Tallstar from Fireheart's side.

"Nightstar is dead," answered Runningnose bluntly.

A stunned ripple spread through the other cats like a

breeze through trees, and Fireheart blinked. How could the ShadowClan leader be dead? He had only recently received his nine lives. What a terrible sickness! No wonder Littlecloud and Whitethroat had been so afraid to return to their camp.

"Is Cinderfur coming instead?" Whitestorm called, referring to the ShadowClan deputy.

Runningnose looked at his paws. "Cinderfur was one of the first to die of the sickness."

"Then who is your new leader?" demanded Crookedstar, emerging from the shadows on the other side of the Great Rock.

Runningnose glanced at the RiverClan leader. "You'll see for yourselves soon enough," he promised. "He'll be here shortly."

"Excuse me," Fireheart murmured to Tallstar and Onewhisker. "There is something I must share with Runningnose."

Fireheart padded to where the ShadowClan medicine cat stood, surrounded by warriors and apprentices, all anxious to discover who ShadowClan's new leader was. He wondered how the old cat would react to hearing about Yellowfang's death. Runningnose had seen so much death lately that perhaps it wouldn't mean much to him anymore, but Fireheart felt he should break it to him privately, before he made an announcement from the Great Rock. After all, Yellowfang had trained Runningnose when she had been ShadowClan's medicine cat. The bond between the two cats must once have been very close, if only for the short time before Brokentail drove Yellowfang out of her Clan.

Fireheart signaled with his tail to the ShadowClan medicine cat. Runningnose looked relieved to be leaving the circle of inquiring faces as he followed Fireheart to a quieter spot beneath one of the oaks. "What is it?" he asked.

"Yellowfang's dead," Fireheart meowed gently, feeling a fresh thorn of sorrow drive itself into his heart.

Runningnose's eyes clouded with grief. The gray-and-white tom bowed his head as Fireheart went on: "She died trying to save a Clanmate from the fire. StarClan will honor her bravery."

Runningnose didn't reply, just swung his head slowly from side to side. Fireheart felt his own throat tighten with sadness, but he couldn't afford to let grief overwhelm him here. He touched the tom's head with his nose and padded quickly away.

The rest of the cats were beginning to weave anxiously around one another, their mews growing louder. "We can't wait any longer!" Fireheart heard a RiverClan warrior mutter to his neighbor. "The moon will be setting soon."

"If this new leader is going to be late, that's his problem," Mousefur agreed. Fireheart knew the real reason for her keenness to get on with the meeting and return to camp. With Tigerclaw loose in the forest, none of the Clans were safe.

He saw a flash of white fur at the center of the clearing as Tallstar leaped onto the Great Rock. He had obviously decided to start the meeting without ShadowClan's leader. Crookedstar started toward the rock. Fireheart braced himself, ready for his first Gathering at the head of his Clan, and desperate to warn the other cats about the threat that lurked in the woods.

"Good luck." Fireheart felt Sandstorm's breath ruffle his ear fur. He turned and gently touched her warm cheek with his muzzle, knowing that their quarrel had been forgotten. Then he threaded his way through the other cats toward the Great Rock.

He was stopped in his tracks by a yowl called from the slope behind him. "He's here!"

Fireheart turned and saw Darkstripe craning his neck beside him, but their view was blocked by the other cats peering and rearing up on their hind legs to get a look at ShadowClan's new leader as he passed through the crowd. Darkstripe's ears suddenly pricked with surprise. The striped warrior was staring up at the Great Rock, his eyes glittering with barely suppressed excitement. Fireheart twisted his head to see what had prompted such a strong reaction from his Clanmate.

Framed by the cold light of the moon, Fireheart saw the powerful shoulders and broad head of the cat who had leaped onto the rock beside Tallstar. The other leader seemed puny and frail beside this massive figure. And with a cold shiver of dread, Fireheart realized that the new leader of ShadowClan was Tigerclaw.

KEEP WATCH FOR

WARRIORS

BOOK 5:

A DANGEROUS PATH

A dark new leader has risen in the forest, seeking only one thing: revenge on ThunderClan. And he's not the only danger: A different kind of wild creature is ravaging through the forest and haunting Fireheart's dreams. Can the young deputy protect his warriors from the threats surrounding them on all sides?